SET IN STONE

SET IN STONE

Kay Stephens

This first world edition published in Great Britain 2003 by
SEVERN HOUSE PUBLISHERS LTD of
9–15 High Street, Sutton, Surrey SM1 1DF.
This first world edition published in the USA 2003 by
SEVERN HOUSE PUBLISHERS INC of
595 Madison Avenue, New York, N.Y. 10022.

British Library Cataloguing in Publication Data

Stephens, Kay
    Set in stone
    1.   Love stories
    I.   Title
    823.9'14 [F]

    ISBN 0-7278-5871-8

Typeset by Hewer Text Ltd.,
Edinburgh, Scotland.
Printed and bound in Great Britain by
MPG Books Ltd., Bodmin, Cornwall.

Author's Note

Among many books studied while researching the background for this novel, the following have been particularly useful: *We Landed by Moonlight* by Hugh Verity, *Masquerade (The Amazing Camouflage Deceptions of World War II)* by Seymour Reit, and *The Week France Fell* by Noel Barber.

One

J ane couldn't bear to watch. 'Leave that for now, Dad,' she said gently, drying her eyes as she turned to walk away.

Alfred Townsend wouldn't cease struggling to compel weak hands to chisel into the Yorkshire sandstone that was his inspiration. While he cursed the fingers causing his frustration, his blue eyes were reddened by tears he no longer hid.

'I am going to fetch him some stone that he could carve,' Jane told her mother when she reached the kitchen. 'I can be there and back in a few days.'

'On your own, love?' Sheila protested, as she had been protesting ever since her daughter first had suggested going to France.

'I am twenty-five, Mum. Didn't I show what I was made of – training until I qualified?'

'How is being an architect going to help you drive all that way abroad? What use will it be to you?' Sheila persisted.

'It will take me to the right place. I explained earlier – where a group of us went as students.'

'A group, aye. Not you on your own. And two years since, not in 1938.'

'There's no more need to worry now. We all heard on the wireless last night, Mr Chamberlain's come back from Munich with the agreement he wanted.' Jane paused, smiled. 'I thought you'd be pleased. I am doing this for my dad.'

'I know you think it'll help. I wish I was half as sure this'll be for the best. He's getting worse with every week that passes.' Sheila swallowed, her quivering chin stopping her mid-sentence. Despite being tall, she suddenly looked frail.

Jane grasped her mother's arm, and steered her to a chair beside the table covered in red chenille. She ached to imbue Sheila with her own optimism. None of the family would ever forget the shock of Alfred Townsend's fall from the civic hall his company was constructing, nor the shattering of hopes when the surgeon declared that he would never stand again, let alone walk. His slow recuperation in hospital had scarcely prepared any of them for those terrible early days after his return home, to life in a wheelchair.

Being obliged to have a bed in one of their ground floor rooms was a mere fraction of the trouble. A master craftsman who'd always lived to follow the family tradition of building, Alfred was bereft, and the rest of them were hurt by seeing how greatly he was hurting.

'He's not yet fifty, Mum, he shouldn't have to resign himself to doing nowt.'

'Alf likes a good read, I can allus fetch plenty of books from the library. That'll fill his time.' Her hazel eyes were resolute. *She* would look after her husband.

'But not his heart, it won't fulfil his yearning to create, to make something beautiful.'

'I won't have your dad upset again, you've seen what he's like when he can't carve that lump of stone.'

'Which is why I'm going to obtain something soft enough for him to work.'

'And how will you bring it back here? You'll not manage to fit much into that little Morris Eight.'

'I shall bring him samples. When that succeeds, I'll arrange to have supplies sent over. You wouldn't believe how beautiful that stone looks when it's carved.'

'That's right, I wouldn't – or that it's going to be worth the trouble.'

'It's me you don't believe in, isn't it, Mum?'

'I just wish – well, that you didn't always want to be right, so

2

clever. Where's that getting you? Young men don't like a woman to be too clever.'

It was an all-too-familiar argument. Sheila Townsend belonged to a generation where marrying, having a home, meant more than any career. Or where a career was made of ensuring their offspring didn't neglect to wear their vests!

Staring through the window towards Oxenhope Moor, Jane fought down the urge to stride off over there and beyond to Haworth. She willed herself to forget her longing for the freedom she always found in all that space. Before leaving on this far longer journey she must ease her mother's concern.

Throughout her training she had resisted Sheila's opposition, which Jane soon understood was simply because her dedication to studying had somehow prevented her from getting to know someone she might love.

'I do appreciate what you're trying to do, Jane. But I won't have your father reduced to tears by yet another thing that he can't manage.'

'It won't be like that, I promise. He'll do us proud again. Even if he can't construct buildings any longer, he can provide carvings to enhance them.'

Ever since he had recovered the bit of mobility he now possessed, Alfred Townsend had set his mind on creating embellishments for the buildings the family firm would continue to erect. He would still make them special.

Today, his concern about her trip shadowed his blue eyes when Jane went through to the living room, where he spent most of his time, and where she often feared he now looked dwarfed by the Victorian walnut furniture.

'Are you sure you meant what you said, and you're not neglecting your own opportunities, just to help me out? I'll not have anybody worse off on my account, and certainly not you, love.'

Jane smiled affectionately. 'How many times do I have to tell you? That latest project was off my hands last week, and the boss is afraid we'll have a long wait for approval of my outline plans for that new school out Illingworth way.'

3

'All right, love, good. I only need one person who understands. Them two lads of mine seem to think that, so long as they keep the business running, nowt else matters.'

'They have their uses though, eh – our Jack and Phil? They'll not let the Townsend reputation be forgotten.'

'They'd better not either, or they'll have me to reckon wi'! And my father, an' all. William Townsend might be turned eighty, he still keeps a close eye on the books. And more – on what's going on around us in the trade.'

Jane smiled. She'd always been particularly fond of her grandfather, and had been immensely proud when he'd approved her choice of career. She could hear his voice now.

'An architect, eh? That's quite something, for a family that started out in the nineteenth century as jobbing builders. And for a lass to achieve it, an' all . . .'

It was being a girl that had impressed her tutors throughout her training, Jane reflected as she hurried to get ready for setting out. Her fellow-students had reacted in various ways, some flirting outrageously, others patronizing her in class, one or two respecting her for making that choice.

Any who were eager to seize the opportunity and philander, Jane had put straight. From the start, she was determined to work. The family business was doing all right, but money wasn't there to be wasted, and nor was her time, she'd always resolved to achieve the necessary certificate by the earliest date possible.

When she opened the door to the lavatory Jane smiled, all seriousness vanished. The stag's head mounted on the wall witnessed that her father's nature had a crazy side. After visiting Scotland he'd brought the stag home to a variety of reactions.

Her mother had protested over the site he'd chosen for displaying it, while one of Jane's aunts confessed to hanging a towel across its antlers to cover prying eyes. Their Jack's first girlfriend had refused to use the lavatory there, cutting short her visits to the house in order to find a public convenience that was less disturbing.

I wish I could make Dad contented enough to laugh again, thought Jane, going to wash her hands. Her eyes reflected in the mirror were a shade greener than her mother's, no less resolute. It seemed years already since he'd shared his enjoyment of the ridiculous. Somehow she must restore that humour to the man they loved.

Jane glanced about her while she drove down from their home overlooking the stone-built houses of Hebden Bridge and then on through valleys and hills that were less densely populated. She was considering how much all the studying had brought her. Not simply in qualifications gained. She had started out from school unsophisticated, naive, lacking self-confidence.

The years in that grammar school had never changed her from the inhibited individual whose scholarship had taken her there. In those days, the family firm had been struggling out of the slump, while her form had contained a preponderance of girls whose fathers were mill owners, or men respected in one of the professions.

Not until she had begun her further education had Jane overcome the remembered dread of having those grammar school girls find out that her uniform was second-hand, that her dad patched her shoes when they couldn't afford the local cobbler.

Things had started to improve as soon as she attended Leeds College of Art, and students and instructors alike recognized that her inherited love of buildings, and of stone, gave her an advantage.

Because of this love, learning had never come hard. The will to succeed experienced at the school she had hated only increased with admission to this college that she could adore. Each examination had proved to Jane her ability, and had generated this essential feeling that she might tackle any new challenge.

To her left, on the summit of a hill midway between Elland and Huddersfield, a large sandstone house gleamed in October sunlight. Jane smiled to herself, delighted as always to see this evidence of Alfred Townsend's skill. Even from this distance and with most of her attention on the road ahead, she could appreciate the carved balustrade surrounding its terrace. She had been no more than a lass of seven when she'd watched her father creating that. When he'd gone on to provide an elegant internal staircase carved entirely of stone, Jane had marvelled. And from that day had resolved to design spectacular buildings. It often seemed to her that the siting of that house, with its widespread views of hills that soared to the skyline, encouraged the belief that possibilities should be limitless.

When planning that particular house, her father had intended it should be their home. Jane had learned only recently that her mother was too fond of the place where she and Alfred first had started their family to be prepared to consider moving.

She recalled now the way that Alfred Townsend had always respected men who beautified stone through their carving. If he hadn't been obliged to keep their building firm going by concentrating on practical constructions, he might have become a sculptor. She'd never forget how he'd taken her all the way to Claydon House in Buckinghamshire purely to admire the intricate work of Luke Lightfoot.

This father of hers had inspired her career, he deserved more than the mere existence of a life without purpose. She loved him too well to shirk the opportunity to offer some chance of his finding an enduring interest.

Her mother's concern was justified though, Jane admitted privately, travelling through Huddersfield and beyond to the south. She wasn't accustomed to driving long distances, even over here. Towns of millstone grit, steeply sloped valleys, wooded hills and moors mauve with heather were all familiar. Her heart felt heavy with the pain of leaving them behind, a pain echoed in the mind that had planned this interminable journey.

Determined, she might be, but she recognized her inhibitions. This route might not be the most direct, but would spare her the most testing situations. Only the outer suburbs of London need be negotiated, and she vowed to avoid Paris. There would be overnight stops on the way, she should not overtax this little car, *or herself.* Jane feared she could be too soft, hoped she was merely being practical.

Her planning had worked, the only misfortune she hadn't contemplated was her seasickness throughout the crossing to France. Mercifully, she had chosen the Dover–Calais route, anything longer might have seemed unendurable. And being obliged to press on and drive once she came ashore provided a distraction. Jane had reserved a room for her first night in France at a small hotel in St Omer. Arriving during the early evening, and hungry for the first time since that crossing, she ate almost at once, then took a stroll through the autumnal darkness of the quiet streets. Next morning from her room, she saw the picturesque ruins of the abbey on the hill nearby, and wished this mission of hers permitted more time for exploring.

St Omer was only the first of many places demanding closer acquaintance, but Jane remained concentrated on her purpose, and resolute in forbidding feelings of loneliness. She might be growing accustomed to driving alone, but here in France, with the everlasting need for observing different rules of the road, she would have appreciated a companion to alleviate the strain.

As she drove eventually through Orléans, she allowed herself to begin to relax. The rest of the journey to Montrichard should take less than two hours. No one would be more relieved to arrive at the hotel there.

The car began to pull to the right on a country lane south of Orléans. Alarmed, Jane slowed to a stop and sprang out to investigate. The only good thing about the punctured tyre was its being on the side away from other traffic.

Thankful the height inherited from her mother, plus experience on building sites, had given her a bit of strength, she got out her tool kit and unfastened the spare wheel. Prepared though she was, and capable enough to change the wheel herself, Jane sighed grimly when the task was completed. The hem of her skirt was dirty where she'd knelt in the road, and her hands were filthy.

She was able to clean herself up a little at the garage where she stopped to have the ruined tyre replaced, but Jane still felt grubby as she embarked on the final stage of her journey. She also was two hours behind schedule.

The riverside hotel in Montrichard looked beautiful in the early evening sunlight, Jane seized her suitcase and hastened up the steps. Approaching the small reception desk, she found her way obstructed by a tall man whose grey eyes warmed with amusement. Dark-suited and wearing an immaculate white shirt and navy blue silk tie, he clearly was going through to dinner.

Aware of her dishevelled condition, Jane gave him a rueful smile as she struggled between him and other potential diners when she went to sign in.

After mustering enough French to explain her late arrival, she dashed to her room. One glance in the mirror revealed that her short sandy hair was untidy, and she had smudges of black oil across her forehead. Washing them away swiftly, she opened her suitcase and found a clean linen skirt.

The man smiled again and nodded as though in approval as Jane entered the hotel restaurant. She noticed that he still looked tall when seated, with a thin face whose severity only seemed brightened by those gleaming grey eyes.

Too tired to do full justice to her meal despite her hunger, Jane soon found that only she and this man remained at their tables. She might have wished him away to his room, but she was already feeling slightly ridiculous eating attended by what appeared to be the restaurant's full complement of waiters.

Jane wasn't surprised to find the stranger seated near the bar when she finally left her table. The way that he stood up as she approached did surprise her, and when he spoke she would have been churlish to ignore him.

'You also seem to be alone,' he began, his English accented but otherwise faultless. 'I am wondering if you might perhaps permit me to buy you a drink?'

Refusing would be more embarassing than to consent, and

Jane trusted her instinct that she'd have no good reason to decline his offer.

'Thank you, although I mustn't sit up late tonight. I've had a long journey.'

'And not without mishap, am I right?' Smiling eyes were fringed with long lashes as dark as his hair.

Jane was compelled to laugh. 'A puncture en route. Didn't help me to arrive looking suave.'

'But much smarter now,' he assured her before introducing himself. 'Henri Bodin.'

His hand was cool on hers as she told him her name, but his grasp felt firm, and those splendid eyes were searching her face. 'And what would you wish to drink, Jane?'

She chose wine, a red that resembled the one of which she'd drunk one glass with her meal. Almost too tired to think, she dared not risk anything stronger.

Henri was sipping cognac, smiling again over the rim of his glass while he enquired how far she had travelled that day.

'And before today?' he asked after Jane had told him. 'You are English, are you not? Do you live in London perhaps?'

She shook her head. 'Miles north of that, in Yorkshire. Hebden Bridge in the West Riding.'

'Where they build in that beautiful golden sandstone.'

Jane was amazed that he should have first mentioned her home county's stone. What of its textile manufacturing, carpets, engineering . . . ?

'You seem surprised,' Henri remarked. 'Is it so extraordinary that I should observe your fine buildings?'

Jane laughed. 'Only that it's quite a coincidence. My family have always been builders, you see.'

'And you yourself . . . ?'

'An architect. So, an allied trade.'

'A *profession*, surely. And one in which it is rare for a young lady to succeed.'

'You could say that. I don't mind admitting I was pleased when I qualified. Lucky, I suppose.'

'Or determined to apply yourself?'

'Well – yes.'

'And so – is it to draw elevations for some building here in France that you are arrived?'

'No, nothing like that. It's to obtain some of your local stone, *le tuffeau.*' Jane went on to explain about her father's injury, and how she hoped to improve life for him.

Henri seemed impressed, and wished her well in completing the mission. 'You do know where you may acquire the supplies you need?'

'Oh, yes. I arranged all that by telephone before leaving home.'

Normally, Jane would have enquired into the purpose of his visit, but she was extremely tired, not fit to be staying any longer to talk. The only thing that Henri revealed was his intention of leaving Montrichard the next morning to attend a meeting so early that the appointment had necessitated this stay in the area.

In her room that night Jane caught herself regretting that she was unlikely to see Henri Bodin at breakfast, or to meet him ever again. Neither handsome nor particularly young, he nevertheless attracted her, and that was extremely rare in any man newly-met.

Studying for years among predominantly male company, Jane had swiftly grown wary of succumbing to immediate attraction. And since her father's accident she felt more responsible towards family, had steeled herself to accept that forming relationships could be a luxury she shouldn't indulge too readily.

Falling asleep with Henri's commanding eyes superimposed on her own mind's eye fitted Jane for awakening with a smile as she recalled the encounter. But that must be all, she reflected ruefully, and she gave herself to fulfilling the purpose of this trip to France.

Monsieur Laigret, from whom Jane wished to acquire the special stone, greeted her as she parked the Morris Eight. He smiled when she went on to address him simply as 'Monsieur', after her one attempt at pronouncing his name. He, meanwhile, managed 'Mademoiselle Townsend', quite creditably as he led the way to show her something of their methods for extracting *le tuffeau.*

Jane was surprised to follow him along passageways leading underground into the hillside. She had visualized that the quarrying might be done in the open by similar means to recovering her native sandstone.

Although the experience was less daunting than had it been mined by, say, the same method as coal, Jane still felt quite uneasy in the cold dampness inside that hill. She made herself pay attention during his demonstration of the technique they used for extraction, but wasn't sorry when Monsieur Laigret led her to the surface and into his office.

Jane was astonished to see Henri Bodin there in intense conversation with someone who proved to be one of the three brothers in business together as suppliers of the *tuffeau.* Henri greeted her with yet another of his smiles.

'It is good that we meet again, I had hoped that this might emerge as the place you had selected for acquiring supplies.'

Jane felt elated to be seeing him again, half-regretful that her own purpose must occupy her when she would have preferred to get to know Henri better. She gathered that his business there was almost concluded, while she had much to discuss, and samples to examine.

Monsieur Laigret was exceedingly generous, charging only a nominal sum for the hunks of *le tuffeau* which he soon was loading into the car for her.

'You have impressed to me your concern that your father may continue to express his love of stone. And if it should prove that you wish to purchase greater quantities, I may assure you that my price to you is fair always.'

'*Merci bien, Monsieur Laigret, vous êtes très bon,*' Jane said, and promised to let him know if she would be able to place an order.

He said goodbye and Jane watched him walking towards his office.

She turned to get into the Morris just as someone spoke

through the open window of the car parked alongside hers. It was Henri.

'I could not depart without enquiring that all had gone smoothly in your transaction, Jane.'

'Very well indeed, thank you. It was kind of you to wait.'

'And so now are you to leave immediately on your long journey to England?'

'Not straight away. I'd like to see some of the châteaux, now that I'm particularly interested in this stone. When I visited the Loire region before it was mainly to study the designs of some of the buildings. And there never really was so much time as I'd have liked.'

'I wonder perhaps if I might suggest something? My reason for coming here was connected with a château – my own, of less grandeur than many, but important to me. Sadly, a part of it is in disrepair. My visit here early today was to consult with Jacques Laigret, whose technical skill normally is employed out on sites elsewhere. I think you could be interested to see my plans for renovation.'

If any other owner of a château had invited her to inspect his home, Jane would have been pleased to accept, when the offer came from Henri she felt twice as thrilled to go with him.

His grey eyes lit with pleasure when she agreed. Checking that she had no further business in the vicinity, he suggested that she should follow his car.

'You will find that I live some little distance away, hence my overnight stay in Montrichard, but I will use my rear-view mirror to keep your car in sight. Now that I find you again, I do not mean to lose you.'

His words delighted Jane. She would not dwell on her suspicion that they could be no more than the automatic reaction of a warm-blooded Frenchman.

Their route took them some distance beside the course of the river Cher before they turned northwards. Between fields and through several of the many hunting forests of the region, Jane drove on, feeling quite relaxed. She had accomplished very swiftly all that she had intended in France; following Henri's car like this she gave her mind to enjoying the rural country-side.

They passed close to the château at Cheverny, and later on the splendour of Chambord. A few miles further on Henri drove off up a curving driveway. When Jane caught him up he was stepping from his car before what appeared to her to be a very grand mansion, with turrets and towers glowing almost white in the sunlight.

'*Bienvenu,*' he said. 'Welcome to my home. Please come into the house now, my housekeeper will reprove me for being late for *le déjeuner.*'

'And on my account!' exclaimed Jane. 'Perhaps you shouldn't have waited.'

'How could I not, *ma chère*, how could I not?'

Laughing a little, Jane preceded him through the door which he had unlocked and held open for her.

'*Monsieur Henri, tu es très mechant!*' an old voice called from somewhere towards the distant end of the stone entrance hall.

Jane recognized in this familiarity of address the affection of someone long-acquainted with Henri Bodin, and when the plump, white-haired woman came hastening towards them, Henri's smile confirmed this conclusion.

'Jane, this is Bernadette Genevoix, who has lived here many years, since she was my – what is your word – "nanny"?'

'And like a mother I am to him now,' Bernadette confided in surprisingly good English. 'With no family remaining in the château, some person must care for him. *Non,* Henri?'

'*Mais oui, Bernadette,*' Henri confirmed and introduced Jane to her.

After pausing only to wash her hands in the tiled cloakroom indicated by Bernadette, Jane followed their voices to find the spacious kitchen, which was stone-flagged with an enormous fireplace complete with ovens. Henri was seated at a long oak table. Her surprise must have shown in her expression, he grinned into her widening hazel eyes.

'When we have eaten and I show you around you will

discover that the dining room is one of the many parts of my home that suffered neglect.'

'You should tell the young lady the reasons for that, so that she may understand,' his housekeeper remarked as she began serving their food.

'If you insist, *ma vieille*.' Henri turned to Jane, spoke reluctantly. 'Although we, in this region, did not suffer to the degree of compatriots in the Somme, for example, this place never was the same after the Great War. My father had to fight, he could not fail our country. And my mother was a nurse, she went to tend our soldiers, you understand.'

'They did not come home,' Bernadette explained when Henri's telling faltered. 'Henri was a boy of fourteen when the war ended, this château ruined by an uncle who should have preserved for the family. Instead the *cochon*, that pig sold off the stones that were falling from the walls.'

'Enough, Bernadette, our guest does not need to know.'

'So, you think? A good young lady like this should understand how you are. *Who* you are. How many years is it that you have brought no young lady to your home? And now all the while Louis is growing, and needs a *maman*.'

'You have a son?' said Jane, and wondered where the boy's mother was.

Henri shook his head. 'His mother worked in the kitchens here. Her husband is Spanish and has gone to fight in the civil war there. Gabrielle left Louis here for safety when she travelled to see her husband. That is one year ago now.'

'We have no word from her, nothing,' Bernadette continued. 'Henri is wishing to trace her, he would like to adopt the boy.'

'How old is he now?'

The softening of Henri's often austere expression revealed his fondness. 'Three years.'

Bernadette chuckled. 'And – how do you say in England – a full hand?'

'A handful, aye.'

'Is he banished to his room again?' asked Henri.

'He is taking a small rest again,' the housekeeper corrected firmly. But then turned to Jane for sympathy. 'Throughout this morning Louis has been running through the house, banging on the drum that some misguided person has give to him. When he insist on rushing out and in of the door, out and in, out and in interminably, looking for his *Oncle* Henri, I decide that Louis must be tired.'

'You shall meet him when we have finished our meal,' Henri suggested.

'I'd love to,' Jane agreed, but wondered how she might relate to the child. Neither of her brothers had any offspring, and spending all those years studying along with men had left her having few of the women friends who might have provided her with their children's company.

Her introduction to Louis occurred spontaneously while they were still seated eating the warm baguettes with cheese to end their meal.

'*Maman?*' the boy enquired, his voice tremulous yet promising elation.

Glancing towards the doorway, Jane was entranced by the sturdy lad whose dark curly hair and brown eyes witnessed to his half-Spanish blood.

'I'm not your mother, love,' she said swiftly, and ached to hug him.

'*Voici mon amie*, Jane,' Henri told the lad, extending an arm towards him.

Louis bounded into the kitchen and was swept up on to Henri's knee.

Bernadette sighed, gazed heavenwards. 'And so, now the two of you will have no peace. Louis is a demanding boy.'

'And has no one else,' Henri reminded her, as he offered the boy cheese from his plate.

Louis was the one who insisted that Jane must be shown around the whole of the château, and took her hand to ensure that she missed nothing during the tour. Only when they reached one carved wooden door that was locked did he hesitate, and gaze up imploringly at Henri.

'My workroom,' Henri explained as he slid a key into its lock. 'Territory forbidden to this young man, for reasons that will become evident.'

Furnished with antique mahogany pieces but clearly as some form of office, the substantial room was dominated by a huge desk where reference books surrounded large sheets of paper. 'You're not an architect too?' asked Jane, realizing that she had no idea of his occupation.

Henri shook his head. 'Nothing so artistic. I am a cartographer, have my own business, working from here is good economics.'

'That's interesting.'

'*Intéressant.*' Louis declared.

Surprised, Jane bent down to speak to the lad. '*Oui, intéressant.*'

Henri sighed when she stood upright again. 'He learns too readily, I fear. And hears too much, which is the reason that Bernadette and I have to use English for certain discussions.'

'About his future?'

'His history also. But all too soon he will be well aware of everything that we know about him. Too much so for his comfort.'

As if eager to change the topic, Henri led her to the desk, and began explaining the map which he'd recently begun to create. Well-drilled on avoiding any potential mishap, Louis hung back from the desk, leaning against one of the leather armchairs while he regarded them solemnly.

'*Vous êtes très jolie. Voulez-vous rester avec moi, Jane?*' the boy suggested.

Delighted, yet embarrassed, Jane gave a tiny shrug as she looked to Henri.

He laughed. 'So – that is aired between us now. I was hoping that I might find some way to ask you that question about staying here. Without risking the misinterpretation of my motive.'

'Wouldn't my staying be a nuisance?'

'You have discovered that I have an efficient housekeeper,

16

you shall see that we have several rooms unoccupied here. Why should you refuse? Or do you have a further reservation in Montrichard perhaps?'

'Nothing booked, no.'

Evidently interpreting their expressions if not their words, Louis appeared to bounce as he rushed to grasp Jane's hand again. His sticky fingers seemed to generate a warmth that fuelled her entire body. Or was that rush of heat connected with her recognition that Henri also was delighted?

Her visit to the château developed rapidly. From an interesting tour of a building where she felt an immediate affinity with the ambience, it became a stay in the home of someone with whom a strong rapport was readily being created.

By the time that she had seen the entire house Jane was empathizing with Henri's regret over its decline. She yearned to have a hand in restoring the place.

Many walls to the rear looked in danger of falling down, while several windows were devoid of glass. To her, it appeared that some error in its original design could perhaps have generated a certain instability.

Eventually, Henri remarked on her architectural training, joked that he might have invited her there for her expertise.

'Use it then while I'm here,' she insisted. Louis had gone to bed for the night, and they were sitting on at the kitchen table following another delicious meal. Jane needed to give a little in return for the welcome she was receiving there.

Henri brought out plans he had drafted for the reconstruction. And Jane soon recognized that his claim to being purely an amateur underestimated his ability.

Studying in detail, she indicated one or two points, safety measures which should not be overlooked, then went with him to look once again at the sections of the château to be renovated.

They talked long into the night until, somewhat embarrassed, Henri apologized for keeping her from her bed. Jane had been too enthralled to care, told him how she felt, and received a long, appreciative look.

'You might be my twin soul,' he said. 'And so clever that I marvel at your understanding of what I am about.'

Henri took her hand, pressed it to his lips, while they stood in the doorway of the old dining room. His eyes were searching her own. When his next kiss was on her mouth Jane could be neither surprised nor dismayed. Kissing him back was as instinctive and as *right* as everything between them which founded this friendship.

She was no more surprised when Henri drew away, his smile rueful, grey eyes revealing neither apology nor regret, but echoing her own latent longing.

'You must go to your room,' he told her evenly, the sudden tension in him witnessing to the power of his emotions.

Throughout the next day, and the one after they continued in perfect agreement – about their feelings unexpressed as much as their delight in each other's company. Jane advised him further on restoring his home, and afterwards he insisted they take time off to visit several of the famous châteaux of the region.

At Chambord, Henri watched as she admired the carved stone staircase, and smiled when she gasped over further examples of the château's intricate stonework. In Chenonceau's long gallery spanning the river Cher he told Jane how his mother had nursed there while it was a military hospital during the Great War.

Sharing the experience of these places that interested her so deeply made her certain that she and Henri did indeed possess a special affinity.

Each night they parted with a kiss, and on the day that she must leave for home Jane felt that his embrace would make her heart sore. Emotions that morning all seemed barely disguised. Louis wept copiously on learning she must depart.

Straightening her back after bending to reassure the lad, Jane glanced to Henri for assistance in comforting the child. Were Henri's grey eyes really gleaming with tears? Shaken, Jane could not fathom how to interpret this evidence of emotion.

It was all due to nothing more than the continental temperament, Jane decided as she drove as swiftly as she dared along the winding French lanes. Yet dismissing the feelings she had read in Henri's eyes proved far from easy. Each château that she neared seemed only to remind her of the one in which she had stayed. Of the man who had relished sharing the love of his home with her. And of the part of her which she felt would remain for always within its walls.

It will be simpler when I'm back in Yorkshire, Jane assured herself as she eventually boarded the ferry. The familiar moors and woods, smoky towns, and mills clacking with machinery would return her to reality.

She had not reckoned with the reminders brought by sudden glimpses of fine Yorkshire stone houses – reminders that over near the Loire there existed homes created just as affectionately. And many with comparable, if different, skills.

The sharpest memories of all arose when she unloaded the pieces of *tuffeau* stone that had been the purpose of her visit. Would her feelings always remain this restless now that she'd experienced for a while the life of that quiet French region?

Her father enthused at once, testing his tools on the stone moments after asking how her journey had been. Alfred Townsend had cherished the urge to carve for so long. He greatly admired Eric Gill whose figures of Ariel and Prospero so impressed him when the new Broadcasting House was finished. Might there be just one compensation now that he himself could no longer increase the success of the family firm by concentrating on more mundane aspects of the building trade?

Interrupting preparation of their evening meal to look into Alf's workroom, Sheila smiled to see him and Jane fascinated by the new materials. Happen this would be better for him than reading. If it kept Alf happy, she'd not ask for more.

Jack and Phil came in together after work, dust from the building site covering them from dark hair to their boots. They won a reproof from their mother for tramping dirt through the house, and ignored her reproach. The whole family were aware that the business would only continue due to their efforts.

'You actually got there all right then, our Jane!' Phil exclaimed.

'And back again,' added Jack, pretending amazement, the blue eyes like his brother's teasing . . . 'Took you long enough though.'

'Got lost, did you?' Phil enquired.

Jane turned to grin at them. 'Actually, no. Matter of fact, I was invited to spend a few nights in one of the châteaux.'

'Oh, la-di-dah!' said Jack. 'Tuppence to speak to you now, eh?'

'Bad enough before, with her having qualifications, an' all,' Phil put in.

In the kitchen their mother was singing 'Just a Song at Twilight', one of her favourites, while the smell of her steak puddding wafted through the house . . .

Jane gazed at her father, towards Phil and Jack, and she smiled. She was home again in the West Riding, back with her family where the evening ahead seemed as predictable as ever. Phil's latest girlfriend would expect him to take her out. No doubt Jack's fiancée Cynthia would call round to see him.

Jane had never really taken to the girl, who seemed very *forward*. Cynthia had confided in her too fully. Surely, no woman who wasn't married yet ought to be advocating the birth control introduced by Marie Stopes! Jane wouldn't quarrel with Cynthia. She'd be glad to spend a few hours in her father's workroom.

She hoped that perhaps it could be that she had made things here fractionally better than they were. She must now apply her attention to settling back into her own routine. She would learn tomorrow from Hugh Dunstan in the office what progress there had been on that school she was designing.

There would be no time – maybe there *should be* no time for looking back to the exquisite few days she had spent all those miles away from reality, from her home. In the valley that she so readily was learning to love.

Two

Alfred Townsend seemed obsessed, spending hours every day conjuring from *le tuffeau* his vision of a magpie, readily capturing the distinctive set of head and tail. His wife was too appalled to appreciate his skill in representing the bird's feathers, 'Whatever do you want to choose a magpie for? It'll bring us bad luck.'

'Nay, lass. We've had our share of that, it's over. Don't take on so. This'll do us no harm.' A country lad reared on the edge of Midgley Moor, he'd grown up with the wildlife among these glorious hills, knew every superstition regarding all their creatures, and still possessed this fondness for many supposed to be unlucky.

'Happen I'm challenging fate,' he continued eventually. 'I feel that I might do that now. Our fortunes are changing, think on. Now our Jane's found summat that I can tackle.'

He knew Jane didn't care what he might choose to carve: she would relish the fact that he was working, rather than question the advisability of his subject. He'd suggested their Jack should find a spot for this bird on the house they'd almost completed. The carving wasn't anywhere near perfect, but this was only the start. Maybe beside the chimney stack or on the gable end somewhere . . . Folk could look at it, puzzle a bit, even have a laugh.

Jack was willing to indulge him. He was twenty-three now, happy to humour the father who no longer prevented him from having his head regarding everything Townsend's were building. And, viewed from the ground with nothing to convey the black and white of its plumage, there was little chance of

21

anyone identifying the creature more closely than as just some kind of bird.

Phil was less happy about attaching it to the new house. Three years younger than his brother and more like their mother in temperament, he wasn't eager to risk encouraging misfortune.

'Don't be so soft, lad,' Jack scoffed, on the day that they took the carving to the site of the new house. 'Just fix it up there by t' gable end, like you would any bit of decoration. And thank your stars that it's not you as is reduced to sitting carving at home instead of building stuff you can take pride in.'

Jack had felt with his father the hurt of limitations so suddenly inflicted. He also knew how alarmed his brother had been by the shock of Alfred's accident. Phil remained daunted still, he might be dreading some additional tragedy.

When Jane drove past the new house, she smiled over the bird perched there as though recently alighted. She became determined to take their father to the site.

'Aye, aye, one day. Thanks, lass,' Alfred responded when she rushed through to tell him.

In his workroom converted from the former wash-kitchen, he was beginning to fashion a large squirrel from the *tuffeau*. He'd suggested Jane might incorporate it in her designs for the school. She had laughed, called the suggestion premature. But she certainly wasn't amused about the delays to having her plans accepted.

'There's no way of knowing yet that it'll be built to my drawings, is there?'

Her great disappointment since returning from France was the evident reluctance of those in authority to press on with any major constructions. It was all on account of the unstable international situation, Jane knew. And that was doing nothing for her peace of mind.

She had received a letter from Henri soon after arriving home, and had written back immediately, elated to be in touch with him. When he wrote again, much of his concern was for young Louis, whose future seemed increasingly uncertain.

Jane gathered that the Spanish civil war was gradually heading towards a conclusion, but instead of easing communications as Henri had anticipated, contact with people in Spain appeared to worsen. He had failed to get in touch with either of Louis' parents, and the three-year-old was growing more and more perturbed by the need to find his mother.

Or a mother, Henri wrote: *He is too young to have clear memories of her now, I hope you will not be annoyed to learn that he speaks often of his "Maman Jane".*

Annoyed? How could she feel anything of the kind? She had taken to the little lad from the moment she'd met him. Jane only hoped that before too long she would have the opportunity to see the boy again. To say nothing of his *Oncle* Henri. Every reminder of the difficult communications within Europe strengthened her fear. One day she could be prevented from contacting anybody in France.

Jane was waiting now for her father to complete this second carving. Much larger than the magpie, the squirrel would take longer, but once it was finished to Alfred's satisfaction she would visit France and select further supplies of stone.

Henri had written insisting she stay in his home. He claimed that he needed further architectural advice concerning reconstruction. Jane would be more delighted than Henri might guess simply to make use of some of her knowledge.

Lacking any decision on that school project, Hugh Dunstan was struggling to occupy himself and his son with drafting plans for buildings that might go forward for construction. He was the boss, and seemed content to overlook Jane's need to be tackling something fresh. She foresaw no prospect of anything interesting.

Autumn had turned to winter, and there in the West Riding the frosts and frequent snow always caused interruptions in work for the building trade. This year seemed worse than many she recalled, Jane was struggling not to feel disgruntled, but she hadn't trained so diligently simply to have time on her hands.

* * *

Christmas became just as subdued as her working life. Jane yearned to escape to Henri. Only the second since their father's accident, the family couldn't avoid looking back to the splendid celebrations enjoyed in the days when he was fit.

Jack was particularly quiet throughout the holiday. Jane wasn't surprised when he admitted on the day work began again that he and Cynthia had quarrelled.

'Don't let on to Mum, I don't want her making a fuss,' he confided as he put his boots on. 'Cynthia wanted to get wed in the new year, but I'm again' it.'

'Are you, love? Why's that then?' She might not get on particularly well with Jack's fiancée, but there was nothing grave to dislike about her. Jane knew that Cynthia would think her old-fashioned for believing girls shouldn't need to even think about birth control *before* they were married.

'I've got to give my attention to seeing the firm keeps going, haven't I? Now it's up to me to make sure jobs are coming in. I'm not in the right frame of mind for marrying, starting a new life, and all that. Cynthia wants us to have our own house, do it up an so on. And then she'll want bairns – at least a couple, I'll bet.'

'But they wouldn't be coming along straight away, would they, Jack? And couldn't you explain about the house – that she might have to wait a bit before you bought one and made it look nice for her?'

Her brother shrugged. 'Eh, I don't know. It just feels like a lot of anxiety to me – a burden, if you must know.'

'But you would want a family one day, wouldn't you?' Since meeting young Louis, Jane recognized that a child made any house feel like a proper home.

'*One day*, aye. But that won't be for a long while.'

And Cynthia is doing something about that, thought Jane, but couldn't mention what the girl had confided. Evidently, the couple hadn't discussed the matter. Jane felt sorry for them both. She was still wondering if there was anything she ought to say when Phil came thundering down the stairs to the hall.

'Not on about that again, are you? You'll bore our Jane to

death with your moaning on, like you have me.' He turned to his sister. 'You tell him, why don't you? He doesn't deserve a lass like her, if he won't pay the price. Of course, she expects a plain gold ring on her finger, they've been courting long enough. If it were me, I'd be off like a shot.'

'If I know you,' Jack chided him heavily, 'it will be like a shot that you get married. A shotgun wedding, you'll be having, if your carrying on is owt to go by!'

Phil laughed, gave Jane a wink. 'Happen so, and I'll not be complaining. The way our Jack dithers, scared to take owt on, he'll be past it afore he makes his mind up. And Cynthia'll have her home that she makes no secret of wanting, and the kids an' all, with some livelier bloke.'

Watching her brothers stomping side by side to the van, Jane shook her head. She'd grown more sympathetic towards Cynthia, if she couldn't condone all her ideas. If Jack really had good reason to believe Cynthia would want to have children, he seemed unable to understand how much the lass wanted *him*. Cynthia appeared ready to consider sacrifices that would spare him burdensome responsibilities.

Jane had always thought it was wicked to deny children their existence, but times were changing, and sometimes circumstances forced different priorities upon people. Today, she was thankful for Jack's sake that the firm still had some work to complete on that large house. She hoped that tackling the job would help take his mind off his personal life. Perhaps endow a different perspective, one that allowed him to acknowledge his need for creating a home with Cynthia.

Glancing at her watch, Jane realized that she was in danger of being late for her own work. Not that there was much joy in returning to the architect's office which not long ago had seemed the most exciting place where anyone could work.

As though to confirm her dread, Hugh shook his head wearily when she asked if there was any news on that school she'd been designing.

'Only that the local authority are not contemplating going ahead, as yet. I've been thinking that you'd best apply yourself to something else. You could read up on what the government have in mind. They announced, didn't they, last March that they've set aside eleven million pounds for RAF aerodromes.'

Jane had no choice but to try and discover what precisely would be required. She couldn't visualize that as being anything more interesting than a lot of concrete runways and hangars for the aircraft. There would be accommodation for their crews, naturally, but she didn't suppose they would be better than functional buildings that certainly wouldn't demand much of anyone's flair for design.

Within the family business January brought even less cause for optimism. One of their clients who had asked them to provide estimates for building a commercial garage workshop announced that it must be postponed. At the first opportunity he would be joining the army, where he intended offering his skills to maintain military vehicles.

During the same week they also were informed that the scheme for a whole succession of semi-detached homes, which in prospect had delighted them, was to be shelved, *indefinitely*. This meant that the large house now virtually ready for occupation had become the last substantial project on their books. Jack and Phil began looking for the repair work which was more readily available than fresh constructions.

Ever practical, and determined he wouldn't allow Townsend's to sink, Jack also followed up rumours of builders being needed to make underground bunkers.

'Whatever for?' asked Sheila when Jack mentioned this over midday dinner.

Alfred gave his wife a look, tried to manage a smile. 'To protect them as will have charge of defending our country, I suppose. There is every likelihood that we're going to be at war, you know, love.'

'I'm not listening to that sort of defeatist talk,' Sheila asserted sharply. 'Everybody had more than enough with that last lot. They'll all negotiate now, there's no country as really wants all that fighting.'

Jane watched their father's expression, and recognized that

he was searching his mind for some reassurance he might offer. He found none. She glanced towards her grandfather who had joined them for a meal.

William Townsend shrugged old shoulders which had remained strong and upright despite – or even because of – all his years spent working on building sites.

'What do you think, Granddad?' she asked him.

'I'm afraid your father's right. Men don't learn, except by experience. And them as fought in the last lot aren't the ones who'll be making the decisions these days.'

Alfred was nodding wearily, his forehead crinkling with concern. Jane saw in that moment how incapacity had aged the man. His lined features and greying hair made him appear as old as his own father. They might have been brothers, she thought, appalled, and wondered what this threatening war would do to them.

The gloomy forecast of impending conflict soon combined with her frustration about having no challenging project to design. There was talk now of fortifications being necessary around many of the coasts, but Jane had no inclination to even find out what exactly the various government bodies would require.

She was making enquiries concerning airfields as Hugh Dunstan had suggested, but they weren't at all the kind of thing that inspired her. Jane wondered how long she could resist being obliged to draw plans for something connected with fighting.

On the day in March 1939 when her brother Jack set out to learn for himself all about government requirements, Jane had taken unpaid leave to embark on her second journey to reach the French countryside.

Today, she was travelling by train – Henri's idea, which he'd expressed to allay his own anxiety about her undertaking such a long trip by car. If anyone else had made the suggestion, Jane would have argued to prove her continued ability and self-sufficiency. Since Henri had come up with the notion and insisted he would be happy to meet her train in Orléans, she was warmed by how much he cared.

Throughout the journey she acknowledged that she wasn't sorry to avoid driving through France alone. Mr Chamberlain may have asserted only the other day that the international situation was 'satisfactory', she couldn't help feeling uneasy. She had left home trying to forget news that Hitler had invaded Prague.

Seeing Henri as soon as she stepped down from the train in Orléans drove from her mind any apprehension about the possibility of war, along with disappointments in her work. His smile was bright, warming thin features until his grey eyes were gleaming.

'Jane, *ma chère*,' he exclaimed, and drew her to him in a fierce hug. 'I have been so afraid this day would never come, that you would not come.'

'For a welcome like this, I'll always come over here to see you.'

He kissed her firmly on the lips then moved slightly away, but only to grasp her hand.

'The car is outside the station, let us go. I am eager to take you home.'

'And how is life for you?' Jane enquired, he had seemed so far from her, she had been worried by not knowing what to believe about events in Europe.

Henri smiled again as they hurried out towards the car. 'Good, in many ways quite good. I finally have contacted Louis' father. I believe that he will agree that I shall adopt the boy.'

'Really? But what about the lad's mother?' Jane couldn't credit that any mother would be willing to let her son go to someone else.

Opening the car door for her, Henri sighed. 'Sadly, Gabrielle did not survive. She died in bombing somewhere in Spain. And so – the father, who you remember hardly knows Louis, cannot comprehend how he might take care of him.'

'Are there no grandparents then, are they dead too?'

'They are alive, I understand, but Louis' father is no longer welcome in their home. He is a communist.'

'And they are not?'

Henri shrugged as he started the engine and moved out into the flow of traffic. 'I can believe that they do not approve his determination which seems to drive him to fight for that cause. I myself can only feel very thankful that he wishes to free himself of responsibilities that could divert attention from his aims.'

'And how will you cope?' Jane couldn't visualize that any other single man she knew would wish to adopt a small boy.

Henri laughed. 'I believe that Louis and I have developed a very good understanding. He is good and I am happy, or he is naughty and I get angry. He does not like when I am angry.'

Jane laughed with him. 'And Bernadette, will she be pleased to have Louis remain at the château?'

'*Mais naturellement*, do not forget that she has cared for children since I myself was a tiny boy. She tells to me that Louis make her to feel young again.'

'Until he becomes really mischievous perhaps?'

Henri shrugged away the suggestion. 'I do not worry so, and Bernadette also, I think. We love *le petit garçon*, that is enough.'

While he concentrated on driving out through the city Jane pondered Henri's decision, and his easy acceptance of a father's role. She wished she possessed one quarter of his instinctive optimism. Maybe growing up among the brooding Yorkshire hills during the deprivation of the twenties and thirties had conditioned her to being cautious.

It was only during the last few years that Townsend's had become a firm of any importance. Until their name had acquired some weight there had been little reason for rash decisions. And they were Yorkshire folk, she reflected wryly, careful with their money!

As Henri spoke of his future plans for Louis while driving along, Jane began to understand that there was little comparison between her family's situation and that of the man beside her. While Townsend's recent success might count for less if current uncertainties in the trade reduced their business, Henri seemed to be in a position where he had no need to dread a massive reduction in finances.

This soon became evident when he spoke of the renovations to his château.

'I have not had very much time to progress greatly, but I do have most of the necessary materials to hand now. Demand for maps relating to various parts of Europe is soaring – a fact which, although alarming in itself, has created the wherewithal to provide the things that my home is needing.'

When he went on to remind her that he required her professional advice, Jane smiled again.

'It seems an age since I tackled anything remotely interesting,' she told him, and explained the delays and frustrations that the threat of war seemed to be creating for some British architects.

When their drive through the frosty countryside ended and Henri parked outside his sunlit château Jane felt her spirits racing. This was such a beautiful place, she could hardly believe that she would have the opportunity to draft plans for part of its restoration.

It was Louis, however, who delighted her even more than that prospect. With Bernadette struggling to restrain him, he was waiting in the large entrance hall. The instant that Henri unlocked the door and ushered Jane through ahead of him, the boy hurtled across the flagstones towards her.

Laughing, she caught him up in her arms, felt eager kisses smothering her cheeks.

'*Bienvenue, ma chère amie,*' Louis exclaimed, and then in English: 'I am so ver' happy to see you again.'

'And I'm happy to be here, love,' Jane responded as she set him down.

Henri had caught up with her, she felt his arm about her shoulders. 'We are all very happy,' he insisted.

Bernadette bustled towards Jane, greeting her warmly as she picked up her luggage.

Set in Stone

'You will follow me, please? I show you to your room, and then the meal will be cooked, I think.'

It was so good to be back. Her room was the one where she'd slept during her previous stay and Jane glanced all around her, smiling. Very little had changed, but she could see that the walls had received a fresh coat of the creamy-coloured paint. It combined beautifully with the stone surrounding windows and door and framing the fireplace. The curtains and bed cover were the ones she recalled, old but clean and bright, of red velvet. Their shade reminded her of the chenille table cover in her mother's kitchen.

Very briefly, Jane felt saddened. That red cover always forced her to face the reality of how greatly her father's accident had altered everything. He so hated sleeping in their former dining room. She supposed her mother must hate that too, but Sheila Townsend didn't believe in complaining. Especially when a situation could not be changed.

It could be improved, though, Jane reflected. And was being already since she had found the *tuffeau* stone for carving. Following this visit there should be greater supplies shipped to England.

Alfred Townsend had plans already. He meant to carve items which were more important than the decorative creatures engaging him so far. He'd so readily mastered working this softer stone that he intended now to create architraves, lintels for doors and windows which might be incorporated into the firm's next building project.

Jane had seen his sketches, and approved the manner in which this special stone would be used. Because it whitened while being hardened by weathering it should become a pleasing feature to offset the varying shades of Yorkshire sandstone.

She was pleased to tell Henri this during their meal when one of his first questions was about the success of her father's new work.

'It has gone really well, thank heaven. He's a different man now.'

31

'And so you must swiftly arrange further supplies of *tuffeau*, yes? In case we find all too soon that war becomes inevitable.'

Jane sighed. 'You do believe that will happen then?'

'I am afraid that it cannot be avoided. However, we must not speak more of war today. You are come to me, and I mean that we both shall be joyful.'

Tired though she was that night, Jane could not doubt that her stay in Henri's home would be good. Whether through their previous meeting or the letters which although never intimate had established mutual understanding, he certainly seemed to know her well. Sensing her lack of energy following the long journey, Henri led her through to a sofa before the fire as soon as they wandered down the staircase together from saying goodnight to Louis.

Handing her a brandy glass, Henri smiled as he sat beside her. 'This should ensure that you relax, and that you will sleep when you go to your room. In the morning you must be refreshed, for I shall wish to show you the work that I have completed here. Together with my plans for further renovations. That is when I hope that you will give me your advice.'

When he went on to insist that he would pay for her expertise, Jane protested.

'I couldn't take anything from you! You've made me so welcome here, twice now. You're a friend, Henri.'

'And you a professional architect, you should learn to accept fees for your knowledge. I admire you very greatly for your skills, you know.'

'Well, I'll have to think about that. I have taken time off to come here. But that was to see about buying more *tuffeau*. And the way things are at present, there's not much call for my usual work. I'm very upset that the school I'd drawn the plans for is extremely unlikely to go ahead in the foreseeable future.'

'And your family business, are builders finding enough work?'

'Depends if you're being choosy or not. Our Jack's gone off somewhere to try and find out what the government want building. From what I've read it's going to be bunkers to protect ministry folk and so on. Plus a lot of defence stuff, and new airfields.'

'Not exactly picturesque, eh?'

'Not exactly, no.'

'All the more reason why we must make your stay here more interesting.'

His words were simple enough, his ideas of how they would spend their time were hardly spectacular, but Jane felt that once again Henri was providing precisely what she needed.

Although he was a busy man, the thought that he'd given to preparing for her visit showed how much she mattered to him. Henri *cared* about her, and Jane had almost forgotten how good that could feel. Since her father's accident everyone had concentrated their concern and their caring on him.

Am I growing soft? Jane wondered, not really understanding this side of her which appreciated a bit of tenderness.

The brandy did help her to relax and sleep that night, just as Henri's company seemed to bestow the necessary calm within her. She awakened in the morning feeling infinitely better than she had for weeks.

After breakfast – a boisterous meal because of Louis' excitement to have her there – Henri took Jane to inspect the reconstruction work he'd completed since her previous visit.

She was pleased to see that one of the outer walls which had threatened to turn into a ruin was now rebuilt as far as the top of the second floor windows.

'That was the easy part, I think,' he told Jane when she complimented him on all he'd achieved. 'The later stages will prove difficult, especially when I have to ensure that everything is correct where it supports the roof.'

'Have you got any photos of what it looked like originally? If you have, I might be able to work out how it was constructed.'

'That would be immensely helpful. I do believe I may locate photographs. Or failing that earlier paintings.'

They continued to walk around the exterior to where he showed Jane the way the stone surrounding the dining-room windows was renovated. 'You may recollect that we had to remove the frames as well as the glass, because I feared that they might fall away.'

'And now they're as good as ever. You have got a lot finished.'

'With help, in this case,' Henri admitted. 'I employed a local glazier, a brilliant man who also confirmed how the surrounding stonework should be completed.'

In search of old pictures, Henri took her through into the room where normally he engaged in map-making. Jane was surprised to see no work in evidence.

'You haven't cleared everything away to provide space for architectural stuff?'

'Not exactly, no. You may not realize that maps of Europe, already much in demand, could prove useful to all sides in any potential conflict. I have removed all my professional work to a secure place, where I am not known.'

'Isn't that going to be awkward for you? Unless it's not far away.'

Henri smiled. 'I can tell *you*. Everything important for my work is in a small home I have, in Montrichard.'

Jane was puzzled. 'I didn't know you had a home there. So why were you staying in the hotel that time?'

He continued to smile. 'I was not. I was merely dining in the hotel. My apartment is the upper rooms above one of the farms just south of the river.'

'Ah.'

'If you experienced my attempts to cook, you would know that I need to eat someone else's cooking!'

Jane laughed affectionately, but she was keen to help plan the reconstruction Henri mentioned. Didn't she already feel it was too long since she'd tackled an architectural challenge, what could be more interesting than this beautiful home?

He had found photographs of the exterior of the château which showed the original roof. Checking that he wouldn't disturb her concentration, Henri drew up a chair beside the one he'd indicated for Jane.

She began to sketch her interpretation of how the walls must be made to support the roof, explaining while drawing the way certain factors must be considered.

'As you may understand, proportion is a matter of relating breadth to height. But did you know that the rules governing good proportion were formed through studying ancient buildings? That should reassure you regarding your own reconstruction – I'm not likely to come up with too many newfangled notions.'

'Your preferred styling is traditionalist then?'

'Old-fashioned, you mean?' Jane teased, with a sideways glance from hazel-green eyes.

Henri met her gaze with his own, and held that link between them. Jane felt her heart rate increasing, heard her own breathing quicken, deep within her a pulse hammered its response to him.

She hauled her attention away to the paper on the desk, checked the shaking of her hand, which threatened to wreck the design she was creating for him. She would be so embarrassed if Henri should guess how fiercely he attracted her.

Her voice slightly unsteady, she began explaining the materials she had depicted.

'The stone you already have, then tiles for the roof – did you say they were slate?'

'I do not know if I told you, but slate has been used originally, yes. Tell me, Jane – do you always have to calculate how much of every material must be used?'

'That's normally the job of a quantity surveyor, but an architect needs to understand what will be needed for a particular construction.'

'And do you attend every site to surpervise?'

'If you mean being there all the time, no. On big projects, a clerk of works is employed to keep an eye on progress.'

'And which part of your work do you enjoy the most?'

'So far, it's really only been the planning I've had much experience of, it's not all that long since I finished as a student and came into the business. But from what I saw during my training I reckon the biggest thrill has to be seeing something you've designed absolutely complete.'

'I am sure that must be so. Let us hope that after my home is restored you may have many opportunities for appreciating this work to which you are contributing.'

Jane contained an excited gasp. She had so hoped that Henri might wish to continue to see her. She could feel his grey eyes searching her face, but she mustn't yet respond as she was longing to. That certainly would prevent her from concentrating on any work. And this seemed so soon – almost too soon in their friendship to be acknowledging how passionately she wanted him.

She could try to ignore this additional dimension and still be happy in Henri's company, be content that her task should be useful to him. Although when Henri so readily understood her completed drawings she wondered if he really needed her specialist skill!

On the following day they returned outdoors to stand in sunlight where even the breeze seemed to carry a hint of early summer. Comparing her plans with the good stone château itself, Jane smiled to see him nodding his approval.

Henri insisted afterwards that it must be his turn to be of use to her. They drove through the countryside to the Laigret brothers, where, with Henri's help, she swiftly made arrangements for additional supplies of *le tuffeau* to be delivered to her father in England.

Before returning to the château Henri drove closer to Montrichard where he relished showing Jane his tiny apartment. Reached by a narrow stair, it was over a farmhouse which appeared to be one of the oldest in the vicinity. The flat itself had the slanting floors and uneven walls so often found in ancient buildings. At the window of its small living room Jane exclaimed, delighted to see the castle keep a short distance away across the river.

'And there is the church of Sainte-Croix,' Henri told her. 'Formerly the château chapel. It was there in 1476 that the future King Louis XII was married to Jeanne de France, Louis XI's daughter.'

They relaxed during the rest of that day, savouring the excellent meals which Bernadette provided, and having fun whenever Louis insisted on being with them.

'I foresee that a certain young man might eventually become more company than we wish during the whole of *every* day, do you not agree, my Jane?' Henri suggested, grey eyes glittering after the housekeeper had whisked the lad away to his bed.

Jane was compelled to smile as she agreed. From the moment those architectural plans had ceased to occupy her, she'd found the passion that Henri awakened so startlingly obtrusive she suspected he might be aware of the tremors pulsing through her.

'Will you forgive me a quite personal question?' he enquired, suddenly serious.

'Go ahead, so long as you'd forgive if I can't answer.'

'Is there anyone special in your life at home in Yorkshire? Any man, I mean, who is important to you?'

Jane shook her head. 'No one at all. I was too busy learning as quickly as I could. When Dad had his accident – well, it didn't put me in the mood for going out a lot.' She didn't bore him with mentioning how her support was needed in the home.

'And for me also, there has been no one who mattered so much to me that I must neglect the rest of my life. Since I completed my education I inherited this house and – the rest you know.' Henri paused, smiled. 'I am thankful that there is no one else in your life. That fact may permit me to hope.'

Those few words were enough for Jane. When Henri kissed her she responded without reservation, felt her own mouth yielding to the pressure of his lips. His tongue was pressing at her teeth, they parted and exhilaration surged through her.

They drew back slightly, but only so that Henri could lead her to a sofa. He pulled her down with him into its cushions. Arms holding her close, he kissed her again, his mouth insistent, demanding, matching the power and urgency of her own soaring need.

The telephone rang on the table near their heads, jolted them to spring apart. Answering the call, Henri listened briefly, frowning.

'For you, Jane. Prepare yourself please, the news is not good.'

Her brother Phil was on the line, sounding agitated. 'I've had such a job getting in touch with you. Had to ring the folk you're getting that stone from. They didn't know where you were, but they did say you'd called on them with Mr Bodin.'

'Henri, that's right. What is it, Phil, what's happened? Is it Dad?' She felt tears choking her already, could not bear the thought that something might have happened to her father while she was so far away.

'Nay, lass, not him. It's Grandfather. He had a stroke last night, didn't survive beyond this morning. I had to let you know. Can't contact our Jack. And Dad's taking it that badly . . .'

Jane was so shocked that she was struggling to force herself to grasp all the details. Phil evidently was too disturbed to be anything like coherent.

'Dad's in a state, you see. On account of not being able to do owt. He wants our Jack home . . .'

'Yes, you said. Never mind Jack for now, I'll be on my way back as soon as I've packed.'

'Aye, but there's such a lot to do. I don't rightly know what, or *how*. And Mum's gone to bed . . .'

Additional alarm rushed right through her. 'What's the matter with her? Don't tell me she's poorly . . .' Jane had never felt this perturbed about being far away from her family.

'No, I don't think it's that,' said Phil, but sounding so doubtful that he did nothing to ease her anxiety.

'Well, what then?' Jane persisted. 'It's not like Mum to take to her bed.'

'She did sit up most of the night at the hospital, happen that's it . . .'

'Naturally, it will be. I think you'd better stop panicking, Phil. That won't get anything done, and it won't make you feel you can cope either. Hasn't Dad told you what needs doing straight away, contacting an undertaker and stuff?'

'Aye, he has. Only he expects me to go and see them, and to

get the death certificate when the hospital release it. You know how I hate them places.'

'Nobody likes 'em much,' Jane responded, then took pity on him. 'Tell Dad I'm on my way. And Mum an' all, when she wakens. If you feel you really can't manage to see to everything, it'll have to wait till I arrive there.'

'But when will that be?' Phil asked, sighing weightily.

'I haven't the slightest idea, but I shan't waste any time.'

Jane hung up feeling quite annoyed with her young brother. She'd always known he was softer than their Jack, but he was a man now, shouldn't need to be relying on his sister.

'Am I right to believe that it is your father who has died?' Henri enquired, his grey eyes solemn.

'No, no, my grandfather. It's still upsetting, though, he's – he *was* such a lovely man. Always a worker, an' all – continued to do the books, keeping an eye on the family firm right to the end. You'd have liked him,' she added, and realized how deeply she was longing to have Henri know all her family.

'I could not avoid hearing that you were arranging to return home. Does that mean you must leave early in the morning?'

'If I can't get a train tonight.'

'Tonight?' Henri was appalled. They were only just beginning to really know each other, he had so much to say. About his feelings for her, about his hopes for the future.

'Would it be an awful nuisance to drive me into Orléans? There'd still be trains for Paris from there, wouldn't there? I'd be that much further on then; even if there weren't trains during the night to take me across France, I'd be able to get the earliest one out of Paris tomorrow morning.'

Henri could only do whatever was possible to help. While Jane rushed off to thrust everything into her suitcase, he told Bernadette what had occurred, and asked her to ensure that Louis was all right during his absence.

The motherly housekeeper hurried to Jane to sympathize, and offer assistance with her packing. Finding that task well on the way to completion, Bernadette hastened to her kitchen.

When Jane was ready to depart the housekeeper presented

her with a small basket containing wine, bread and cold ham for the journey.

Jane thanked her warmly, and kissed her on both cheeks. 'Please hug Louis for me, tell him I was sad to leave without saying goodbye.'

Frowning anxiously, Henri settled her into the passenger seat of his car. He did not believe Jane's leaving at night was a good idea, but he hadn't known how to prevent her without appearing inconsiderate of her grief. As he saw it, the only redeeming factor in this situation was the drive to Orléans. He was relying on their remaining time together for an opportunity to speak of his growing love for her.

Turning off from his drive into the quiet lane Henri began to talk. 'It is very unfortunate that your family loss has – has intervened at this moment.'

'Because you'd more plans you wanted me to draw?' asked Jane, sounding quite vague.

'Not that only, no.'

She interrupted swiftly. 'I can post some drawings to you with a few notes.'

'No, Jane, you misunderstand. I was speaking of *us*, of . . .'

When she spoke again, it was clear that she was not listening, or certainly not heeding him. 'It won't be until after the funeral that I can post anything off to you, but I shan't forget.'

'Jane *ma chère*, I am not concerned to have those plans, that is not worrying me.'

'That's all right then. It's going to be awkward, you see. Our Phil's surprised me, you know. I thought he'd more about him nor that. I know he doesn't like hospitals, who does? But he could have gone to the office or whatever there, and asked about that certificate. My dad'll be that upset because he can't get out and sort everything himself. And he – Dad – will be heartbroken about his father, they were always that close.

'It was working together like that, you see, expanding the company. And the whole family's got such strong ties. Grandfather was forever coming to the house for his dinner. I'm going to miss him so much . . .'

Her tears weren't unexpected, indeed Henri felt that she might later benefit from the release of weeping. But this did create within the car emotions which precluded speaking of the passion that was his need of Jane.

'I am so sorry about your loss,' he said, 'I wish I knew how to comfort you.'

'Thank you. I'll be all right, I suppose, once I get home.'

Henri nodded, quelled his sigh. It was rapidly becoming evident that Jane truly felt that she belonged only with her own family. How could he even have fantasized that she might one day come to him? Make her home here?

In the station at Orléans, the Paris train stood waiting at the platform. Jane thanked Henri again, kissed him on both cheeks. He might have found reassurance in the kisses, had he not seen her treat old Bernadette in precisely the same way.

'We'll keep in touch,' said Jane, noticing the misery in his grey eyes. As she turned to board the train, though, all she could feel was a heart-rending sense of loss, and not only concerning her grandfather. All at once the feeling of war being imminent overwhelmed her. Nothing was certain any longer. This weighty foreboding seemed to express her greatest dread. She might have seen Henri for the last time ever.

Three

T he spring sunlight glinted back from the wind-rippled surfaces of the canal and the river Calder while her train rattled along the line towards Hebden Bridge. It wasn't a bad day for this early in the year, but Jane expected to feel cold after the balmy temperatures of the Loire valley.

As she left the station and hurried to find a taxi she gazed out over the stone buildings of the town towards the green of its surrounding hills. Nothing about the West Riding seemed at all special to her today. Was it only because of dreading what she might find in the home altered by bereavement that Jane felt uneasy here?

She couldn't blame her long journey for this disturbance, travelling had proved smoother than she'd thought likely. She ought to be feeling thankful to have arrived back in Yorkshire.

Jane soon was reassured when her mother seemed as energetic as ever. Sheila came rushing from the kitchen, followed by the smell of freshly ironed bedlinen prepared for the visitors who would arrive for William Townsend's funeral.

'Eh, Jane love, it's grand to have you home so quick.'

'You're all right then, Mum?' Jane checked and hugged her.

'Aye, lass – I've had a right good night's sleep. Your dad's recovering from the initial shock an' all.'

Wheeling his chair through from the workroom as soon as he heard Jane's voice, Alfred began telling how he'd made numerous telephone calls to help his younger son cope with the necessary formalities.

Listening, Phil looked towards them from the kitchen table and the notes he was making, he appeared eager to tell her how much he'd achieved. Jane sensed that dealing with funeral arrangements had matured him. Phil no longer was quite the same young man who'd always leaned on his older brother at work.

'I got the death certificate soon as I could, then I saw the registrar, and the chap at the funeral parlour. None of it were that bad, certainly not as difficult as I expected.'

Jane smiled her understanding. 'That's good, Phil. Dad must be relieved. So, what else needs organizing? Have you managed to contact our Jack yet?'

'Not so far. Once the parson's been to see us – he's coming tomorrow first thing – there'll not be much more to see to. Mum'll have the catering organized.'

'Naturally. And now I'm here, I'll give her a hand. And what about flowers, has anybody done owt about ordering any?'

'I couldn't, the shops were shut when I'd seen to everything else.'

'We've decided what we're going to have, though,' Sheila added. 'When the details of the service have been settled tomorrow, I'll go down into Hebden Bridge and see they're ordered.'

'Or I can do that, Mum,' Jane offered. 'Unless there's other jobs you'd rather I was tackling.' Tired though she was, she felt desperate to be occupied with something useful. Something, she hoped, which might restore the familiar feeling that she belonged here.

The long train journeys had furnished too much time for thinking, and not only about the grandfather she would miss and the terrible effect his loss would have upon all the family.

William Townsend's death didn't feel real to her yet. But nor did the emotions she'd been experiencing in France moments before that news reached her. How true was all that enveloping warmth? Had she been right to suppose that Henri was about to reveal the depth of his feelings for her? Cut off abruptly from their relationship, Jane couldn't be sure that what Henri felt was more than desire. Had she herself really believed she was beginning to love this man she scarcely knew?

Right from the start she had been flattered by his interest in her and – could this be because he was foreign? – Henri seemed more exciting than any man she'd met. When he'd taken her to his château and invited her advice on his renovations she'd been thrilled that he valued her knowledge. And then she had met young Louis. Learning his history had revealed Henri's kindness expressed in determination to adopt the boy. Everything she knew about Henri Bodin convinced Jane that he was a very special man.

Were all her reactions enhanced by the physical attraction drawing them together though? Jane freely acknowledged that it coloured their friendship. And she was old enough to be aware that such a fierce longing wasn't necessarily any guarantee that a relationship might prove lasting. She supposed, grimly, that was likely to be tested now. She shouldn't actually be even thinking about Henri.

Tomorrow she would be busy with practical arrangements for her grandfather's funeral, she'd be compelled to shelve all memories of her visits to France.

Even before going to bed that night Jane was shaken into pushing every one of her more personal concerns to the back of her mind. Exhaustion was already inducing a light-headedness which made her afraid she might faint when her father reproved her. Alfred Townsend was sounding unlike his usual gentle self.

'You've been in the house how long?' he demanded. 'And you haven't even asked where your grandfather is. I thought the first thing you'd want to know would be when you could see him.'

Whether or not it was because of her tiredness, Jane was bemused. She caught herself staring at her father while he stared back, his blue eyes hard.

'He's upstairs, naturally. Resting in the master bedroom. They've made him look very nice, they showed me when they brought him home again.'

'I'll go up straight away,' said Jane hastily, and hoped Alfred didn't realize that she hadn't even thought that the old man might be kept in the house.

'I'll go upstairs with you, if you like,' Phil offered. He read Jane's shaken expression, and he was beginning to relish his new, helpful role.

'No, I will,' their mother interrupted. 'There's something I want to fetch from the bedroom, any road.'

As they went up the stairs side by side, Sheila slid her hand on to her daughter's arm.

'He doesn't look too bad at all, you don't have to worry. And you needn't spend so long with him. Your father'll not know if you escape to your own bedroom for a bit afterwards.'

'I suppose this is how it's done, I never thought,' Jane admitted quietly. 'It was just rather unexpected. But I don't want to upset Dad any more than he's upset already.'

'I know, love, I know. He did take it hard at first, happen we all thought William Townsend were that strong he'd last for ever. We don't like being reminded that none of us will always be alive.'

Still aware of Sheila's hand on her arm, Jane entered the bedroom she remembered as the happy place where on so many childhood mornings she might find her parents. Breathing deeply, she willed herself to walk unhesitatingly towards the coffin, which seemed to be placed on some kind of table.

'Do you want me to stop with you?' asked her mother softly.

'No, it's all right. I'm not going to pass out or owt. You get whatever it was you came up here for, Mum.'

Sheila switched on the light, went to the mahogany wardrobe that stood behind Jane, and took out her summer coat.

'This'll have to do, it's navy, the only dark thing that I've got.'

Jane listened to Sheila's footsteps crossing the linoleum, and the door closing behind her.

She had no alternative now, no reason to delay. Never having seen a dead body was no excuse, but she'd been only about eight when her grandmother Townsend had died. At that age she had been considered too young for including in any mourning.

The stark, glass-shaded overhead light didn't help. Over-bright for this situation, it threw every line of Grandfather's face into strong relief, emphasized the cheekbones, made his nose look sharp.

He *was* old, Jane thought, and wondered if he'd been in pain. *Her granddad.* They had been such pals while she was small. She yearned to have been here for him during his last hours, to have been able to hold him. Her arms ached now with the need to hug the old man.

It was too late.

He looked so stiff, he might have been starched, like that white material surrounding his face. How could you hug anybody who was arranged to appear so dauntingly formal?

She bent to kiss his forehead. It wasn't as cold to her lips as she expected. No doubt these upstairs rooms drew some heat from those on the ground floor. Aware that she might seem foolish, Jane was glad the place wasn't icily cool for him.

'I loved you, Granddad,' she murmured. 'I hope you knew that we all did.' It seemed to Jane an unforgivable number of years since she'd told the old man she loved him. 'We've been busy, so much of the time, all the lot of us.'

The horror surged over and right through her. It was too late to tell William Townsend anything ever again. Alarming in its intensity, being confronted by the finality of death scared her.

We ought to remember this throughout every day, thought Jane, tears tumbling down her cheeks. We need reminding that too much gets crowded out, that there never is enough time to *appreciate . . .*

No time for showing people how much we love.

Any people, anywhere . . .

She had been concerned for Henri in the past, had wondered previously how he was or what he was doing. Today recognizing what death can do made her terribly apprehensive. Loving someone wasn't enough. It was no protection. Henri could be taken from her.

And she hadn't yet really tried to show him how much she cared.

* * *

The following day was only fractionally better. Joining her mother and father for the vicar's visit, Jane listened attentively while they expressed their thoughts about the service, and she made notes of all that was decided.

Walking down into Hebden Bridge to order flowers was a relief. The cold March wind blasting down from Blackshaw Head helped to clear her mind, and made her speed her pace until she was invigorated by the exercise.

The respite was brief. The woman in the florist's shop knew the family, but not their news. When her eyes filled sympathetically Jane couldn't help weeping.

Ordering flowers on behalf of her parents and more from each of her brothers and herself was an ordeal. A struggle to hold on to sufficient composure. Unable to speak, she had to write out each message word by word – words which induced what Jane felt was embarrassingly excessive grief.

The woman understood, tried to reassure her by reminding her that she frequently had to deal with similar requests.

Drying her eyes, Jane tried to smile back. 'Aye, I dare say you do.'

'Did your grandfather suffer a lot?'

The question gave Jane a jolt. 'Do you know, I don't really have any idea.'

And that is awful, she thought. I haven't even asked anyone how much pain he had. That showed how preoccupied she was. With her personal reaction to his death. And with that other sense of loss – the result of leaving Henri?

Jane walked through the streets between soot-darkened sandstone houses in Hebden Bridge, crossed the river to stride out uphill towards the house. She was battling to order her thoughts. She needed to be of use to her family here, must give herself to considering how best to remember the old man, and how to look after those who were left behind.

Phil was working that day, and wouldn't be back at the house until his normal time just before their evening meal. Jane glanced up towards the wooded slopes, the fields beyond embraced by drystone walls, and mauve-tinged moors at their summit. She'd give anything to be free to continue up those hills, to trudge on right over the horizon, to reach some place where she might find her peace.

These hills always had seemed so *healing* for her, always used to provide a kind of solution for past troubles. She must not seek that luxury today, and Jane suspected anyway that no absence from home would really help. Old William Townsend's death weighed heavily. Perhaps solely by concentrating on what she must do for him now could she begin to solve anything.

Her father was in his workroom, her mother snatching a moment to savour a cup of tea.

'Your dad was asking if I knew whether you'd ordered that stone afore you had to leave France,' Sheila told her, pouring tea into an additional cup. 'He must be feeling better about his father if he's thinking of summat practical.'

'I did order it, yes,' said Jane, 'I'll tell him now before I sit down.'

Alfred was relieved. 'For a day or two yet we'll be busy with the funeral, but I do need to be sure that stuff will come. I've barely enough for Father's headstone, and we can't be certain how long we'll manage to contact anybody over there. Ever since Hitler's lot invaded Prague there's been no doubt that war's coming.'

Those words remained in her mind, no matter how hard she tried to concentrate on getting the house and themselves ready for the funeral. Jane had known about events in Czechoslovakia, of course, but while she had been with Henri she'd been too happy to permit such gloomy news to depress her. Confined in her home with the family she loved enveloped in grief, refusing to succumb to utter hopelessness was difficult.

The one good thing was discovering a means by which they might contact her brother Jack. Recalling that her boss had spoken about some of the possible plans for war defences, Jane telephoned the office.

Hugh Dunstan expressed his surprise that she was home

48

from France so soon, quickly sympathized about the family bereavement, then heard out her request for information:

'As I may have told you, our Jack went off to try and learn more about the stuff they're going to construct, like bunkers and that. Trouble is, he didn't let us know where he was going or anything, and we need to get him to come back home.'

'Naturally. Hold on a minute, Jane, I have the names of a few contacts somewhere on my desk here.'

Hugh supplied several telephone numbers, and Jane immediately began to call them. The third place she rang had been visited by her brother the previous day, fortunately someone had noted a number where he could be reached.

When she got through to the boarding house where Jack was staying, their father insisted on taking over to explain what had happened. From Alfred's end of the conversation Jane gathered that her brother was as shocked as anyone by their grandfather's death.

'. . . Just look after yoursen' mind, on the way back home,' Alfred finished. 'So long as you're here for t' funeral, nowt else matters now. Everything else has been attended to.'

Jack's arrival during the evening of the following day made Jane feel slightly better. Although Phil had done so much before she had come home, she was very conscious of being the eldest. She must keep an eye on both parents. Even though Jack was her junior by a couple of years, he was the older son, and he'd always been serious enough to share responsibilities.

The funeral was to be one week after William Townsend's death. During the preceding day several relatives arrived to stay in the house. Content to be helping their mother to cater for this enlarged family, Jane devoted her time to making and serving meals, clearing away afterwards, and all the while trying to prevent aged aunts from becoming too melancholy.

Great Aunt Maud, always a favourite of Jane's, seemed the most likely to surrender to her grief, but was grateful when it was suggested that she might enlighten them further about the Townsend family grave.

'It was *my* grandfather invested in that,' she began telling Jane as they sat in the front room that night. 'I'm glad it's to be used again. Even if Mytholm church is a bit of a way from here. You'll know, of course, that it was when most of t' family started going to Cross Lanes Chapel that they stopped using that grave.'

'I didn't know, Auntie, actually,' said Jane. 'We were brought up to go to Mytholm Church, I never thought about it only being us lot as went there.'

'William's side of the family, you mean? I recall it caused a bit of a stir when he said he'd had enough of chapel, like.'

Just as well Father has made certain that he will be buried in the most appropriate place, thought Jane, and wondered how much was understood of past differences within the family.

She herself had never really questioned her Church of England allegiance, but then she had been so busy throughout her teenaged years and early twenties that she admitted religion had somehow got crowded out.

'Do you attend Mytholm church regular yourself?' Aunt Maud enquired.

Jane was compelled to be honest. 'I have to confess I don't go there as often as I ought. Christmas and Easter, and maybe once or twice during the year.'

'I expect you got out of the habit when you were studying so much.'

'You've always been generous, Auntie, but I'm not sure I deserve your understanding over this. I have neglected God, I'm not certain being busy is sufficient excuse.'

On the day that she entered the church behind her grandfather's coffin Jane was feeling even more positive that nothing did excuse her neglect of regular worship.

She had loved coming here when small, sitting with her parents, and with William Townsend and his wife in the days before her grandmother became ill.

The hymns and the psalms had brought her particular enjoyment, and if the sermons seemed over-long, she had whiled away time by letting her eyes roam about the calm interior.

That interior felt less calm today, as was likely from the perspective of a funeral. There was a great deal to disturb her. Even while the organ played, the wind beyond its surrounding walls wailed its own dirge, increasing their solemnity. But the family were concerning her far more than any external circumstances. Jane had seen her dad's hurt expression when he had watched *his* father's coffin being carried by Jack and Phil together with other, more distant, relatives. She knew Alfred Townsend, and the way he would have given anything to be able to do this last service in respect for the old man he loved.

I can't bear death, thought Jane, even of someone as old as Grandfather. And nor can I bear the knowledge that I should have done more to hold on to all that I once acquired through coming to this place.

The thought that she didn't deserve the comfort that might be found within this church coloured her emotions when the vicar began the service. She hadn't expected to feel cheered, but nor did she anticipate experiencing this sense of having cut herself off from everything valued here.

Concentrating seemed difficult, the greater her effort to absorb all that was said the more Jane's ears took in only occasional sentences, a mass of words that sounded disheartening.

'Behold, thou hast made my days as it were a span long: and mine age is even as nothing in respect of thee; and verily every man living is altogether vanity . . .

'For I am a stranger with thee: and a sojourner, as all my fathers were.

'O spare me a little, that I may recover my strength: before I go hence, and be no more seen . . .

'Thou hast set our misdeeds before thee: and our secret sins in the light of thy countenance. For when thou art angry, all our days are gone: we bring our years to an end, as it were a tale that is told.'

Only when they all stood at the graveside did she find any sense of peace as the vicar began speaking of resurrection, and a life beyond the one which her grandfather had surrendered. Turning at last to leave, Jane felt even that brief peace evaporating. No matter what anyone believed concerning William Townsend's soul, the man they had loved was absent from their daily lives now, and always would be absent.

Helping to organize everyone into cars for returning to the house, and being responsible there for looking after so many people was good for her. Jane didn't let up until only immediate family members were left to tidy away all remaining evidence of the meal they had provided.

Phil and their father were even discussing football again, Jane was glad to hear, while she helped Sheila return clean dishes to their cupboards. Jack was walking Cynthia home, but with promises not to be late back. Cynthia's arrival had surprised Jane, but she'd been pleased the girl had cared enough about Grandfather Townsend to wish to show him respect, despite disagreements with Jack.

Jane suspected that Jack had been more than pleased to see Cynthia again, but he patently was hanging on to his reservations about marriage. His manner towards the girl throughout that day had seemed cool, perhaps more so than Cynthia's response to their bereavement warranted.

Jack ought to have shown he was thankful to have someone who cared beside him. Jane would have given anything to have Henri there for *her*. Even if knowing him for so short a time made her wonder how and why he'd become so vital to her.

Alone in her room that night, thinking about Henri became more disturbing than yearning for the comfort of having him around. No longer occupied with the funeral, the distress of leaving someone interred hit her. Jane recognized how greatly Henri Bodin mattered to her. She would be inconsolable if he were to die.

If fighting broke out in France he could be in real danger. Exhausted though she was and desperate for sleep, the dread of losing him would not shift to give her quiet. Amid relatives and friends that day, rumours of impending war had surfaced all too often, many nourished by conjecture that Britain would soon be called to aid Poland against a seemingly inevitable onslaught by Hitler. By the last day of March rumours about such an enemy attack on Poland seemed confirmed when Mr Chamberlain announced that an Anglo-French-Polish military alliance would be sealed the following week.

'That means we're pledged to defend Poland against attack, doesn't it?' said Jack.

They had all listened to the wireless report of the Prime Minister's statement.

'I think it's time we had a talk, Dad,' Jack went on. 'About what we're going to do. When the war comes, and that.'

'How do you mean? Get it off your chest . . .' Alfred prompted.

Jack hesitated for a moment, sorting his words. When he spoke again he was frowning, but his blue eyes held a glint of excitement. 'What I want to know is how much you reckon there's going to be for us to do here – in the business, I mean. It's clear enough there's not going to be any fresh building schemes on the cards, not the sort of stuff that interests me.'

'There'll be airfields all up and down the country, won't there? And the government must have plans for various defences.'

'And bunkers, Dad – like the ones I went to find out about, aye. I'm afraid none of that thrills me. Matter of fact – so long as you think the firm will keep ticking over without me – I'm keen to fight properly, to enlist in the army.'

Sheila had been listening gravely. As Jack's last words emerged she dropped the sock she was darning and one hand flew to her mouth.

'Don't look like that, Mum, I only want to do my bit. I might not even get sent out of this country.'

Alfred seemed serious, but not displeased. 'If that's what you've a mind to tackle, son, I'd not hold you back. As you say, there's not going to be the same quality of skills in demand:

more basic jobs, and later on, keeping up with repair work perhaps. There'll be plenty of older chaps around, them as are past joining the forces. I reckon we could manage with them till the duration.'

'And there's our Phil, don't forget,' Sheila put in, desperate to be reassured that one son, at least, would be remaining at home.

Jane caught a glance passing between her father and brother. Did they know something of Phil's intention, something neither she nor her mother had learned?

'Phil fancies himself in the navy,' Jack announced. 'Think it's the uniform – he always was one for dressing up.'

When Sheila gasped in alarm Jane steeled herself not to go and hug her. They would all need to toughen up, this wasn't the day for anything that encouraged giving in to crying. In fact, any reassurances Jane might offer could soon prove insubstantial. The prospect of avoiding war *was* slim: sooner or later radical changes in their family life would follow. This could be the time for Sheila to accept that Jack and Phil were old enough to make their own choices – a time for facing the truth more easily than a day or so before they eventually left to fight.

'But your dad needs you at home, needs you both,' Sheila insisted.

'Nay, I'll hold nobody back,' Alfred contradicted. 'Since my father passed on I've already taken full control of the books, and happen our Jane'll give a hand with the office side if we do get busy again.'

'Our Jane's got her own job,' said her mother firmly. 'She has enough on.'

'It's not quite like that, Mum,' she responded gently. 'Architects, round here at least, recently seem to have less than enough to do.'

When she returned to work after her grandfather's funeral Jane was indeed disappointed by the situation in their office. The best suggestion Hugh Dunstan made was to reiterate that she

54

ought to give her mind to discovering more about the airfields which would be needed.

Jane was willing herself to go and investigate that when she heard that drill halls were to be built for training the men aged twenty who were to be conscripted into the forces. Expecting architects would be needed to design such places, she made enquiries of the various local authorities responsible for construction. This should be more interesting, and the family firm might also become involved in this work.

All too soon she learned that those drill halls to be newly built already had planning in hand, and most of the ones in her area were to be converted from existing premises. Unable to believe she'd missed out, Jane felt obliged to try and learn more about military airfields, but she was discouraged by more than her lack of enthusiasm for such sites. Fewer airfields appeared to be needed in the north of England than the south.

Amid all the changes and uncertainties, Jane had become inhibited by feeling she ought not to stay away from home for any length of time. Both of her brothers were joining the forces at the earliest moment possible. Her mother's alarm had not waned at all, and her father was suffering because of believing he was unable to contribute anything to the war effort.

'I felt useless afore, Sheila,' Jane overheard him saying one morning when she came down to breakfast. 'How do you think I feel now that the country's relying on able-bodied men to come forward?'

'You'll be keeping Townsend's going, like you said,' Sheila reassured him.

'And for what?' Alfred wanted to know. 'I can't *do* owt – if I set on a few labourers, how will I even visit sites to supervise their work?'

Jane decided it was up to her to introduce more optimism. 'But you'd be employing older men, Dad, that was your idea, wasn't it? They'd be experienced.'

'And wouldn't need me to keep any eye on 'em? Is that what you think? It'll still be Townsend's responsibility, don't forget – and when did men work their best in those circumstances?'

Jane thought Alfred was doing the majority of the building trade workforce an injustice, but she would say no more. For the present. She could understand his genuine regret that he could do so little, but she suspected he might be allowing frustration to colour his judgement.

Fortunately, Alfred had his fresh supplies of *tuffeau* stone to provide inspiration for carving and to distract him. That stone also had an effect on Jane, from the day of its arrival just before William Townsend's funeral. Cut off as she felt from Henri, and from France, she could have done without anything that rekindled fears that all her dreams seemed to have foundered.

The letter she'd received from Henri shortly after returning home appeared quite formal in tone, almost an obligatory commiseration on a bereavement rather than the warm sympathetic note she'd expected from the man who'd not only held her to him, but who she had felt to be close in so many ways.

Jane delayed replying, she hoped time might provide words that could restore the relationship she believed they enjoyed. No amount of time helped, Jane grew desperate to avoid writing anything which suggested she was assuming too much about Henri's feelings. The note she finally sent seemed no less cool than his own.

And so now here she was, more concerned than ever for Henri's safety amid the threats of war, and surrounded by the dust and fragments of his native stone which each day increased the reminders of her private disappointment.

Left with no alternative, Jane eventually spent several weeks visiting potential sites for airfields, and found at each in turn that any constructions were already in hand, or so basic as not to require an architect's services. Disappointed, she resigned herself to working instead with her father.

She had never been exactly fascinated by the practical side of building work, now that all of Townsend's really interesting schemes were suspended she couldn't get excited about the job. Helping to keep the books did provide something to stimulate her mind, nevertheless, and the ability with figures which always facilitated her professional drawings proved useful.

Throughout that uneasy summer Jane read newspaper reports of everything happening across the sea, and listened regularly to wireless bulletins. Word from France was not good, and elsewhere in Europe the threat of conflict increased.

No one could be surprised on 3rd September when war was declared, but Jane found no consolation in having been at heart prepared for this announcement.

'Don't worry, we'll come through all right, somehow,' she told her anxious mother and father that night. 'I'll be here to see that we survive.'

What she couldn't bring herself to tell them was her dearest wish, her strongest determination – that she would find some means of playing her part in this war.

Her life *once* had seemed to hold such promise – and if today, career, her family, her half-formed relationship with Henri, all were altered – she must find a way to fight until she could restore them.

Four

J ane's first opportunity to use her architectural training to aid the war effort was such a long time coming through that she became thoroughly discouraged. She felt at times that she must be the only person not actively engaged in resisting Hitler. Her boss seemed only too ready to leave her free to work with her father.

'If there was anything any better with some other practice I'd leave altogether,' Jane told Sheila when she heard about yet another job for which Hugh Dunstan *wouldn't* require her. Knowing the war was curtailing normal work for many architects didn't compensate her for having no new designs to draft.

Her mother smiled reassuringly. 'Happen it'll be different when the war's over, love. You can't blame him for wanting to keep him and his son busy. After all, men aren't the same. They have to provide for their families.'

And I wish I was able to contribute more here, thought Jane, but said nothing.

She was taking very little pay for the work she was doing for the family business, and was earning only a minimal amount from the bit of architecture she was given.

Since Phil had gone off to the navy and Jack had begun training for the army, Jane knew their mother was finding it harder to pay household bills and provide good food. It seemed to her the rationing soon to be introduced might not make too much difference where they already seemed to be living less well than ever before!

Alfred Townsend had remarked that the Fuel and Lighting Order insisting that they should consume only 75 per cent of the previous year's usage in coal, gas and electricity ought to be met with two fewer people in their household.

'Aye,' Sheila agreed. 'And that might save us a bit towards the cost of all those blackouts I've been making for the windows.'

Jane had offered to help making up all the yards of black material, but when her mother tackled the task alone it became evident that Sheila needed to keep busy in order to avoid dwelling on the future safety of her absent sons.

Another war precaution had upset Alfred for several days after they were issued with a stirrup pump and long-handled shovel to protect their property against incendiary bombs. He was close to tears of frustration because he was unable to carry them upstairs and install them in the attic.

He refused to listen when Jane assured him she had put them in place alongside a bucket of sand as recommended, just as capably as anyone else might have done. She wished she could remember that he didn't want anyone but *him* to be capable!

Jane also was missing her brothers, but couldn't say much about that while her mother needed no reminders of the fact that they could soon be in danger. Most of all, Jane was missing the happiness created whenever she met Henri.

Following her sudden return to England after William Townsend's death, she literally had prayed that Henri might suggest she should return to continue her aborted stay in his château. Their initial exchange of letters had been so brief, and so cool, that she still had difficulty equating them with the feelings they had shared. She had written to him again, wary of "throwing herself at him", yet yearning to restore the affection that she was so sure had existed between them.

Henri had replied eventually, but again with no suggestion that they meet. This left her feeling dissatisfied, and plagued now by the anxiety that she must have said or done something to disappoint him.

Seeing Jane with that further letter from France, Sheila had noticed her expression, and privately sighed with relief before speaking.

'You look as if you'd lost a ten bob note and found a sixpence, aren't things so good between you and that French chap, these days?'

Jane tried to conceal what she was feeling. 'He was never more than just a friend, you know, Mum. And he'll be busier than ever now.'

'He'll be glad to know you're safe over here, if he's so much to occupy him.'

Jane wondered just how safe England would be in the future, the vast numbers of children being evacuated indicated considerable alarm. Even though many people were heartened by Queen Elizabeth's assertion that *her* daughters would not be leaving. The Princesses Elizabeth and Margaret Rose would not go without her, she herself would not leave the King, and His Majesty would *never* leave London.

Jane longed to have a job she could throw herself into and forget everything else. Yet during the first few weeks of the war even the time she spent working for the family firm seemed to decrease.

Her facility with arithmetic meant that keeping the books and also sending out invoices were always up to date. The older men they employed now, being so experienced in the building trade, needed little organizing. In the main, an occasional discussion with her father was enough to agree details of their jobs.

There were rare occasions when Alfred was needed on a site, and Jane was happy to drive him there. Her father, who'd never enjoyed being driven by anyone, was less happy. Quite often he would protest that they should conserve petrol instead now that there was such a shortage.

When the opportunity to use her expertise again finally came, Jane heard of the work in a call from her boss who contacted her so infrequently that she'd almost forgotten what it was like to have a desk in his office.

'I've just heard about something should interest you,' Hugh told her over the phone. 'And I've recommended that you go and take a look. It's down in Middlesex, you'll have to stay there for a while if you get taken on.'

Jane felt excitement surging through her at the prospect of travelling again, if only in her own country. When she went into the office to learn more she came away with exhilaration increasing.

The task was to be partly a conversion rather than designing a construction from scratch, but sounded no less interesting for that. An eighteenth century building was being recreated as a headquarters for Fighter Command, complete with an underground operations room. Her role would be to ensure that all the reconstruction was in accordance with the principles she had learned throughout her training.

The result might not be stylish, Jane reflected, but meeting all the necessary criteria would be a challenge, and she would enjoy becoming involved in something so different from anything she'd attempted previously. Something for the war.

Jane's elation was dimmed hardly at all when her mother protested on hearing that the task would mean staying away from home in Middlesex.

'That's near London, isn't it? Have you thought about that? You do know there's a lot more going on down there – because they're expecting attacks?'

'Oh, Mum – I do wish I could stop you being such a worrier! This is nowhere near the centre of London.'

'It's a darned sight nearer nor we are. And you know how things are down there – when our Jack came home on leave, he were telling how his first job training with the Territorials was filling sandbags to protect places down that way.'

'And, so far, those sandbags haven't been needed, have they?'

'Somebody believes they will be, else they wouldn't have gone to all that trouble. And anyway, this thing you're going to help with is for the RAF, isn't it? You can't tell me they aren't preparing for the worst.'

After failing to reassure Sheila, trying to get her father to understand was Jane's final effort before setting out. Whilst Alfred could see how eager she was to use her knowledge and contribute to fighting the war, he didn't attempt to conceal his concern that she was going so far away.

'Since the lads went off, my only consolation has been having you at home, Jane love.'

'I don't expect they will want me down there for long. They'll already know what they need, it'll just be a matter of sorting out the practicalities.' And nothing, she thought, is going to prevent me from doing precisely that.

The journey south by train was slow and uncomfortable. Jane had never seen so many uniformed men, and women too, some of the latter quite mature and in ATS uniform. She remembered that experienced ATS women had been called to report in as soon as war was declared. She had gathered that they were needed to cope with the influx of men into the Territorial Army.

I might find out more about joining the ATS if this work now doesn't lead to more jobs in my own line, thought Jane. She already appreciated getting away from the confines of home. No matter how greatly she loved her part of Yorkshire, she had felt there that they were rather out of touch with the war. And there was no denying she herself was no longer challenged by her career.

Getting off the train that dark evening in an unfamiliar, blacked-out station was unnerving enough; when Jane stumbled from the platform and out into the street without seeing the man due to meet her, she felt her heart racing agitatedly. With a car promised for the remainder of her journey, she hadn't asked for any directions, and none had been offered.

She had been told that she would be accommodated in a local pub somewhere near the building where she would be working, but no one had even told her the name of the pub.

Jane had been standing out in the cold autumn air for several minutes when a sports car zoomed towards her, and stopped with its wheels about an inch from her toes.

'Jane Townsend?' the driver enquired.

When she said yes he told her to hop in, and she noticed his strong Scottish accent. 'Toss your case in the back, will you?' he added, briskly. 'Daren't take my foot of the accelerator, damned car's playing up. Reason I was late.'

As he started off at speed Jane grabbed for the hat she'd worn in the effort to impress. Another second and it would be lost for ever, somewhere over that wall she could just about discern through the darkness.

Her companion laughed. 'Should have warned you – causes quite a breeze, this beauty, once she gets going.'

'What make of car is it?'

'An MG, what else is worth buying? Trouble is, no time to get her serviced, and a shortage of spares now, I'll warrant, until the duration. Normally, see to everything myself, but that's no longer a priority.'

'How far is it? I gather I'm putting up at the local pub?'

Again, he laughed. 'What's wrong? Don't you like the car? You can't be finding fault with my driving!'

Jane laughed with him. 'Not with either of those. It's just me – tired out, I've come all the way from Yorkshire, you know.'

'You don't have to tell me – that accent explains the lot. Packed trains again – and too much stopping en route?'

'That sort of thing, aye.'

'Aye,' he agreed, exactly replicating her accent.

Jane turned to give him a sideways look, didn't he know that he'd no room to mock the way she was speaking? All she could discern was his strong profile. She swivelled back her gaze to where their dimmed headlights revealed a few feet of roughish road surface, and nothing beyond.

The inn was reached and his car parked neatly before Jane recognized that the building she could barely distinguish was indeed a public house.

'They're efficient with their blacking-out here,' she remarked as the car engine died. Uncertain how to extricate herself from the tiny vehicle, she was expecting to be offered a hand.

'Don't forget your baggage, Yorkshire,' the driver called over his shoulder as he leapt from the car and strode towards what had to be the entrance. 'Take your time, why don't you?' he shouted back. 'No good opening the pub door more than once.'

He was by now waiting, impatient for Jane to join him, before opening the outer door of a tiny porch.

'That's it, in here with me, shut that door behind you.'

Jane realized that only when all possible light was contained would he open the inner door. Crammed in beside him, she grew aware of how tall he was, and broad-shouldered too in a flight jacket that smelled of new leather. He used expensive soap as well, if she was any judge.

The door opened on a low-ceilinged bar packed with the predominately male clientele which Jane might have anticipated, if she'd been accustomed to drinking in public houses. With the exception of half a dozen or so women, some in WAAF uniform, everyone was talking at the tops of their voices, apparently determined to be heard over the noise from an overstrung piano.

'Wait there, Yorkshire – I'll find the landlord,' her escort ordered.

As he began to push his way through the crowd Jane noticed his hair was a quite beautiful, a slightly wavy, golden shade that gleamed beneath the light.

'I bet he doesn't half fancy himself with that,' she thought, and wondered if his face was equally attractive. She hadn't had an opportunity to see more than his profile. Not that it mattered, this could be their only encounter.

They were an age before coming to rescue her – an age during which she began to feel increasingly awkward and embarrassed. The glances being sent her way – and they were many – were all too readily interpreted. I know now why young women don't go into pubs on their own, thought Jane, and was thankful that her mother couldn't see her. Sheila Townsend rarely drank, even at home, and had probably never entered a place like this in her entire life.

'It gets better when you know a few of the lads.'

The airman who had driven her from the station had ap-

proached her unnoticed from the left, startling her so that she
turned sharply to face him.

His eyes were blue, yet the smile in them reminded her
forcefully of Henri's. His features were strong, especially the
jutting chin, but with eyebrows and lashes the shade of his hair
the whole effect was pleasing. Extremely pleasing.

'I'm to take you round the back, Tom's busy as you'll guess,
but his wife has your room ready. She does all the cooking, we
don't see her during opening hours.'

Scotty – as she thought of him – took her case, and slid his
other hand through her arm to press through the throng. He
was greeted from one side and another, and responded with a
grin and a nod, plus the occasional 'Hello there!' The geniality
made Jane wonder if some innate reserve really explained his
initial brusqueness with her.

They had almost reached the door leading through to the
rear. A lusty voice hailed him. 'Doing all right for yourself
again, Adrian – how come you're the one always locates the
choice talent?'

Her companion's face clouded. Jane expected him to give the
cutting reply evident in the sharpening of blue eyes. Instead, he
hustled her through the door ahead of him.

'You couldn't have missed that,' he said as he indicated the
narrow staircase in front of them. 'Trouble is, Yorkshire,
there's too many of us away from home. That makes for folk
being overcurious about other people's private lives.'

Jane ignored his observation, and dealt instead with a habit
which was beginning to irritate her. 'Do you have to keep
calling me "Yorkshire", all the time? You know my name.'

'My apologies, *Miss* Townsend – or have I got that wrong
too – is it Missus?'

'It is not, I've concentrated on studying.'

'You'll have me know!' Adrian exclaimed, taking her aback
by making her realize how assertive she sounded.

They had reached what appeared to be the door of her room.
Jane relented and turned to smile at him. 'Do I sound that
forbidding? I'm Jane to my friends, any road. And I suppose I

owe you sincere thanks for meeting me tonight, and helping me find my way around here.'

He nodded his acknowledgement. 'If thanks is all I'm getting, I'll be on my way then. Unless you'll join me in the bar for a nightcap?'

'I'm much too tired, honest. Perhaps there'll be some other time,' she added, thinking she didn't wish to seem ungrateful.

'There will that! Did no one tell you I'll be showing you round while you're on site? Making certain you understand all our specifications.'

'I'll look forward to it,' responded Jane swiftly, and wondered immediately if she would. This young man was rather too disturbing for her comfort.

'Tom – the landlord – says to make yourself at home, he'll be up to welcome you when he can spare a minute. See you tomorrow morning – seven sharp. Goodnight, Yorkshire.'

'Goodnight, Scotty!' she called after him. Tired, she might be, but not beyond joining his little game.

The landlord when he came to knock on her door was older than Jane expected, sixty at least, grey-haired and with a stomach whose shape witnessed to liking the beer that went with his job. He looked exhausted, but managed to smile.

'I just wanted to assure you we'll do our best to see you're all right while you're staying with us. Eileen – my wife – will have breakfast ready at six thirty, so you'll meet her at last then. We'll see you have a key for our private entrance, that way you can come and go whenever – not only when we're open. And you needn't come in through the bar each time – unless you've a fancy to.'

'Thanks, I might have the odd drink when I'm not tired out. I used to enjoy going out with the lads when I was a student.'

'The lads, eh? Because it was architecture you took, I suppose?'

Jane grinned as she nodded. And then she saw, beyond their landlord, that Adrian was passing along the landing as he hurried towards a further flight of stairs. She was surprised

66

that he was staying there rather than on an RAF base somewhere. Jane wasn't displeased to have him near at hand.

'I didn't know if you'd prefer your own company first thing,
Miss Townsend.'

Eileen had greeted her at the foot of the stairs, and was
indicating beside the bar the two tables each set for one person.

Adrian was already seated at his, and appeared to have
devoured most of his breakfast. After nodding in Jane's direction, he swallowed a mouthful of tea before speaking.

'What's it to be, Yorkshire? How sociable are you in a
morning?'

'As amiable as you, Scotty. I'm used to having a couple of
brothers around first thing.'

Eileen was smiling. 'I'll push your tables together then, and
let you get on. There's porridge in your dish, dear, and your
bacon and egg's keeping hot.'

'Sleep all right?' Adrian enquired casually while she began
eating.

'Fine thanks, and you?'

He shrugged. 'Much as usual. So – soon as you've got
through that lot we'll be on our way. Since I've been delegated
to provide the grand tour, it'll be as efficient as possible.'

'That's good,' said Jane, spooning down porridge.

Eileen smiled as she brought her cooked food the moment
Jane had emptied the cereal dish. 'I couldn't help hearing
Adrian getting on at you about timing. He does get better –
mostly evenings, with a few pints inside him!'

'You can't know that,' he reproved their landlady with a grin.
'You never dare to emerge from tending your stove.' He turned
to Jane. 'If I didn't know her better, I'd say our lads scared the
pants off her!'

Although pleased to witness the jocularity between them,
Jane didn't know how to react. In her student days there'd been
plenty of ribbing, but among young folk, contemporaries with
much in common. She concentrated on finishing breakfast.

Adrian checked Jane was carrying the pass she'd been given.

They hurried out to the car while he enlightened her a little regarding the situation at the pub.

'Eileen's a good sort, so's Tom, and I try to jolly her along. Tom's her second husband, her first died in the last lot, likewise her only son. He must have been the age I am now.'

And she's acutely aware of that, I'm sure, thought Jane. Being surrounded by young chaps can't be helping.

Jane was glad the confidence that Adrian had shared with her revealed a more considerate side to him than some he'd shown her. She would be happy to bear that in mind while they began this task together. Hadn't his manner the previous night left her wondering how she would get along with somebody who could sound so offhand?

'How long since you qualified then?' he asked her as they approached the large house that was their destination. 'I am right thinking you *are* qualified?'

'If you'd said, I'd have brought the documents to prove it!' Jane retorted. Once again, she relented and grinned. 'It wasn't all that long before this war began threatening. I'd hardly got my teeth into any good solo jobs when all the talk turned to likely hostilities.'

'Bad luck. Still, your boss thinks highly of you.'

'Really? There's a surprise!' She shrugged. 'Trouble is, he's already got his son in the practice, can't blame Hugh for making sure they have all the interesting work. What little there is now.'

'I'd have thought there was plenty of construction work going on – fortifications, aerodromes . . .'

'They're not really interesting, though.'

'They are to me.'

'Because you're into flying, I suppose.'

'You could say that.'

They left the car and Jane began following him towards the large building that dominated the site. Adrian had snatched up his uniform jacket and was putting it on as he strode ahead. It was the first time in daylight that she had seen him in full uniform. Jane noticed as she caught up at the entrance that he wore the pilot's wings she'd expected. What she couldn't identify was the significance of the rings circling the sleeve of his blue jacket. For the first time Jane began to wonder if she ought to have been feeling in awe of this smart airman.

The salute he received from the very young looking serviceman at the door increased her impression that she owed Adrian a touch more deference. Too late now, though, she feared – and it was too late also to pay attention to anything but their descent into what seemed like a badly illuminated cellar.

'I didn't know work here had begun already,' she remarked, puzzled about her intended role there.

'Think this was just conventional storage,' Adrian told her over his shoulder. 'Until we decided it must be utilized. But this is only the start, a tunnel, if you like.'

'Ah.'

Jane ceased talking to concentrate on where she was placing her feet. The ground was anything but refined, mainly of earth, with here and there the occasional slab of concrete or stone. The lighting too was haphazard, and she stumbled more than once when she trudged through a pocket of darkness.

Eventually, Adrian sighed, and waited until she reached his side.

'Can't you manage?' he enquired, though not unkindly.

She grinned. 'Not at your pace, unless you're prepared to restore me to my feet if I trip up!'

'Heaven forbid!' Even in the dim glow from a lamp nearby she could see he was smiling. 'Never let it be said that I neglected my duty.'

He offered a hand. Jane toyed with the idea of proving her self-sufficiency, but decided that if he was prepared to be accommodating so was she.

His hand was firm but smooth. Reared in a family of builders, she relished that smoothness just as much as the steadiness of his grasp.

'That seemed to take an age,' Jane exclaimed when they finally emerged into a massive underground chamber. Her hand felt cold immediately he released it.

'Takes ten minutes, I suppose, but the idea is that all personnel should be secure down here.'

'Quite. So, where do we start?'

'Well, I'm about to outline our requirements, and then we shall need your knowledge to assess the practicalities. You'll have to bear in mind, of course, that we're faced with potential enemy invasion. This place will have to withstand attack by ground forces, and from the air. I trust you're familiar with the stresses a construction could face?'

'Yes, if not precisely those connected with war, explosives and such.'

'Fair enough. We no doubt have specialists who can add in their particular expertise. When we leave here I'll show you the plans we've drafted.'

'Oh.' Jane was crestfallen. 'I understood that planning was my job.'

'To modify them perhaps. Anyway, to business. We're intending to divide the available space according to our needs, you'll have to suggest materials for that. Again, keeping in mind we should ensure that in the event of attack one area, at least, must remain operational. Then there's the actual layout of each sector. The larger of the two rooms will be this end, and we want a – a sort of gallery, I suppose you'd call it. Glazed perhaps, so that operations down below will be visible, and a degree of soundproofing would be preferred.'

'Any gallery has got to be designed to be totally safe, there'd be a catastrophe if it collapsed under bombing.'

'You're catching on. Ensuring the safety aspect is one of the main reasons for employing you.'

Adrian was smiling appreciatively. This was more than Jane had expected. Despite the chill of standing about somewhere deep underground she felt warmed.

'We have all the existing internal dimensions, you won't be obliged to clamber up the walls to measure, nor to crawl around the floor. What you will need is the ability to calculate if further excavation should be required to fulfil our expectations of the place.'

'You seem to have already worked out what you want here.'

'I personally haven't, but the powers that be, yes. Does that disappoint you?'

Jane shook her head. 'Only a little, most people who employ an architect do so to interpret their own ideas.'

'In every case?' Adrian asked her. 'I'd have thought that didn't apply with, say, new estates of houses. And what of public buildings, schools, and such?'

'There was a school I worked on once, seems ages ago, I was allowed my head to some degree. Mainly, because they knew my boss and his style of work. Unfortunately, that was in 1938 – the school hasn't gone ahead.'

'Your first major project?' Empathy was darkening the blue of his eyes.

'Should have been, aye.'

'Let's hope the work you tackle during the war will further your career.'

'Wish I thought it would. Trouble is, jobs of this sort – even if I'm offered another – are hardly going to recommend me for peacetime constructions.'

'Don't put yourself down – doing a thorough job, *any* thoroughly good job speaks volumes for your abilities.'

'I hope I don't have to remind you you've said that if I get stuck on sorting out the requirements here.' Jane's hazel-green eyes were rueful.

She repeated that sentiment within her head an hour later when they were in an upstairs room where Adrian was showing her their early drafts of how they anticipated the finished control centre should look.

Her feelings about the work were confused. In part, she *was* disappointed that so much of the planning had gone ahead without her input. She preferred to assess a site herself, checking measurements, allowing inspiration as well as her knowledge to provide answers. And she was accustomed to cooperating directly with quantity surveyors and eventually with builders.

Here, it seemed, she would work differently, offering specifications and suggesting materials perhaps, but never participating beyond the planning stage. From what Adrian was saying, all the actual construction work would be taken from her hands. It would be beyond her reach. As was becoming evident, confidentiality and security were paramount.

'How soon can you go through all our drawings, and give an opinion as to their viability?' Adrian asked her. 'As you'll soon discover, time is of primary importance. One of the reasons we've had to engage someone from outside.'

'I'll tell you that tomorrow, when I've taken a first look through all this paperwork. I'll do that tonight.'

She could have a quick snack at the pub, they'd had sandwiches this lunchtime while Adrian had explained certain of the drawings.

He was shaking his head at her. 'Correction, you've earned yourself a break tonight. In any case, all our documents remain on site, and you surely don't wish to stay here. We could eat out, there's a place I know in Stanmore. Or Eileen does a meat pie that's brilliant when you allow for shortages.'

Jane wanted to change rather than dine in clothes that she'd worn throughout the long day. They ate quite early nevertheless, and she was pleased to see that the bar was nowhere near so crowded as it had been the previous evening.

Being obliged to suspend most matters relating to the reason for her visit, Jane decided that she must make an effort to be congenial. Adrian had surprised her today by being quite complimentary about her work, and never once had he reverted to calling her 'Yorkshire'.

That changed the moment that she reappeared in the bar of the pub, when he glanced up and nodded his approval of her navy blue dress with its printed design of tiny pink and white flowers.

'Wow, Yorkshire – you certainly look feminine tonight!'

Receiving another compliment pleased her, even made her blush slightly – not something that she relished – but 'Yorkshire?' Again?

'Thanks, Scotty.'

He grinned. 'I'm afraid I could only change the shirt. Don't have anything but uniform stuff here.'

Looking as smart as that, I'd not be surprised if you chose to wear no other outfit, thought Jane. She could believe Adrian was well aware of the impression he created.

'Is it the pie you'll choose?' he asked her. 'I've told Eileen that's what I'm having, but she also has sausage toad on tonight.'

'The pie would be lovely.'

Eileen had listened from the door of the kitchen which led off from behind the bar. She gave them a thumbs up sign, and disappeared from sight.

'What're you drinking, Yorkshire? Do you like beer, or a shandy perhaps?'

'If there's any port here, I'd love that with masses of lemonade.'

Adrian smiled to himself as he stood up to go to the bar, she suspected he thought her taste old-fashioned. Jane was merely being cautious; she was tired again and needed to be comfortable with the effect of a drink that was familiar.

Even before their meal was served the pub was growing busier as several airmen and others in civilian clothes surged in. The WAAFs from the previous night reappeared shortly afterwards along with three further colleagues.

'So, whereabouts in Scotland is your home?' Jane asked as they started to eat.

'Hamilton – do you know Scotland at all?'

'I've been to Edinburgh, and to Dunoon once for a holiday, that's all.'

'And where in Yorkshire do you live?'

'A place called Hebden Bridge, in the West Riding.'

Adrian smiled. 'I've stayed there, one time when I walked part of the Pennine Way.'

'Really?' Jane smiled back at him, and wondered why she felt so pleased that he knew her home territory.

'And aren't your family builders?' he went on, his blue eyes

seeking her gaze intently. 'You all must love your good Yorkshire sandstone . . .'

'Oh, we do,' Jane responded swiftly. All at once she shivered.
Speaking of stone was all it had taken to remind her of the stone
she really loved, *le tuffeau*. To remind her of the man in France
of whom her thoughts were very close to loving.

'Are you cold?' Adrian asked, sounding quite anxious.

Jane shook her head, but even late into the evening while they
remained chatting to his friends near the bar Adrian continued
to appear concerned about her. He made her uneasy, as though
she ought to explain that she wasn't going to encourage any
man here to become interested in her. Yet why should she feel
this way, was there really anything in Adrian's manner to imply
that he wished to be involved with her?

And realistically, what made her suppose she had some
commitment that prevented such a relationship? Since the
war began she had received no assurance from Henri that
she would even see him again.

Five

A drian still drove Jane to the site each day from the pub and picked her up in the evening on the way back there, but she no longer saw anything of him while she continued her task. She gathered he was stationed on some airbase quite near to the house being converted for Fighter Command, but he told her nothing about the position he held in the RAF.

Jane didn't ask him the nature of his work, she never had. The first thing she'd learned on beginning to draft revisions to those plans was the emphasis on security. The people she met during the course of a day were few, and she herself the only exception to their having a forces or ministry background. Initially, the aura of secrecy was intimidating, but Jane quickly became absorbed in interpreting requirements in order to ensure structural safety, and accepted the situation.

If her days tended to provide a shade too much isolation, her evenings compensated very fully. Once or twice Adrian drove her out into the countryside in Hertfordshire to dine at some wayside inn or hotel, but much of their free time was spent in the pub where they were staying.

Jane was befriended by the WAAF girls who frequented the bar, and felt envious of their very evident comradeship. Their lives seemed full of as much fun as sheer hard graft, and the diversity of their training sounded stimulating. She began to wonder whether she might be happier among their ranks if her own kind of work evaporated yet again after her present job was completed.

In the meantime utilizing architectural principles was enjoyable, even though she still tended to feel that more of the work should have been left to her. She tried to rationalize that RAF Fighter Command knew what they needed, it was to be expected that they would get everything they could down on paper to enable precise interpretation of their needs.

With few distractions, Jane was working quickly – almost too quickly for her liking when she recognized that she soon would be returning to Yorkshire. She would be pleased to see her parents again, of course, but telephoning had assured her that Sheila and Alfred Townsend were all right.

The two of them certainly were well away from the constant reminders of being at war which proliferated further south. The barrage balloons being manufactured with all possible haste had become a feature of the skies over and around London. The Local Defence Volunteers enrolling throughout England were turning out in greater numbers in the home counties. Jane was compelled to believe that people there supposed Hitler's threat of invasion was indeed likely to materialize.

When the plans she had drawn for providing the underground command centre were submitted for approval she became decidedly uneasy. So far as Jane knew, she had never met the man who had first contacted her civilian boss, and she'd have been a deal happier if they had been introduced. She hadn't as yet had sufficient experience within her profession to endow complete confidence in her own ability. If for some reason she were to fall short on this assignment, word would go back to Hugh Dunstan, and might ruin her future career.

While awaiting the verdict on her work, Jane tried to set aside her anxiety but Adrian was too concerned about her to fail to notice. And he did know that her contribution to the job was finished, even though she hadn't told him.

'You shouldn't be worrying like this, you know, Yorkshire,' he said one evening over dinner. 'They're anxious to have construction go ahead, and have their own experts who'll check out the details, but you'll still be allowed room to suggest any necessary amendments.'

'But I don't want there to be any, I like to get things right at the first attempt.'

'I know you do,' said Adrian, his eyes confirming that he approved this quality in her. 'We all like to get things right straight off. But we have to allow others their bit of input.'

Adrian was so understanding he made Jane realize that once she was free of all worry about those plans she would have further cause for unease. Despite all her early reservations, she was dreading the time when she'd no longer see this man who had become a valued colleague.

The details requiring redrafting were few and none of those major. When she had completed her additional work to everyone's satisfaction Jane was immensely relieved. But she could not deny feeling at the same time deflated. Once or twice during her stay in the south Hugh Dunstan had rung through to ask how things were progressing, but he had no offers of further work for her.

'You might try to discover if there are any more constructions for the RAF on the cards,' he suggested, but clearly had no intention of putting her name forward again with whoever had sanctioned this particular job.

Adrian refused to allow her too much time for becoming concerned regarding her future. 'We're going to celebrate all that you've achieved,' he told her as she got into his car in the evening.

After driving to the pub to change they rode off again, towards the centre of London.

'We're going to make the most of it now entertainment places are opening again, after closing in the initial panic when war was declared. Who knows when they'll be compelled to shut their doors again.'

The night was cold and Adrian had relinquished his love of fresh air to put the hood on the car. A full moon hung in the starlit sky while more than a hint of frost on the road sparkled back from even the dim beam of masked headlamps.

The darkness within seemed to hold them to each other as though bound by more than the narrow confines of the interior. The now-familiar leather scent of his coat and the car's upholstery blended with the aroma of the soap Adrian favoured.

All at once Jane felt reluctant ever to leave, saddened by the prospect of arranging her journey back to Yorkshire.

'What are you thinking?'

Startled by his question, she wished he hadn't asked. How could she reply without seeming to attach too much significance to their situation – a significance which Adrian surely would not intend?

'Just that this is very nice, Scotty – that I owe you a lot for making my stay down here so good.'

'Excellent. You've certainly turned my preconceived notions on their head. That first night I had you down as some old spinster, at least fifty, living only for her career.'

Jane laughed. 'Not sure women trained in architecture that long ago.'

'Or only really ambitious ones, a generation or more ahead of yourself.' He grew silent for a few moments, then asked what made her choose that career.

'Loving the idea of working with stone, originally, but without possessing the slightest inclination to become a builder.'

'Fortunately. You'd have ruined those lovely hands. And I'd hate you to risk your neck scrambling about on scaffolding.'

'I'd never contemplate that, not after Dad's accident.'

'How did that happen, was it serious?' his voice deepened in concern.

'Wasn't sure if I'd ever told you. I try not to lumber everybody with family problems. He was up on scaffolding against the gable end of a civic building. There was a fierce wind that day, but then there often is near us. No one's ever been sure if the wind was partly to blame. Or if one of the scaffolders failed to check every metal joint. End result was the platform collapsed, Dad fell with it.'

She heard Adrian draw in a sharp breath.

'He must have been badly injured.'

Jane nodded. 'We almost lost count of the weeks in hospital. We'll always be thankful we didn't lose him, but his worst hurt was facing life in a wheelchair.'

78

'How distressing. For you all.'

Adrian reached out sympathetically, and grasped her knee. Through the soft texture of her skirt his touch felt reassuring, but awakened more, an intense assertion of an inner yearning. A longing to seek a solution to a need greater than any she should be experiencing here with this man.

I wish he'd move his hand, thought Jane, while her pounding senses craved its remaining there. Neither spoke for what seemed protracted minutes of soaring attraction, an insistence that she could not bear, but one which she only reluctantly would relinquish.

A darting cat as they drove through the suburbs demanded his full command of the wheel, and left Jane feeling deserted.

Adrian's laugh was rueful. 'Thank heaven puss didn't pay the price of my inattention.'

When he drew up outside one of the London clubs he appeared totally at ease. Jane hoped that she might become equally relaxed. What was wrong with her, she could not imagine. She and Adrian had got along perfectly happily, being companionable and no more. She had no right to spoil everything by beginning to fancy him. How could this be happening while she thought the world of Henri?

The club looked elegant, so smart that Jane wished that she had brought an evening gown away with her. Once inside however, where uniforms seemed in favour alongside more elaborate dress, she soon felt easier.

They ate at a table for two where Adrian selected for her when asked, and then teased that she might again wish to drink port with lemon.

'I'll leave the choice of drink as well to you, Scotty,' she responded firmly. 'Just remember I'm relying on you to get me back to our base tonight.'

'If much later,' he added, smiling mischievously.

I love you in this mood, thought Jane, before mentally correcting 'love' to 'like'. He was a dear person, though, despite the teasing.

'Let's see how you cope with dancing, Yorkshire,' he suggested when they had eaten their first course.

'Afraid I'm not very good.'

Adrian seemed not to hear her; and in his arms she appeared to lose the first fraction of misgivings. The tune was a quickstep, which might have been worse, she'd never been very swift at adopting intricate footwork.

He danced like a star, one who had mastered every nuance that might contribute to showing his prowess. Holding her, guiding her, his firm thigh directing each step, Adrian had all the power to make *her* accomplished.

'I loved that, thank you,' Jane told him, returning to their table for their next course.

'My pleasure,' he said, his tone making the words far more than a cliché.

'What exactly is your work?' asked Jane, thinking to break the sexual tension that threatened to overwhelm every one of her pulses.

'I fly 'planes,' he told her solemnly.

'Even I could have guessed that one.'

Jane sipped her drink, tried to avoid his disturbingly amused eyes. Adrian had chosen well from the wine list, something pale and smooth, neither sweet nor dry, and French.

Memories arose of other wines, other days, of another man, the one she might always love.

'Let's dance again,' Adrian insisted.

The foxtrot was slow, quite the slowest ever, providing time in which to fit her steps to his, to yield all resistance and relish the arms that held her. Sensuous as a caress, the music fuelled her desire, evaporated her unspoken, private protests.

'You, Yorkshire Jane, have restored my sense of joy.'

Against her ear Adrian's words were a shock, the very last she'd have expected from this man she'd thought the epitome of self-possession. Jane was unprepared for accepting his admission as utterly serious.

'That has to be your line with every girl!'

'Actually, it's not. But I will allow you might have someone in your life who would prevent me from pursuing my feelings to their conclusion.'

Jane would not say, could not spoil this dance with words to destroy emotions.

As the foxtrot ended she prayed to be left unquestioned.

Adrian was not deterred. A few sips of wine, and he refused to have her escape without answering.

'Some Yorkshire squire, is he perhaps? Or a mill owner who seeks to make you his wife? There again, could be that you'll only be satisfied with a man in a familiar line – is there some husky master builder? Perhaps a fellow architect?'

'No one like that, not like any of those.'

Adrian relented. The night was theirs, and must not be destroyed. Jane could not know that he dreaded the threat that it might be his last in her company. He was no fool, rarely had been one, and could not doubt that this war would soon enough remove feelings of permanence. If it should be that Fortune – or Whoever – favoured them, there might be further chances. And if that were not to be – he had never previously failed – however reluctantly – to find consolation . . .

His brief seriousness made Jane think, overlaying desire with the need for consideration. She never teased, except innocently within the safety of her own family, and now she would not. Adrian had been good to her, and good *for* her, he did not deserve the complexity of her feelings.

This is ending now, she reminded herself, while trying to sort her own emotions without seeming to ignore him. Adrian couldn't be giving her a happier climax to the work that she'd completed, but how could she show appreciation and not risk his misinterpreting that as encouragement?

Away from here, tomorrow or the next day, she would be back to normal. Jane sensed already that whenever family concerns weren't preoccupying her she would revert to her perpetual concern – for Henri Bodin.

They danced again and the wine she'd drunk freed her feet to follow Adrian's lead quite stylishly, and freed her anxious spirit of the instinct to be cautious. The music was good, made her relish dancing until she surrendered to its beat, to the nearness of her partner.

Jane had been aware of him during the outward journey. On the homeward run she was conscious of nothing beyond the pulsing in her veins, that deep resonance generated by Adrian.

They kissed in the car park of their darkened inn, each reluctant to end the night, both acknowledging the need surging through them.

At the door of her room they kissed again, pressing close, desire willing away inhibitions yet still they each steadfastly respected their individual conventions.

'Do you have to go home to Yorkshire?' Adrian's voice was husky.

'You know I do, my work here's finished.'

'Then delay another day. I have leave owing me, plan to go north to Hamilton. I'll drive you home, it is on my way, after all.'

Agreeing might appease her urgent senses. And would bestow time in which they both might consider if there was some place for these confusing emotions.

The alacrity with which Adrian arranged immediate leave made Jane wonder again what precisely his work might be, it also made her concerned. There could be no denying they were fiercely attracted to each other, Jane hoped she'd been as careful as she'd intended to avoid convincing him that their relationship had a future.

On the day they set out she nevertheless couldn't help feeling happy, and Adrian was in high spirits. He offered to let her drive his car.

Jane refused very swiftly. 'Thank you, but I couldn't. Your MG's much smarter than my little Morris Eight – it also seems a lot more powerful.'

'As you wish. But it will be a long journey, you might get bored.'

'You don't have to tell me how far it is – I have driven down south in my own car, even as far as Dover.'

'Ah – an experienced motorist!' he teased.

'Happen so, and one that knows her limitations.'

Adrian laughed. He did a lot of laughing on that cold but dry winter's day, calling her 'Yorkshire' until she was obliged to retaliate with 'Scotty'. He kept asking about her parents, and was eager to meet them. Jane had telephoned her mother to say she was coming home and, perhaps unguardedly, had agreed to Sheila's suggestion that Adrian must be invited to have a meal with them.

En route they paused for lunch in a Leicestershire village, but both were hungry by the time they were driving through the West Riding.

'Tell me about that,' Adrian demanded, pointing to the Wainhouse Tower.

They were taking a short cut Jane had recommended up Skircoat Moor Road in Halifax.

'Do you want the truth, or the fantasy? One story goes that it was constructed for some businessman who wanted to overlook his neighbour's place, and spite him. Otherwise, it was started as a chimney for a dyeworks. It was never used as a chimney, I do know that. I think the dyeworks had been sold by the time Wainhouse Tower was completed.'

'That must have taken some time.'

'Four or five years, I believe. It certainly bears witness to the stonemason's craft.'

'And to some architect's. More interesting than working on an underground control room, eh, Jane?'

'There would have been some underground construction involved in this case, had it been utilized as a chimney. The dyeworks was down in the valley, there was to have been a flue deep in the earth to connect them.'

'What use has been made of the tower then?'

'Not a great deal – it was sold just before the end of the nineteenth century to a chap who intended letting people go up to the viewing area. I think now there's talk of the ARP adopting it as an observation post.'

'The tower certainly commands an excellent vantage point. I take it that you can confirm that?'

'Aye, I've been to the top – all four hundred-odd steps! Part of any local architect's training.'

They were journeying along Burnley Road, passed through Luddenden Foot and were soon heading through the valley towards Hebden Bridge. Jane was beginning to feel a shade uneasy, wondering how Adrian would fit into her home. Good though he had been to her, she knew very little about him, and nothing at all about *his* family.

'Another tower?' he remarked, indicating the pinnacle on the crest of a hill to their left.

'A monument, and rather older – Stoodley Pike, it was built after Napoleon was beaten. There's a grand view from up yonder.'

'I do know that, I passed quite close when I walked that way.'

It would be interesting to walk these hills with you, thought Jane, and willed herself not to permit the words to trip off her tongue. She must do nothing that could be construed as leading him on.

They had reached the house. Before she got out of the car and found her key, Jane saw her mother was at the door, opening it wide, smiling.

'Come on in, both of you. It is good to see you. Adrian, isn't it, have I got that right?' Sheila added, shaking his hand before ushering them indoors.

Alfred Townsend was waiting impatiently, his wheelchair near the door that led from the hall into the kitchen.

'Eh, Jane love, it is grand to have you back home!' He looked up into her eyes, his own suddenly moist.

The moment she had hugged her father, he was smiling towards Adrian. 'How do you do, young man? I see you've managed to bring my lass home to us – and I hear tell you looked after her fair champion. I hope we shall be able to do the same for you, if only for a few hours.'

The 'few hours' extended into an overnight stay when their evening meal became as protracted as it was proving convivial.

'Do you have to be home tonight specially?' Sheila asked him. 'We've got more than one spare room ready, to say nothing of the couple more as is empty now our lads have joined up.'

Adrian needed little persuading to stay the night, and appeared delighted when Alfred offered to show him the stone he was carving.

'He seems very nice, a lovely man,' said Sheila while she and Jane were washing the dishes. 'And no side on him either, he might have known us for years.'

Jane rather wished that Adrian had done so. As a family friend, he might have seemed less exciting, nowhere near so great a threat to her tranquillity.

'And he seems to really appreciate you,' her mother continued. 'What you can do, and so on. Happen because he's clever himself, he can recognize a soulmate.'

Jane would have queried the expression 'soulmate', but she was determined to say nothing to either parent which might encourage questions about her feelings regarding Adrian Stewart.

Before she waved him off the following morning she learned that by going down early for breakfast Adrian had ensured a private chat with Sheila.

'Your mother has clarified one thing for me, which you declined to elaborate on,' he told Jane, his blue eyes glittering. 'I'm very thankful to learn that I've a clear field. You can be confident that I shall be in touch with you again.'

'If it's to take me to see round that command centre when it's finished, I'll be ever so grateful,' Jane said quickly. She had wondered quite how to extract his promise to arrange for her to see the place.

'That could make a focal point for one meeting. If that's the best you're offering.'

After she had said goodbye to Adrian as he finally drove away, her father had something equally disturbing to say: 'I'm right proud of you, our Jane, you've made a hit with that young man – and him a squadron leader an' all. Not that you'd believe he had that much standing, he's such a *genuine* bloke. I told him I'd taken to him straight away.'

Jane might feel pleased the few hours Adrian had spent in her home had passed quite smoothly, but her father had shaken her. She couldn't believe that she had known Adrian so long without finding out he was a squadron leader.

Learning his rank immediately made her struggle to recall her initial attitude towards him. Hadn't she issued retort for retort, even been quite impertinent?

As for her father's assurance that he had taken to the man, she'd have preferred that to remain unspoken. If she'd been bringing Adrian home for parental approval, Sheila and Alfred Townsend couldn't have done more. Unfortunately, that was *not* the case. Jane could only hope now that ensuring he didn't return there would prevent Adrian from believing their ready acceptance of him mattered.

Jane was still feeling uneasy a few hours later when her mother remembered a letter recently arrived for her.

'I didn't post it on because I was expecting you home. And then yesterday I knew you wouldn't want me to be on about that chap in France while Adrian was staying here for the first time.'

Jane sighed. 'There was no earthly reason for you to conceal Henri's letter, Mum. Adrian's a friend, that's all. And with Henri miles away in France while there's a war on it's surely to be expected that I'm desperate for news of him.'

'I hope you're not playing one young man against the other, those aren't our ways. I brought you up to know better.'

'Of course I'm not.'

'Then what is going on? What am I to think when you don't tell me what there is between you and that squadron leader you brought home?'

'Nothing. Like I said, there's nothing between me and Adrian. We were doing a job that entailed his taking me to the site. We got on all right.'

'He seemed very smitten with you while he was staying here.'

'That's just the way he is,' said Jane, and hoped that it was. With the exception of the remarks from his RAF colleagues about girls he acquired, she had learned scarcely anything about Adrian's personal life.

'Are you sure? You can't tell me he'd have brought a girl he hardly knew all these miles, just to see her safely home.'

'This was on his way – to his own home in Scotland,' Jane reminded her mother sharply, and turned to hurry upstairs to her room to read Henri's letter.

The address at the head of the page was the Bodin château. Jane was quite surprised, and also relieved: if he hadn't moved to the apartment where his maps were kept Henri must feel safe enough.

This was confirmed as soon as she began reading.

For the present the situation here remains quiet, I sincerely hope that also is true for you in England. We worry, naturally, about the threat to our peace, but life here is not as yet substantially different since events of early September.

Louis is planning excitedly for Christmas, and dear Bernadette is working determinedly to produce treats enough to convince us that we must celebrate.

The two of them send you their love, and hope that you are well.

Louis has grown considerably taller, and looks older than he is, something that is substantiated by his vocabulary, which is peculiarly mature – no doubt on account of his spending too much time with adults.

I trust that this looming war will not hinder his eventual commencement at school, or I fear he will suffer the lack of children who are around his own age.

I hear on the radio and read in the press of the English children who are evacuated from their homes. Are any of these arriving in Yorkshire? It seems to me that your county will be more safe than other areas of England. I tell myself that you should find that it is so.

Jane read on, expecting to learn of his deep concern for her safety, if not of his love, and found no mention of either. The final paragraph referred to the renovations of the château which Henri had been obliged to suspend while he fulfilled orders for the maps which were his business.

He signed off, *Votre affectionné*, but still left Jane disappointed. Only on rereading the letter did she reflect on the fact that he *had* expressed the hope that the situation in England remained quiet.

Jane shook her head dismally, feeling confused. They seemed to be skating on the surface of their friendship, avoiding any indication of its depth. Was her own reticence responsible for eliciting these somewhat cool words from Henri? The work she had done these past few weeks had driven from her mind any clear recollections of their earlier correspondence. She could read his letters again, as she would, but she suspected she would need something concrete to convince her she hadn't been wrong originally to believe Henri might be beginning to love her.

She could write back straight away, Jane resolved, and smiled. She'd have so much to tell about her work on that control centre. Only then she shook her head, remembering the confidentiality concerning that task. But this still could be the time to confirm how greatly she was missing Henri. Since there seemed to be no immediate danger in his part of France, this should be an ideal opportunity to visit him again. She would suggest that to him, seeing each other again ought to put everything right between them.

During breakfast the following morning Jane was working out in her mind what she would write back to Henri.

Suddenly Sheila's hand flew up to her eyes and she moaned. 'Oh, not again!'

'Whatever's wrong, Mum?' Sheila was so rarely ill, and certainly not given to reacting with the alarm now so evident.

'It'll be another of them migraines,' said Alfred 'I had to get her next door to fetch the doctor last week. That's what he said it were - and she's had 'em afore.'

'I didn't know you were subject to migraine, Mum. Why haven't you said?'

'You weren't here. T' first in recent years were when your grandfather died.'

'They've come more often sin' our Phil and Jack joined up, though,' Alfred continued.

'Hadn't you better take a Cephos tablet or something for the pain?' suggested Jane anxiously.

'I will in a bit. Trouble is I can't be sure I shan't be sick, that's what happens sometimes. I'll have to have a lie down though, it's affected my eyes badly again like last time.'

After helping Sheila up the stairs to her room and using the blackout curtain to exclude all daylight, Jane went to find her father.

Alfred was in his wheelchair precisely where they had left him beside the kitchen table. Jane could see he was too perturbed to wheel himself anywhere, or to do anything.

'You ought to have told me that Mum was getting these bad heads, Dad.'

'There's more to 'em than a headache, you know. They really lay her low, and you know my Sheila – she isn't one for giving in. It's not being able to see proper as does it, then there's the sickness. That last time it were a sort of – well, a paralysis in her arm, an' all. I were terrified she were going to end up like me.'

'But the paralysis came right again, surely?'

'Oh, aye. Like the doctor said it would. Worst on it is, when she's like that neither of us can do owt.'

'I can understand that must make it more worrying. Still, I'm at home now, and I don't know that I'll be sent to work away again, do I?'

Jane needed to think this through, try to discover some solution which enabled her father to do more towards coping if her mother suffered further attacks.

Certainly, for the present, she should not contemplate suggesting to Henri that she might visit him. There would be enough of a problem about leaving her parents if she were again expected to travel anywhere in connection with her work.

The awful thing was that suddenly Jane felt she was being trapped there. *But this is my home, that feeling is ridiculous!* she told herself. She shouldn't be needing to get away.

Six

Christmas 1939 wasn't an occasion that Jane could feel excited about. Butter, bacon, meat and sugar were all likely to be rationed before the month was out, reminding families that any celebrations should be curtailed because of the war. Her mother had tried to beat the scheduled rationing by stocking up on provisions before the official restrictions.

That had been one day when Sheila Townsend came home in a temper from her visit to the local Co-op. Her grey head tossing in annoyance would remain a vivid picture in her daughter's memory for a very long time.

'I was mortified,' she told Jane, shaking with such indignation that she was fumbling to unfasten the buttons of her winter coat. 'Nobody's ever talked like that to me before, and there was no need for it now. Telling me I ought to have more thought for them as brings food to this country. Reminding me that there's a war on. *Me* – that has two sons away in the forces, and a daughter who has to help plan buildings and – and stuff for the air force.'

'What's all the to-do about, love?' Alfred enquired softly, wheeling his chair through from the workroom.

'Yon manager at the Co-op – and I shan't want serving again by him in a hurry, I can tell you. All I wanted was to be able to give my family a bit of a treat this Christmas.'

'They're applying their own form of rationing already then?' Jane suggested.

'That chap back there certainly is! How dare he imply that I was seeking more than my fair share. There'll be five of us if the lads can get leave, them mouths take some feeding.'

*   *   *

When Christmas approached it became clear that Jack would be home for a day or two, but Phil would not. In a rare letter he'd told them he wouldn't be coming to Hebden Bridge. Jane noticed he didn't say he was unable to get leave, and wondered if he was enjoying himself too much where he was.

From the start of his service in the navy everything that Phil had told them showed that he was relishing the life. He'd always got along well with people of a similar age, and had a talent for socializing. If the training was proving tough he'd had enough of a grounding in physical work to give him some advantage now.

'I wonder if there's a girl he's met there,' Sheila remarked.

'Trust you, Mum, you're always trying to fix us up with partners.'

Jane had reason to feel embarrassed about that. She could still picture the whole episode after Adrian Stewart had telephoned to check that he might call to see her on his way south again.

'It's only a matter of days since he dropped me off here, but I've still found myself inviting him for lunch,' she observed bemusedly to her parents.

Her father chuckled. 'Got to admit he couldn't be more keen, our Jane.'

Sheila's enthusiasm went even further. 'I reckon he's the one – and such a gentleman too. I'd be so proud if this came to something.'

'Mother!' Jane interrupted sharply. 'There's not going to be anything like that between us – I'm not in love with Adrian, nor likely to be.'

'You could look further, and fare a hell of a lot worse,' her father asserted.

Adrian's visit wasn't a success. With both parents looking for signs that they might believe Jane was merely concealing her true feelings about the man, she felt totally inhibited. Having seen him only so recently, and with no prospect of her own work providing fresh interest, she'd scarcely anything to dredge up to discuss.

Sheila and Alfred compensated, or overcompensated – disturbing Jane by hauling up memories of her past which she would have chosen to leave interred.

Her unease made her abnormally clumsy, and she spattered soup down her clean white blouse.

Her mother smiled confidingly towards their guest. 'Our Jane allus were dirty with her clothes, she never ought to wear white. There was once when she was a little lass and I'd got her dressed lovely ready for going out. Then her next door went and gave her a chocolate biscuit. I had to bring her back in, and wash her face and hands, change her frock and cardigan . . .'

Adrian's amusement was ill-concealed. 'But she has grown up to be very smart, a credit to you both.'

'We like to think so,' her father confirmed. 'And she has such a way with her – always was the favourite with her grandfather Townsend, you know. He was highly delighted when she qualified. There aren't many women architects, even these days.'

It went on and on, until Jane was desperate for release from being the focus of attention. Even if she'd been trying to attract Adrian, and she wasn't, she'd have felt horrified. Totally unable to behave naturally.

Seeing him to his car, her smile was rueful. 'Sorry you had to endure that.'

'Worth it, to catch up with you again. I hope this won't be our last meeting, you know, Jane.'

'Depends where this war sends us both, doesn't it? There is one thing, though – if it's at all possible I really would love to see that control centre when it's finished. Do you think you might be able to arrange that?'

'I'll do my damnedest. Keep in touch then. Take care of yourself, Jane.'

Adrian kissed her, full on the lips, and before she'd considered if that were wise she was hugging him. Her parents had been such a bore. Even though surprised by how soon he'd wanted to see her again, Jane couldn't help wishing these few hours could have been less awkward.

Two Christmas cards arrived from Adrian, one addressed to her parents, the other for Jane herself, and both were delivered early. With Jane's he enclosed his RAF address, she would have been churlish to ignore that and refuse to post a card to him. And he had said to keep in touch – if she really wanted to see how her architectural drawings had been interpreted, Adrian's assistance could provide the opportunity to view the place.

There was no Christmas card from Henri, but she did receive a short note, with which he enclosed a letter from young Louis. In painstaking English the boy explained that he was helping Bernadette to cook a special cake. They were to have fun on Christmas Eve, and he wished that Jane could stay with them.

Grimly, she reflected that his *Oncle* Henri might have been the one to express such a wish. Without *his* suggestion that she visit, she could do nothing.

Jane still thought of Henri a great deal throughout that Christmas holiday, and longed for him more than ever because of her brother's surprising news.

Jack arrived home on Christmas Eve, thumped down his kitbag in a corner of their hall, and called to them cheerfully.

'You'll never guess what's happening – me and Cynthia's getting wed! On Saturday.'

Sheila came running out of the kitchen. 'Next Saturday, you mean?'

'The thirtieth, aye. Booked the registrar and everything.'

'Eh, love, I am pleased. Wish you'd given us a bit more notice, though. I'll have a job getting something new for t' wedding. And then there'll be the catering.'

'That's down to Cynthia's folk, isn't it. Her mother's got it all in hand. Besides, it won't be a big do. Just us lot, and a few from their family.'

'Do you hear that, Alfred?' Sheila called.

Her husband was already trundling through to join them.

'Hello, Jack lad – that's champion news. We must have a talk

94

when you've settled in again, like. You'll have to tell me all about it.'

'Tell us both, more like,' Sheila added firmly.

Joining them from Alfred's room where he'd been showing her his latest work, Jane kissed Jack, and gave him a searching look. She'd heard little enough about Cynthia since Jack and the girl had had that difference of opinion around a year ago. What had brought them back together, and suddenly eager to marry?

'Aren't you going to congratulate me, Jane?' he demanded.

She grinned. 'Sure, it's good. Glad you've made your mind up, both of you.'

The rest of the country, if not most of the world, was experiencing such an upheaval she could be glad for any couple who found their own kind of security.

Jane wondered during Christmas where Jack and Cynthia would make their home. His being in the army made a difference, of course, but they would need a base. Perhaps they would have his old room, or somewhere in her parents' house, although that didn't seem to provide much spare accommodation.

When Cynthia joined them for dinner on Christmas Day she was so elated that she brought a sparkle to the celebrations for which Jane had felt no enthusiasm. Jack's evident happiness relieved any anxiety about his side in the decision.

On Boxing Day the family were all invited to have tea with Cynthia's parents, and plans for the wedding were discussed excitedly while the gramophone provided a background of Christmas carols.

Driving her parents back to the house afterwards Jane felt thankful that her brother's marriage seemed to be lifting any possible gloom from this first wartime Christmas.

The next few days were hectic with preparations. Although their parents would have been happier if a church service had been envisaged, both families were determined to give the couple a day they would always remember. As soon as the shops opened after the short holiday Jane took her mother to choose a fresh hat. Sheila was resolved to mark the occasion with at least one thing new, and was reluctant to invest in a coat while this war seemed to preclude extravagance.

Jane herself had looked out a hat and coat she'd bought only the previous winter and would wear them with a frock purchased a month ago. Despite her own determination to buy nothing, she enjoyed the shopping trip with her mother, something they didn't recall doing together since before Jane had begun studying.

The day of the wedding was wet, and while Jack bemoaned the dismal weather others reflected that winter in Hebden Bridge might have meant coping with snow.

Jane smiled to herself while she and Sheila were getting ready to go out. She could hear Alfred somewhere downstairs giving Jack his 'little talk'. Most of the words were inaudible from a distance but now and then she caught odd phrases.

Much of it seemed, predictably, to involve 'providing a good home', and 'keeping sober now he must remember his responsibilities', until Alfred's voice lowered and he began speaking of the wedding night.

Jane glanced towards her mother, wondering how much she had heard, but Sheila was concentrating, having trouble combing her hair which was freshly permed for Christmas. Jane herself wondered how Jack would keep a straight face during the lecture: from what Cynthia had revealed, neither of them had needed much education regarding sex for some long while.

Despite the brief amusement, Jane felt quite emotional by the time they were assembling before the registrar's desk. Cynthia looked stunning in a pale cream woollen dress and coat whose fur collar perfectly framed her dark bobbed hair.

Her face was made up, but not too heavily, it was the glow of excitement more than any artifice which enhanced her.

I wish I'd made myself look better, thought Jane, She didn't often spend a lot of time on her appearance, but today was one occasion when she might have done something different with her hair. There had been a last minute rush, her dad had mislaid his Sunday tie, Jane had sped to search for it.

Alfred was very smart now, though, looking much like the father she remembered, despite that wretched chair. At least it wasn't as obvious today as it would be if his daughter needed escorting down a church aisle somewhere.

Thinking that way began from a feeling of relief, but suddenly Jane was overwhelmed with longing. Sitting behind their Jack while he made his vows, she'd noticed already that his army training was thinning him down, tall and with dark hair he reminded her someone. Realizing who that was made her heart lurch, she could never forget Henri Bodin. This focus on weddings made Jane sure that, foolishly or not, if she didn't marry Henri she wouldn't wish to marry anybody.

She suspected she was being an idiot to feel so certain about her future. Such an idea was founded on nothing more substantial than a dream. The reality was harsh – Henri hadn't even suggested that she should visit him again.

For Jack's sake and for Cynthia's, Jane made herself smile and be sociable while, along with her new sister-in-law's family, she passed around plates of food at the buffet meal in their hired hall.

Cynthia was delighted with her, said how much she was going to love having a 'sister', while Jane silently thanked the circumstances that now removed her private disagreement with the girl's attitude to sex.

Jane wondered if Cynthia could be expecting, although she'd heard other guests holding the war responsible for the unexpected decision to marry. She rather hoped that Cynthia's slender figure really did witness that there was no baby. And she did hold the war responsible for *that* reflection. There was so much uncertainty in all their lives.

Jack brought home his bride that first night to the room where he'd grown up, and which his mother protested should have been thoroughly redecorated.

'You ought to have let me know your plans,' Sheila reproved him. 'It's years since that room was done before, and with

Christmas and that I haven't had time to wash the draw-on curtains. I did the nets the other week, though, and the bedspread's clean on. But I'm not happy about that eiderdown.'

Cynthia and Jack looked at each other and laughed. Jane wondered if Sheila couldn't see that their Jack wouldn't be worrying about having a lot of smart covers on the bed.

From that day it seemed that her brother ceased to worry about anything. His decision was made, his and Cynthia's, and they both were all the better for having stabilized their future.

Even the thought of his returning to the army appeared to do little to dim the satisfaction so evident in the pair. Jane was surprised that Cynthia didn't look upset by the prospect of a parting which must seem hard to bear.

The reason for her sister-in-law's equanimity emerged while they all sat around the kitchen table for their last meal before Jack's departure.

'Are you seeing him off at the station, love?' Jane asked. She could drive them down into Hebden Bridge, but wouldn't they prefer to be alone together? The last few minutes before parting for an unspecified length of time would be precious.

Cynthia swallowed a mouthful of tea, set down her cup, glanced towards Jack and then across at Jane.

'Actually, I'm not seeing him off. I'm going back with Jack, it's all arranged. I was down that way until we came home for Christmas. I've got a job in the NAAFI, not on their camp there's an RAF base quite close.'

'Oh, I see, that's nice,' said Sheila.

'Aye, aye. Well done,' Alfred added.

Jane didn't know what to say. Only eventually did she manage, 'You must be very pleased.'

For some reason which she couldn't immediately identify, she felt peculiarly uneasy. Why should she sense some threat to the family was being generated?

The conversation turned to more general matters, as the war obtruded on their conversation. The people of Finland claimed to be reinforcing their border, pushing back the Russians with whom they had fought for the past month. And the wireless had news that Hitler had spent Christmas with his troops on the western front. Jack's theory was that Hitler needed to boost their morale after the Graf Spee was scuttled by her crew when trapped by British warships in the River Plate.

'So you think you'll enjoy working in the NAAFI, Cynthia,' said Jane hastily.

The word 'warships' had made Sheila frown, reminding Jane how she had struggled to keep back news of the Royal Oak being sunk by a German torpedo at Scapa Flow much earlier, during October. With Phil putting to sea somewhere, their mother was agitated by any word about U-boats, shelling or bombs.

Cynthia was smiling again. 'I dare say the NAAFI will suit me, for a while. Until we know where Jack's going to be sent. And I like it down south.'

'We both do,' said Jack. 'It's so much livelier down yonder.'

'Happen they didn't go short like we did up north, during the Depression,' Sheila remarked. 'You young folk don't know one half of it.'

'Nay, don't go bothering them wi' that, not today,' Alfred reproached her. 'We managed, and Jack knows we got the business back on to a better footing again. Once this lot's over, he'll be glad to come back to run Townsend's.'

'Er – well, that's what I was going to say,' Jack began. 'There's so many more opportunities will open up round London, places like that. You should see some of the grand housing they've put up – for ordinary folk, not just them as are well off.'

'I'll bet they're not built of good Yorkshire stone,' his father observed.

Jack laughed. 'You and your stone, you'll never come round to considering owt else, will you? Don't forget there are brick works round here an' all – some of them bricks will be going into buildings down south.'

Alfred shrugged, but his son hadn't finished.

'Any road, that's where our future's going to be, mine and

Cynthia's. Soon as the war's over, we shall buy our own place, move on from where we're renting. And there'll be plenty of work, I'll warrant.'

'And what about Townsend's? Don't sit there with that self-satisfied grin and tell me that you can disregard all the work we've put into the firm!'

'Alf . . .' Sheila interrupted worriedly, but was silenced by her husband's impatient gesture.

'We'd better hear what the lad has to say for himself.'

Jack shrugged. He was still smiling. 'There's only one answer, isn't there – move.'

'Move the business away from Yorkshire? You're wrong in your head! We belong here, always have done, allus will. Nay, lad – you'll do what you've a mind to, after this war's over. We're stopping where we are, and we'll manage wi'out folk that're eager to turn their backs on us.'

'Don't you see, Jack,' his mother intervened. 'We love this house, everything round here, we couldn't leave.'

Jack nodded. 'I see that's how you feel, aye. What I can't see is your logic.' He glanced at his watch. 'Time we were off for that train, Cynthia.'

He thanked them for all they had done towards the wedding, gave Sheila and Jane a hug, and Cynthia hugged them too. He grasped his father by the shoulder, but neglected to apologize or explain further.

'There's nothing to stop you two moving after the war, you know, Dad.'

'Never!'

It was an uncomfortable leave-taking, one to be regretted. Jane felt even worse when her mother complained of a migraine as soon as the three of them were alone.

Coming back to her father after taking Sheila to her bed, Jane felt drained, more than a little alarmed.

Alfred Townsend's words soon confirmed her alarm as reasonable. 'There we are then – at least we know where we stand. Until our Phil is home again, it's going to be up to you and me, lass.'

'Just a minute, Dad,' she interrupted gently. 'I don't want you forgetting that I have my own work. I'm hoping to get involved in other building schemes for the forces, and then there may be something that Hugh Dunstan will put my way.'

'All right, love, all right. Happen I was tending to forget. Any road, I'm not finished yet, not by a long way. I can do the books, all the ordering, I've done invoicing in the past. And that team of chaps I brought together when the lads joined up are getting used to the way I want the work done.'

Her father's plans sounded over-optimistic to Jane, an instant reaction in defiance of the blow Jack had rendered. She had a nasty feeling that she could be committed to tethering herself to the business, if not to her parents, and potentially for even longer than it took to win this war against Hitler.

'I don't suppose I'll be too far away to keep an eye on things here,' she said. Trudging back upstairs to discover if Sheila needed anything, Jane resigned herself to adapting to a life swiftly developing additional limitations.

1940 began badly for France with a German onslaught along a front north of Paris. Amid news of shipping losses, anxiety about men at sea intensified, and the weather contributed its own disturbance. For the first time since 1888 the Thames froze over.

Alfred laughed. 'Wonder where the army's sent our Jack now? Hope he's enjoying the freeze down yonder.'

'It might not be as bad as what we're getting up here,' said Sheila reasonably.

The whole of Europe was suffering bad conditions. Towards the end of January Britain began to endure terrible storms.

Alfred smiled no longer when the men he employed couldn't continue to work. Jane thought about Henri and his Loire valley home, where no doubt reconstruction had ceased. If that hadn't already been suspended completely. He had said something about needing to concentrate on his map-making. Who is he selling to now, she wondered, praying that it wasn't to the Germans. Jane wished yet again that she knew. Needing to know what Henri was doing, where he was, or if he was well seemed constantly to gnaw into her.

What did anyone do when the things that they produced might become a means of advancing a battle front? How did one square the need to keep a business running with the demands of conscience? The only thing Jane discovered from pondering this was her own allegiance, which seemed to remain with Henri, no matter where his actions placed him.

This absence of regular contact with him was making her concern for his safety obsessive. At the time when she'd rushed home on her grandfather's death, Henri had given her the telephone numbers of both his apartment and the château. He, however, had never called her, and Jane's inherent reservations always made her hesitate to telephone him. Even if the uncertainties of wartime might have made enquiring after his well-being acceptable.

Jane supposed there were girls now who rang a man up when they felt they'd been out of touch for too long. This was something she'd never done, Sheila Townsend had always asserted her belief that the man must do any chasing.

Henri was on her mind so much that Jane's anxiety on his behalf surfaced whenever she had trouble sleeping. He also featured in frequent dreams where, along with young Louis, the three of them felt to be a perfect family. So perfect that she would awaken to ever greater dissatisfaction.

This was alleviated slightly when Jane became busier. Calling in at Hugh Dunstan's office in that February of 1940, she learned that he had further projects for her to look into.

'There's a lot of construction going on all up and down the country, as you'll probably be aware. Much of it's hush-hush, of course, but you'll have experienced that aspect with the job you've done already.'

'I know when to keep quiet about what's being developed, if that's what you mean,' said Jane, hoping the work might prove at least as interesting as before.

'There are airfields, and new stations for this radar that's going to make such a difference to the war,' Hugh told her.

'Speedy construction is the essence, naturally, but somebody still has to confirm that the buildings will be safe.'

'Do you mean I'd be involved from the design stage?' Jane began to feel a surge of anticipation. It seemed such a long time since she had drafted any plans from scratch.

'Hardly that, I'm afraid. These chaps know precisely what they need – it's more a matter of making sure most of our principles of construction are adhered to. Any road, Jane, they've passed on to me this list of sites. Do your best, eh?'

During Jane's first assignment on that control centre for Fighter Command, her only regret had been having too little involvement in what she considered any *real architecture*. She soon discovered that these later tasks offered even less scope for utilizing her skills. To make matters worse, starting with her first visit to one of these sites, Jane received the impression that her presence was largely seen as a nuisance.

Equipped though she was with knowledge gained through lengthy training, her embarrassment increased when it seemed *yet again* that she'd had the misfortune to try to help in places where she wasn't really required.

In more than one area people seemed already to have received enough expert advice, and didn't welcome more. Least of all from a woman. This was no one's fault, as Jane quickly recognized, but brief inspections of their plans – of constructions already begun, even of some actually completed – were doing nothing for her need to help fight the war.

Travelling on crowded, often delayed, trains to sites that frequently were in remote areas of the countryside was disheartening, but might have been compensated had she felt she was doing useful work at any one destination. Those winter months early in 1940 only endowed Jane with deep discouragement.

On several of the bases already operational she met girls who were training in the WAAF, and again envied them their sense of purpose. This seemed far preferable to visiting places where, if anyone had time to listen to her advice, she was afraid that urgency might not permit full compliance with her recommendations.

Jane hated feeling trapped into travelling up and down to places that weren't offering what she would call satisfying work. But she still needed to comply with Hugh Dunstan's suggestions or she might risk jeopardizing her post-war career.

She envied the men who appeared to join the services with some kind of guarantee that peacetime positions would be kept open for their eventual return.

In the family home the situation was little better. With Jane away quite frequently and both sons in the forces, Alfred was obliged to put in long hours to organize his employees and to keep the paperwork up to date. Days, and sometimes weeks, went by without there being time for returning to the stone carving which he loved. His escape from reality. Frustration over this added to the frustration of his disabilities, making him short-tempered with his wife.

Sheila was accustomed to seeing her menfolk exhausted and irritable, and a part of her was glad simply to have Alfred at home with her, and to see him fully occupied. Since the days when she had been afraid finding books for him from the library would be the best way of filling his time, she now relished the knowledge that he was able to do a proper job again.

Each time that Jane came home dissatisfied with whatever it was that Mr Dunstan was sending her about, Sheila failed to comprehend why her daughter couldn't just be thankful that she wasn't working in some munitions factory.

After one particularly trying journey from Kent where, once again, she seemed to have contributed precious little, Jane flared at her mother who'd remarked that it was nice that she could get about and see so much of the country.

'Nice? Happen it might be, Mum, if I weren't expecting I'd contribute to preparing to beat the Germans. As it is, I feel I'm not doing nearly enough. Nobody has time to listen when I've struggled across miles of countryside on trains and buses, and nor is there time for them to do more than throw together the buildings they want. Dad would be appalled to see what they look like.'

'I'll bet it's not really as bad as that, you've always exaggerated. Especially when you're upset.'

Being made to feel that she might be misjudging her work situation did not help. But Jane was getting used to holding her tongue where a disagreement might make matters in the home uncomfortable. Her mother was healthier than she had been, and only rarely experienced a severe migraine. Aware of her father's dissatisfaction when he could not pursue his carving, Jane had no wish to create more tension there. She understood what frustration did to people.

One night Jane had unpacked her clothes after a trip and was sorting anything that needed washing, when an unexpected appearance on the doorstep shook all three of them.

Opening the door in her nightclothes, Sheila found Phil standing there, leaning against the door frame and looking as though he was in pain.

'Hello, Mum, have you any change? There's a taxi in the road, had to get one from the station, the buses have stopped running for the night.'

Jane ran down the stairs opening her purse, then eased her way past Phil as he limped into the house. She paid off the driver, then hurried back indoors as Sheila was asking her son whatever was wrong.

'Have you been wounded, love?'

'Don't ask, Mum, just don't ask.'

'Well, of course I want to know, I'm your mother, aren't I?'

Phil sighed, shook his head. 'I feel so stupid, that's all. Fell, didn't I – one night when it was icy. Cracked a bone in my foot. Top and bottom of it is, they say I'm no use to them till it's healed. Don't want me cluttering up the place in Portsmouth.'

'Well, it's lovely to have you home again, Phil love,' Sheila exclaimed, theatening to destroy his remaining equilibrium with a massive hug.

'Wasn't there a desk job or something you could do until it's right again?' asked Jane.

Phil grinned. 'Might be, later on. Matter of fact, our petty officer was that irritated with me for doing this in, I think he wanted me out of his sight.'

Jane smiled. 'Oh – well, you'll be able to make yourself useful here, I dare say.'

And, she thought, your being here might allow me to feel free to take off somewhere. She was beginning to believe the WAAF was beckoning so forcefully that she ought to find out more about signing up. She couldn't hold back for ever for fear her boss might become convinced that she was losing interest in architecture.

Seven

J ane laughed out loud after the telephone call, which came on the following day and seemed to provide immediate relief from feeling discouraged. The caller was Adrian Stewart, and although sounding tired he also appeared elated.

'How are you doing, Yorkshire?' he began. 'Keeping busy?'

'Not exactly. None of the work I've been tackling has been very satisfying. I'll tell you later.' If there is a 'later', she thought, while realizing how much hearing his voice cheered her.

'You said you wanted to see the command centre when it's completed. Well, it's now or never – the place'll be operational in next to no time. When can you make a trip to see it?'

'I'll wangle it somehow whenever you suggest.'

'Tomorrow? I'm down here again, could meet your train as before. You'll need to sort out travel arrangements etcetera, then phone me through. I'll fix accommodation for you.'

Jane began by speaking to her boss. No matter how much she wanted to see how the control centre had turned out, she'd only yesterday reflected that she should ensure nothing she did during wartime jeopardized her eventual career.

Hugh listened sympathetically while she reminded him how little she seemed able to contribute to the jobs on which he had sent her out.

'Not my fault, Jane, I hope you realize that. You must know by now that there isn't much going in our normal line of business.'

'I do, that's why I need confirmation that you'll keep my position open for me after the war. If I find there's something else I could do meanwhile.'

'Such as . . . ?'

Jane took a deep breath. 'Well, I am drawn towards the WAAF, but before I make any sort of definite decision there's something I'd like time off for. You remember that underground construction, the conversion for Fighter Command?'

'Yes, yes. If there's something similar on the cards, I've heard nothing.'

'No, it's not that – but the command centre is almost up and running. I've been asked if I want to see it completed.'

'You'd better go along then. There's the chance contacts there might lead to further work. Are you sure about the WAAF, though, Jane? Whilst I'll certainly keep a desk for you here for after the war, I've no wish to lose you now.'

Despite feeling just as unsure of what war work she ought to try, Jane was too elated about her trip to be other than excited as she travelled south again. For once, the trains were running quite well, she was only ten minutes late when she emerged from the station.

Adrian was waiting already in the familiar MG. This time, he sprang from his seat and came round to take her case and open the door for her.

'Hello there, Yorkshire.'

'Hello, Scotty.'

Adrian stood there holding the door until she'd eased herself into the passenger seat. He kissed her then, full on the lips although without lingering. When he had returned to the driving seat, he reached across and squeezed her hand.

'It is lovely to see you, Jane.'

'Thanks. You too.' Suddenly, she didn't know what more to say. It seemed such an age since she'd last seen him, and that had been in her home surrounded by other people. Alone with Adrian like this, she felt unsure of what he expected from her. Their relationship had at times been intense, with attraction a strong element, but there had been nothing to indicate that either of them seriously wished it could endure. And she was more than ever conscious of his being a squadron leader, she'd preferred the days of not being daunted by knowing his rank.

'Afraid you're not staying in the pub this trip,' he announced as he drove off. 'They've always got an overplus of folk there. Mostly potential WAAF personnel, hanging on to learn if they're being taken on.'

'Pity – I thought I might sound a few of the WAAF girls out – fact is, I'm not happy with the jobs I've been doing recently. None of them really need an architect, you know.'

'Why's that – too many of the military buildings being temporary constructions, Nissen huts and . . . ?'

'And aircraft hangars, concrete blocks that look like they're built out of scaled-up children's bricks. That's more or less it. Unless I'm being too choosy.'

'There must be something that'd use your skills to the full.' Adrian sounded so positive Jane wondered if her own attitude was diminishing her opportunities.

'Such as . . .'

'What do you do best – aside from architectural design? What've you always been good at, Jane?'

'Drawing, and I've quite a head for figures, calculations don't worry me.'

'There's one thing springs to my mind, something that's only now being developed fully – camouflage.'

'Painting aeroplanes, and that? Is that what you mean?'

'It's a part of it, but there's going to be much more entailed. There has to be if we're to avoid having the Luftwaffe destroy what little we possess in the way of equipment.'

'Sounds interesting.'

'I can find out more for you, if you really are interested. You'll appreciate that all this is confidential – but I know you already understand what that means. I gather that they're looking into disguising airfields, vital factories as well, so that from the air such installations become concealed from enemy attack.'

Jane turned to him and smiled. 'Could be fun, more importantly it'd be better than trying to force my two-penn'orth on people that'd much rather build what they need as swiftly as possible.'

'If you're seriously considering it as an option, remind me to discover all I can before you set off for Yorkshire again.'

They had driven a further few miles when Adrian pulled off the road in front of what appeared to be a fairly large house.

'We've plenty of space here, we've allocated you a room.'

We? thought Jane, and wondered if he had married. Confused, she tried to remember – hadn't he said there was no one? How much of a difference had Adrian's single status made to her? How much should it have . . . ?

'A couple of the lads from the base are renting the place along with myself. It seems ideal, so far. Near enough to the airfield, can get there as swiftly as from the accommodation on site. And that's in short supply since the latest influx of airmen, no one's opposed our sleeping out of camp.'

Adrian seized her case with one hand, grasped her fingers with the other, and led the way up a narrow path to a door. Jane was steeling herself for meeting his fellow fliers, rather intimidated by what they might think of her.

With the door closed behind them Adrian flicked a switch and the hall was revealed in the beam from a naked bulb.

'Few refinements, I'm afraid. Only moved in a couple of weeks ago. But the beds are fine, we made sure of that.'

Jane was listening for sounds of the others approaching from elsewhere in the house. The place seemed exceptionally quiet compared with the noise she usually associated with having men the age of her brothers about.

'I'll show you your room, and the bathroom.'

Adrian released her hand to lead the way up uncarpeted stairs. The room she was given was large, and its double bed surprised her. Again, the light bulb wasn't enhanced by a shade, and its illumination was meagre, in consideration perhaps of the blackout. Glancing to the window, she suspected the darkly-painted board that had been fitted inside the frame would contain any glow lower than a searchlight.

'Sorry, it's so gloomy. Never enough time to get the place as we want it. Change light bulbs and so on.'

'I thought you were conserving electricity! This will be all right, don't worry.'

'I'll leave you to freshen up, and – whatever. Bathroom's the next door along. Then I'm taking you for a bite to eat.'

Jane wondered if they would be dining at the pub which had been such a feature of her previous stay in the area. Instead, Adrian drove for what seemed like several miles, and parked outside an hotel which looked large from what she could judge in the moonlight.

The food there was as good as, if not better than, any that Eileen had provided. Jane tried to work out how whoever cooked there managed so well now that rationing created so many limitations.

Wine was still available, and not being accustomed to drinking it she felt her head going quite light – not an unpleasant feeling, so long as little was required of her. Adrian appeared to have taken charge to the full, of their conversation as well as of ensuring that she had all she wished.

Letting him lead in whatever they discussed suited her slightly woolly head, and helped Jane to relax and enjoy being with him. He surprised her with talking about her home county, and the walking he had done along the Pennine Way. This led to his further confession that he loved the position of her home with its extensive views over valleys and surrounding hills.

'Did I say that I'd love to walk those hills with you, Jane? I certainly would relish the opportunity to have you show me all the places that you love.'

Jane smiled. 'And what of your home? I don't believe you've told me much about it.'

Adrian told her little now, and left Jane suspecting that there might be some flaw that marred his life in Scotland.

'How are your brothers coping in the forces, are they finding it gruelling?'

She told him about Phil's damaged foot, and then of Jack's return home to marry Cynthia at Christmas.

'There's a lot of that about,' said Adrian. 'Wartime pairings that seem intensified when there's this real threat of partings.'

He was gazing intently into her eyes, his own darkly blue and looking so solemn that Jane supposed there must be some woman somewhere from whom he was separated by war.

Riding back to the house afterwards Jane felt sleepy, but also aware of the attraction that had drawn her towards Adrian during their previous meetings. Beside her in the car every movement he made, turning the wheel or changing gear, became an insistent reminder of how close he was, how very appealing.

I shouldn't be thinking like this, she told herself silently, he might be appalled. In any case, back at the house, she would need to summon some composure while she was introduced to his fellow tenants.

Once again, the place appeared very quiet. Jane wasn't surprised when Adrian said his friends were out.

'They're on "ops" – operations to you.'

'But you're not.'

He shook his head. 'Different sort of job – for the present, at least.'

'Connected with the new command centre?'

'Not really, or only for a couple more days.'

'And you can't tell me what you will be doing then.'

'Better not.' Adrian smiled down at her, asked if she wished to have a hot drink.

'No, thanks – think I've had all I want tonight.'

He was still gazing at her as they stood in the hall before mounting the stairs.

'Why did you ask what I shall be doing? Does that worry you, Jane?'

'Well, of course.'

'Glad to know you care.'

Adrian drew her to him and leaned back against the wall. His face felt cold still from the night air, but his lips grew warm as he covered her eyelids and cheeks with kisses. Her mouth felt his touch tender at first, then bruising. Her lips parted readily for his tongue.

His arms were powerful around her, one hand was pressing hard at the region of her spine, his hips stirred, willing her to move with him. He tasted of their wine, some aromatic spices from their meal, totally delicious. The strongest sense of all was the desire that might answer an everlasting yearning deep within her.

Very gently, Jane drew slightly away from him.

'I really must go up to bed.'

Adrian looked down at her, his blue eyes affectionate. 'And alone,' he added for her, ruefully. 'Whatever you say. Sleep well, my Yorkshire.'

Jane did sleep well that night, all the better for Adrian's easy acceptance of her decision. She'd heard other women telling the names they'd been called for stopping a man before he went too far. She was utterly relieved that there was no such complication here.

Young and healthy and far from home, and from friends, they shouldn't be surprised about the attraction that had thrust them into each other's arms. It was a factor of being alive, one that she might remember for a long time, but something which need not assume too great a significance.

At breakfast the following morning Jane met the other two, and tried not to laugh when they roused themselves from exhaustion to rib Adrian about her presence.

In the car on their way out he said she must not mind their remarks. 'Many of the chaps take whatever they can get while there's so much uncertainty about. I don't trouble to correct their impressions of me. Makes for easier relations.'

What little Jane had noticed about the other two had confirmed that they were of lower rank than Adrian. She thought this might be good for him, a means of lightening his responsibilities, however briefly.

They arrived at the command centre so quickly that there wasn't much opportunity for conversation. Striding along the underground tunnel she was pleased by the addition of further lighting, but the ten minute walk still felt long, quite daunting.

'The men who will work down here are going to find this a nuisance every day,' she remarked.

'And the women – there'll be plenty of them on the teams here.'

Workmen were still engaged on fitting out the principal rooms. Jane noticed some wore air-force blue, others overalls which appeared civilian.

Adrian had taken her first into what he termed the Filter Room.

'Strictly for your ears only, I can reveal this will be the exchange for telephoned intelligence,' he told her softly. 'Personnel will be employed full-time checking everything out before information leaves the place.'

The Operations Room was more interesting to Jane. She was taken up into the gallery which she had helped to design while Adrian explained the significance of the mass of desks, radio and telephone equipment. At the surrounding rail, he pointed out the huge table in the area beneath them.

'The technicians are wiring up below there also, headphone sets will bring in all the information. They're completing the map intended to fill the whole of that table. I believe WAAFs will be used here to plot enemy raids.'

'However will anybody reach to the middle of that massive map?'

'We have magnetic rakes, they'll place arrows according to the grid references.'

'Where does the information come in from, anyway?'

'A lot from the Observer Corps, some from coastal rada— er . . . *experimental stations* as well.'

'I'm glad you've given me the chance to see all this, Adrian. Makes it come alive – and *one* of my tasks seems to have been worthwhile.'

'Are you really that sick of the limitations of what you've been doing?'

'Are you kidding? I won't bore you with how long I spent training, but it sure as hell wasn't to be made to feel I'm just marking time now.'

'Well, I've looked up a few addresses and phone numbers, if you do want to see what's going on in camouflage. Can't take you along myself, but I can provide names of contacts you might find useful.'

'And who might find *me* useful? That would be wonderful, thank you so much.'

Adrian explained he was on duty later that day, but he drove her back to pick up her things from the house, and then on to the station for a train to London.

Jane had decided she mustn't delay if she was going to follow up the possibility of working on camouflage. Some airfields in Kent currently were being disguised by the construction of decoy dummy airbases close by.

From London Jane took a train as far as Maidstone, where she would locate a room for the night.

The profusion of barrage balloons en route alarmed her into staring, badly shaken, from the carriage windows. There seemed to be more, if anything, than she had seen over the Middlesex area.

In Maidstone itself, County Hall stood packed around with hundreds of sandbags. Walking out of the town to find some-where to stay, she found one road blocked with a row of concrete blocks, taller than any man.

'They're reinforced with iron bars,' a passerby paused to tell her. 'Hitler might get as far as this if he invades, he'll never get much further.'

Perturbed by so much evidence of preparations for an enemy onslaught, Jane managed to telephone through to her home that night. She hadn't known how long she might be away, and now she must not reveal the seriousness of these precautions. Her mother would worry too greatly. But she would at least reassure her parents that she was safe.

Sheila answered, sounding unperturbed by Jane's absence and more preoccupied by Phil's damaged foot.

'He might be at home for a while the doctor says, unless the navy find work for him that doesn't involve drilling and stuff. Anyway, it's nice that you decided to talk to me, Jane love. Did you like that place you went to see?'

'Oh – yes, yes thanks.'

'It'd look lovely, I'm sure.'

Lovely was hardly the word, but Jane was thankful for this indication of her mother's lack of comprehension. This war was an unpleasant experience, and likely to become seriously hazardous.

'I was interested to see how it looks now they've almost got the place operational.'

'And how was your squadron leader?'

'Tired, busy, otherwise all right.'

'Is he there with you now, love?'

'Oh, no. He had to go off and do something else. I was lucky he managed to spend a few hours with me, showing me around.'

'Well, remember me to Adrian next time you see him. He's a lovely man.'

Jane didn't explain that she couldn't feel absolutely certain that she would see Adrian again. There seemed no point in a convoluted discussion with her mother, who patently believed there was some romantic relationship between them. She asked instead how her father was, and was pleased to learn that having Phil there to help with the firm's bookkeeping was freeing Alfred to devote some time to his carving. Everyone benefited from fulfilling the occasional dream.

After ringing off, Jane wondered if she ought to have said more to put her mother right about her friendship with Adrian. If she'd told Sheila about holding him at arm's length, there'd have been less scope for future conjecturing. But then, *some* girls might speak about such intimate matters at home, Jane wasn't one of them. Her upbringing had never encouraged open discussion about sex.

Setting out the following morning from the rather dismal lodgings that she had found, Jane was feeling disturbed. She had been welcomed warmly into the tiny house, and soon was listening to her landlady's distress on account of the absence of her children. A boy and his sister, the seven-year-olds were twins who had been evacuated to what sounded to Jane like an extremely remote region of Wales. Unfortunately, an unsympathetic organizer had allocated the children to different houses. In villages some miles apart, the twins were now suffering the agony of separation from each other in addition to being parted from their parents.

'I'm lucky in one way, I suppose,' the woman had added eventually. 'My husband's in the police so they're not going to send him off to the war. Still, he has his work, and seems busier than ever now, doesn't understand why I should be so upset about the kids.'

'At least they're safe, one less worry for you,' Jane had tried to reassure her.

Talking about evacuees reminded her of the period in 1939 when people in the West Riding were taking in children from the south. At that particular time, before Phil and Jack had enlisted, there had been less space in their house, but having her disabled father only fit to work at home had seemed a factor in deeming their house unsuitable. From what Jane had read, anyway, lots of children had since returned south to their own families. This had happened during the time when it had seemed there was less immediate danger than the authorities originally had anticipated.

Thinking back over the months as she walked into the town centre must have prevented her from paying attention to where she was heading, Jane supposed. She reached the bridge over the river before realizing that she ought to have turned off in order to find the station on the railway line for West Malling and the airfield she was seeking.

Vowing that she must take more care in the future, she retraced her steps, but still experienced some difficulty before she located the railway. Here in the south the removal of signposts which might aid an enemy invasion had been thorough, and while waiting for her train Jane watched an elderly man painting out the name on the station platform. There soon would be worse confusion than her own about locations.

The drone of an aeroplane made her look up, her stomach tensing with apprehension until she saw its RAF markings.

Even reassured of its identity, she didn't quickly let go the panic that might have endured had the aircraft been German.

Counting the scheduled stops, Jane managed eventually to alight at her intended destination and began to walk in the direction of another aeroplane which, coming in to land, indicated the end of her journey.

The man whose name Adrian had given her as a contact wasn't on the site, Jane wished that she'd telephoned ahead before rushing to leave Maidstone. The pass which she'd possessed since working on the command centre was scrutinized minutely, renewing her unease. At last, however, the man in overalls who had listened to her explanation of why she was there returned to her from speaking with the uniformed guard.

'Sorry about that, Miss Townsend, can't be too careful. You'll understand our work is hush-hush, to put it mildly. If you'll come along to the workshop, you can begin telling me what you can do.'

The workshop was so far away from the operational sector of the airfield that Jane wondered if he was taking her beyond its perimeter. When he led her inside and she looked around, she had to contain a gasp of amusement. She hadn't known what to expect, but was totally unprepared for the jumble of apparently unrelated objects which resembled nothing more than a load of junk.

'I know,' he agreed ruefully, acknowledging her expression. 'My name's Tommy, by the way. Well – this lot's more useful to us than it looks, but we'll go into that later – always assuming that we decide you're likely to be just as useful. You're an architect, I understand – not many female ones to the pound, I'll bet!'

He was grinning, Jane grinned back at him. 'One reason why I resent not being used to the full now there's a war on. Never realized that when speed's the essence in a construction, someone in my profession can be less popular.'

'You understand that then – so what's so special about your skills that we might want you here?'

'I can draw, I can calculate . . .' Jane paused, watching his eyes which were incredibly green and very sharp. 'I'm used to planning elevations of buildings while visualizing how they will look. I thought that might help me draft designs of – well, of how something will appear viewed from the sky.'

'You're getting warmer,' said Tommy nodding. 'And your practical experience – how good's that? We work in small teams, don't carry folk who don't muck in on the actual construction.'

'I've been on plenty of sites that were filthy. And my father and brothers are in the building trade – I can't remember a time when I wasn't wandering round one after my dad. But I don't imagine you'll accept how much I can manage until I've shown you.'

He nodded. 'Right then – without breaching too much security, I can tell you that what we're tackling now is disguising bases like this, misleading the Luftwaffe about them. From the air, of course – that's what we've always to bear in mind. There's a lot been done already, at several nearby airfields.'

'Are you permitted to tell me more?'

'The basic idea is we disguise the hangars, runways and so on, usually so they're barely discernible from countryside. Then there's the decoy aspect that's the favourite now – taking a place that wouldn't be gravely harmed under aerial bombardment, and recreating there an airfield in mock-up. Draw the enemy away from their intended target.'

'Sounds brilliant, but I don't quite understand how . . .'

Tommy laughed. '*How* is something you'll learn later, if you fit in. To bring you more or less up to date – so far, we've done a lot to conceal places like this from night-time flying. That's involved blacking-out completely on site, and staging "activity" a short distance away.

'It's amazing what you can do with structures comprised of a metal skeleton covered with canvas or the like, coloured suitably. You soon appear to have a range of hangars, accommodation for aircrews. Dot around a few aircraft that have had it anyway, or gliders, light the dummy runways, strew a few motor vehicles about the site, complete with headlamps showing . . .'

119

'I had no idea any of this was going on.'

'You're not meant to know, no one is who's not working with us. Anyway, that's how we're taking care of the night threats. It's somewhat more interesting providing similar protection through daylight.'

'I can believe that.'

'The boss is taking a look at a few notions today. A big airfield which is going to become crucial. We've found a location close enough to mislead enemy bombers, and we're going all out for a thorough representation that, day and night, ought to fool Jerry. We've even been promised a supply of inflatable trucks by one of the motor manufacturers, it all aids authenticity.'

He turned aside and led Jane to a trestle table on which were several drawings, some no more than sketches, others in colour.

'If we were to decide to take you on, you might be useful for getting the proportions right when we create a dummy airbase near the original.'

Jane remained fascinated while she was shown some of the canvas, fibreboard, paints, and even foliage waiting to be utilized.

'You need a lot of branches, even whole shrubs to help disguise a hangar from the air. Then there's concealing aircraft themselves, military vehicles – again, we can use foliage, often over nets – anything to make the shape of the thing indiscernible.'

Jane was enthralled, very eager to take part in something which had ignited her imagination. She was disappointed when Tommy didn't have the authority to give her a job there. She had to be content with his promise that he would put her name forward, together with an outline of aspects of her experience which they could use.

'If your boss is at Biggin Hill, isn't that in Kent? Couldn't I go and see him while I'm down here?'

'I wouldn't recommend it, sorry. He's just so heavily involved there, any interruption is likely to meet with his disapproval.'

'I just want to get cracking.'

'Good. We need enthusiasts, folk that don't think we're barmy. Just leave me your address, and a contact number. In the meantime, you could maybe find out what's going on around your home county.'

'There's not a lot happening in Yorkshire.'

'For all you know. There are fake gun batteries going up along the coastline, did you know that? To say nothing of dummy docks and supply depots. And you'd be surprised how well we disguise gun posts to resemble other things.'

Leaving him, Jane thanked Tommy profusely, even though he'd been unable to set her on to work with him. She had a purpose now, was praying again – this time, that by some means she would be employed to do such fascinating work.

Eight

R eturning to the West Riding felt a terrible anticlimax. Jane was so eager to try the work that Tommy had described, and there seemed little she might do in order to make that happen. When she received a note from Adrian she replied immediately, he would understand how she would love to tackle the job which had been his suggestion.

Adrian didn't respond as soon as Jane had hoped, she began to wonder if thinking that he might help her get taken on was over-optimistic.

Nothing at home cheered her. Phil had been recalled to base where it seemed, despite the injured foot, he could be of some use. Lacking his son's help with the business, Alfred was obliged to neglect his carving again, and grew morose. Sheila was far from happy, losing Phil once more to the navy brought home the reality of being involved in an escalating conflict. Knowing that other mothers must be experiencing similar alarm didn't make her feel any better.

Yet again, Jane turned to her boss for advice on securing her some kind of work that would use her training. Hugh Dunstan suggested travelling to a place on the east coast where fortifications were under construction.

When she made the journey it was only to find neither Jane herself nor the man in charge at the site could feel she would serve any purpose there. If any architects had been engaged in the work, their contribution was already completed.

Visiting that coast made Jane particularly aware of what was happening across the North Sea in that April of 1940. Germany had begun the invasion of Norway. It seemed as though Hitler was encouraged by having overrun Denmark, where – threatened with the bombing of Copenhagen – agreement was reached that Denmark should provide a German base.

By the end of that month the British and French were combining in the fight to control Norwegian ports and prevent Swedish iron ore going to the Germans.

A month later Belgium and Holland were suffering along with France as German armies pressed on towards the coast. No one had heard from Jack for weeks, when his vaguely-worded phone call was understood to mean he was likely to be with the British Expeditionary Force somewhere across the Channel.

Jane began to feel too concerned for her parents to pursue the possibility of more interesting work which could take her away from home. Sheila was growing increasingly anxious with every news bulletin that told of the Allied forces being forced into a narrowing strip of land surrounding Calais and Boulogne. Alfred, meanwhile, was feeling ever more greatly the frustration of being unable to help the war effort. His enthusiasm about the business declined until Jane was compelled to take over from him, and supervise their workmen as well as ensuring that the books were kept up to date.

When Calais and Boulogne fell, their alarm grew even more intense. On the day that news filtered through of the evacuation of Allied forces from the beaches at Dunkirk the three of them prayed that Jack would be among the thousands to be rescued.

The wait for definite news was long, and they all spent restless nights in their West Riding home which felt uncannily detached from the war engaging the rest of Europe.

That wait for news seemed endless and unremitting. When at last Jack arrived at the house their relief was tempered by seeing that, although not gravely injured, he was barely able to stand through exhaustion.

Only several days afterwards was he ready to speak of the ordeal of waiting for the boats which had taken them off the beaches amid terrible scenes of destruction.

'I was wounded, while the Germans were forcing us towards the coast. Could have been worse, I suppose, it was no more than a piece of shrapnel. I had it removed at a bit of a field hospital over there.'

He had suffered torn ligaments in his leg, sufficient to have ensured him this brief respite from active service to recover from the hasty surgery.

'The pain from this lot didn't help while we were stranded there on that damned beach, left to wonder if we'd ever be taken off.'

Even now, whenever he closed his eyes, Jack could see that mass of weary men, many of them more frightened than they'd ever admit as they endured the everlasting bombing and shelling. For him, the worst had been wondering what it had all been for.

They seemed to have achieved hardly anything at all, had been obliged to watch while towns blazed amid smoke like an awful fog which hid the skies from them.

'But I counted myself lucky when I finally clambered aboard the boat that ferried us across the Channel. A pleasure craft it was, from Kent somewhere, we all crammed on somehow, and I saw then how bad lots of the other lads were. I won't trouble you with their injuries.'

Jack only knew that he vowed to remember whenever his own bit of a wound ever plagued him in the future.

'You – you have seen Cynthia since you got back?' asked Jane eventually. She was surprised that he hadn't chosen to spend some time with his wife, rather than in Hebden Bridge.

'I've spoken to her, of course, told her I'm all right. She's working in the NAAFI in the Portsmouth area, living on site, she let out the rooms we'd rented.'

'I'd have thought she'd have been keeping your little home nice for you,' Sheila remarked, wondering what sort of a wife Cynthia was going to make.

Jack shrugged. 'There's that much accommodation needed in the south, and with me abroad that made more sense. Oh – and she bumped into our Phil, you can be proud of him again,

Mum. He's back on active service. So far as I can make out, his vessel would be among the navy lot that were making crossings to get us out of that hellhole called Dunkirk.'

'Oh, no!' their mother exclaimed. 'I thought he was going to have a shore job for a while. I did think I could believe one of you was safe.'

'And so you can, Mum,' Jack assured her. 'You've seen with your own eyes that I'm still in one piece. And fretting won't do anything to help our Phil, will it? You'd best look on the bright side, happen you'll hear summat afore long.'

Several days later they received a telephone call from Phil to say that he was fine. He clearly had no idea that they had been worried about his safety, and whilst, of course, he could tell them nothing about his ship's next destination, he was looking forward to further action.

'I might sign on in the navy when this lot's over,' he confided to Jane who took the call. 'It's exciting, but more than that it's good to feel you're doing summat so worthwhile.'

'Just don't let on to Mum or Dad that that's how you feel,' she warned him, and hoped this sense of adventure was something he would get out of his system.

By the time that they had this news from Phil, Jack was about to return to his battalion. Jane was dreading his departure for their mother's sake, but Sheila surprised her by putting on a smile, and waving him off cheerfully.

If Jack himself had any inkling where he would be serving next, he hadn't given them even a clue, had talked instead of the fresh kitting-out they would all require after arriving back from Dunkirk in uniforms that hung in tatters.

Alfred had listened without saying very much throughout his eldest son's accounts of that evacuation, but he now was following each news broadcast, and cutting out from the newspapers any maps depicting the latest action.

'I hope that somehow these lads that are fighting for our country's sake will sense that we're willing them on, striving to boost their morale.'

Jane could believe that morale would be weak, very little

seemed to be going well for the Allies. British troops had been evacuated from Norway only days after Dunkirk.

To her personally a worse shock came later, in June when the news was full of events in France. The German army had ridden into Paris. The French government swiftly had evacuated to the safety of her beloved Touraine. She could picture so much of that region. Their Premier Paul Reynauld had taken over the château at Chissay above the River Cher, a picturesque home set among trees which she recalled Henri had pointed out to her. The Ministry of Finance was now at Chinon while the British ambassador was in a château at Clere.

So far as Jane could gather, while the Germans occupied the whole of France that lay north of the Loire, to the south there appeared to be more freedom. But where did this leave Henri, she agonized, and old Bernadette, the boy Louis? From what she recalled, she suspected the Bodin château now lay in border country, right on the edge of the German-occupied zone.

Jane was deeply moved when on 18th June, in a stirring BBC broadcast, General de Gaulle called on loyal Frenchmen to continue the fight. 'Whatever happens, the flame of French resistance must not be quenched and will not be quenched.'

Jane's need to put some effort into the Allied cause was renewed while the gravity of the situation in France made her as anxious as concern for her own family. Even when a bomb dropping near Gorple reservoir brought the war closer to home, she couldn't remain where she was. She had to try to join one of those 'disguise and decoy' teams. In July she set out again for airfields in the south.

After telephoning around she'd succeeded, at last, in contacting Tommy. He delighted her by remembering all that eagerness to utilize some of her skills. This time, she was fortunate that his boss was on site with him on that particular day.

Following a chat over the phone she was directed to an airfield in Sussex, and told to report to a team constructing a decoy airstrip a short distance away.

The work was less imaginative than Jane might have hoped, but it *was* a vital part of the effort to protect the crews and the aircraft which otherwise could become ready targets.

During her first day David Grant, the man in charge of the group, showed her rough plans of the existing airbase. He explained how they were used in reproducing its general outline and various features for the dummy. I could draft plans like these, thought Jane, but was content to do whatever was asked of her.

At the decoy site she was introduced to several members of her team, and found she again was the only female. As the hours passed she was thankful for her early student days, which not only conditioned her to coping among a group of men, but also provided the ability to tackle physical work.

They were laying out rows of runway lights, a laborious task which the men decided to brighten by ribbing Jane, a tedious practice but one which she knew would only ease when she managed to convince them she could be useful.

The next task was setting up fake truck headlights which were rigged up on trestles. Trained to be good with her hands, Jane proved to be as swift as anyone, by the time they finished for the day she was beginning to enjoy the comradeship.

They returned as a group to the airfield itself, where David Grant offered to show her the genuine airstrip. Telling her that she might well be expected to prepare a similar decoy elsewhere, he walked with her to the end of the runway.

They were obliged to wait there while an aeroplane was circling ready to land. Her companion sighed and gave a shrug.

'Sorry, your inspection of this lot will have to wait till tomorrow, I'm afraid. This guy coming in is here to see me, he may keep me for some time. Make your way back to wherever you're staying, eh? You do have somewhere to sleep?'

Jane assured him that she had, and turned to walk away. The aircraft was making a tremendous din, she turned to see it touch down, and felt compelled to watch as it taxied to halt. As the power cut, it was so close to where she was standing that she felt a breeze as the propeller slowed to a stop.

Turning again to leave the men to their business, she was startled to hear her name.

'Jane! What on earth are you doing here?'

Swinging round, she saw that the pilot emerging from the cockpit was Adrian Stewart.

'You two know each other?' The incredulous question came from David Grant who hurried now to greet the squadron leader.

Adrian was laughing. 'We're old friends, aren't we, Jane?'

He shook hands with the other man, then smiled towards Jane again. 'I shan't be long over this, say half an hour. Could you wait by the mess or something?'

Jane was only too happy to agree. Although they had worked a long day there, the summer evening stretched ahead, she'd been wondering already how she would spend the time when she didn't really know anyone on the base.

She was reluctant to go into any of the buildings on site while she knew nothing about which might be reserved for senior officers or aircrew. Waiting in the warmth of the summer evening was no hardship, she could sit on the grass with her back against one of the Nissen huts used for accommodation.

During her wait Jane received curious glances from several airmen as they passed, and a friendly smile from a couple of WAAF girls who paused to ask if she was to become one of their number.

She smiled back. 'I might at that, one of these days. Today, though, I'm just waiting for someone.'

'Want us to get a message to him, love?' one girl enquired. 'What's his name?'

'No, it's all right, thanks. He knows I am here.'

'Just watch out. If you don't have a pass, some of them here are sticklers for regulations.'

'I do have a pass, actually. But thanks for the warning.'

Adrian came striding towards her considerably less than thirty minutes later.

He drew her to her feet, and pulled her to him before kissing her on the mouth.

'Well, hello there, Jane!' he exclaimed. 'I certainly am delighted to see you. I gather you've just arrived to assist with the camouflage unit. So you did get taken on for that sort of work.'

'Only just, it's my first proper job with them. Had to spend much too long hanging around for something to happen, as per usual.'

'Where are you staying – anything fixed for the night?'

'A bed in the nearest village, somewhere recommended to me by one chap on the team. What about you?'

Adrian gestured over his shoulder towards the airstrip. 'Got to get my kite back to my own station to report in tomorrow. Otherwise, I'm free to catch up on your news. What do you say to having a meal together?'

He took her arm as they walked through the airbase and out along the lane towards the village. Jane wished there was time to dash into the house where she was staying for a hurried wash, but she didn't wish to keep Adrian waiting around. Their time together would be too limited to deny him one minute.

'So, tell me, how're things at home?' he asked in the local inn after buying Jane a shandy and beer for himself.

'Settling down again now. Did I tell you Jack came home for a while, wounded? That was after Dunkirk.'

'Badly wounded?'

'Could have been worse, he said so himself, caught some shrapnel in his leg.'

'And your other brother – where's he? Or don't you know?'

'We're probably better *not knowing*. Worrying doesn't do a scrap of good. But Phil was back on active service with the navy around the time of Dunkirk. He'd had an injury too, did I mention it? That was something accidental, though, hardly a war wound. Made him fed up more than anything. He loves service life.'

'Good for him. It does provide an admirable comradeship, in any of the services.'

'And what about you?' Jane asked. 'What are you doing?'

'Today? I'm here to look into lighting – runway lighting. Special kinds.' Adrian glanced around the bar, which was quite crowded. 'Can't tell you more, certainly not in here. Perhaps if we find somewhere more private.'

They had been too busy talking to decide what they would eat, but made their selections now from the inevitably limited menu.

'I suppose your parents will be anxious about both your brothers, one's folks do become understandably concerned,' said Adrian while they waited. 'How are they standing up to the stress?'

'Mum seems in danger of going to pieces whenever she suspects one or other of them is involved in fighting reported on the news. Dad doesn't show what he's feeling in that way, but you can see how much he hates being unable to do anything from that blessed wheelchair.'

'I'm sure.'

'That's why I tried not to mind too much when I couldn't get in on any work that was helping the real war effort. I could keep an eye on the family business, and keep an eye on the two of them. But that's not what I want at all.'

'Only now you're down here, getting your hands dirty, doing your share.'

Jane grinned. 'Want to know what I've been doing so far? I don't expect it's a state secret.'

'And you can trust me, I've been vetted very thoroughly.'

She was explaining the tasks which had occupied her out at the decoy airstrip when their meals were brought to the table.

'Important work, don't knock it, Yorkshire,' Adrian told her. 'We pilots appreciate anything that prolongs our ability to remain active.'

Warmed by his pet name for her as much as by his words, Jane smiled across the table. His answering smile seemed to convey a special intimacy.

'Look at me like that with those glorious greeny eyes, and I'll be compelled to ensure we find somewhere for a bit of privacy,' Adrian whispered. 'You are one lovely lady, and I am aching to hold you in my arms.'

Their time alone came afterwards, strolling through a wood

that ran behind the pub and alongside a tiny stream. The sun was sinking beyond rolling hills over to the west while a gentle breeze stirred surrounding trees and wafted to them the scent of grain from a recent harvesting.

'Kiss me, Jane.'

Adrian leaned her gently against the sturdy trunk of an oak, his arms cushioning her from the roughness of its bark while he pressed close until the buttons of his coat felt hard against her breast. A further hardness gave her no room to doubt his desire, and sent her own emotions soaring. How would it feel to love him?

But it would not be *love*, thought Jane and, recognizing that fact, knew that she shouldn't let the surge of attraction drive away all reason.

'Pity I have to fly back tonight,' Adrian sighed into her hair.

Jane began feeling torn. A part of her was delighted that he needed her, while good sense rejoiced that she wouldn't have occasion to deny him anything.

But nothing would stop their kisses. She might have reservations, but the passion Adrian generated thrilled her, she loved this feeling of coming alive through every nerve in her body.

Adrian stirred, his hips willing her to be one with him. His urgent tongue was parting her teeth, summoning some strong internal pulse deep within her. Jane could have cried out with the fever of her own longing.

'God, but I wish I'd come by car,' he exclaimed. 'There we'd at least have found some way to ease this yearning.' He drew back his head, inhaled deeply. 'Never have believed in being uncivilized,' he admitted. 'Wouldn't take any girl outdoors somewhere, least of all a girl as great as you.'

His fingers cupped her breast and his lips found her mouth again, arousing her more urgently. And then suddenly he released her, stepped back, met her gaze ruefully.

'Say something, Jane my sweet, distract me somehow.'

Adrian took her hand as they walked on, she felt his fingers moving restlessly in the caress that echoed her own, now tender, emotions. Quietly like this, Jane felt differently towards him – less *challenged* by desire, aware of increasing fondness.

'Can you really not tell me about your work?' she asked. 'I'd feel better knowing what you do.'

His laugh was sharp, so harsh that it shook her. 'You wouldn't,' he said hastily.

'Don't you trust me?'

'With my entire being, if we're both granted the chance to prove that. And this isn't merely something I say while circumstances prevent commitment.'

The alarm created by his thoughts of deepening their relationship was brief. Jane's need to know all about Adrian was growing. She liked him so much. They both knew this war could prevent their meeting again, tonight she couldn't face the prospect of never understanding more of what made him the person he was.

'You seem very conscious that your task's out of the ordinary,' she prompted. 'Is it something that's making you anxious?'

'Every new mission should evoke anxiety, unless you're a fool. But, yes – some new thing that's got to be done. I'm one of the first to try it out – I can't send anyone off to face situations I haven't tackled myself.'

'You don't mean – you'll not be flying alone?' Jane didn't like to think of him on his own in those vast skies with the Luftwaffe appearing from all directions.

'I managed to arrive here like that today.' He made a joke of it, unsurprisingly. Jane could not laugh.

'Actually, that's not the bit that worries me,' Adrian confessed. 'The worst's knowing nothing about the territory.' He swallowed, considered, decided to tell her the rest. 'I'm testing routes which will be needed shortly, for conveying people, equipment too, into France. It's all got to be covert, trouble is, it's so confidential to date that we don't have all the necessary information.'

'What sort of information?' Jane didn't understand.

'The kind that only comes through experience – the sort of

experience that I hope to gain. Concerning the lie of the land out there, especially now about the part of France remaining unoccupied, from the Loire south.'

'I do know what's happening over there. I took notice, of course, when I heard where the boundary of the occupied zone was. Didn't I tell you the Loire was where I went – to purchase Dad's stone for carving?'

'If you said, it wasn't significant then. Pity you're not a navigator,' he joked.

'How soon do you have to go? I could send you the maps I've got, that could help.'

'Thanks, but they're unlikely to be more detailed than those we possess. It's familiarity with the actual contours on the ground that we need, plus an awareness of potential difficulties.' They would be landing on remote fields, at night, must take advantage of any grains of information they might glean.

'I remember my visits very clearly, and I drove around there a lot the first time, it couldn't fail to make an impression.' It was all so wonderful. If most of the wonder was because of Henri Bodin. Jane was very thankful that Adrian seemed set to assist the people of Henri's region.

'How soon do you need to have any information that would help?' she persisted when he said nothing. 'If we get together again, after I've collected my thoughts a bit, I'm sure I could describe what it's like over there.'

'No time, I'm afraid, but thanks for the offer. I'll remember you wished to help. We need a moon to fly by, you see, and clear weather. That only gives me another night or two.'

'If I hadn't taken on this new work only today, I'd be saying take me with you. I would recognize the rivers – the Loire and the Cher – even from above.'

'Jane, Jane, I couldn't let you. You mustn't go taking chances.'

'Aren't you a safe pilot?'

'I like to think so, naturally.'

'You wouldn't be doing this if those in charge didn't have faith in what you can achieve.'

'What do you know about it? Nothing. And nothing about the odds that have to be weighed.'

'If you're merely gambling with your safety, shouldn't you shorten those odds – equip yourself with all the information you can muster?'

'I cannot delay this trip until you come up with maps, drawings, or whatever, Jane. And that is the only assistance that I could even consider having from you.'

Adrian closed the subject by giving her another kiss, but one which felt different, charged with affection that seemed stronger than their earlier desire.

His arm around her, they walked slowly, reluctantly back towards the house where she'd booked a room. Its windows blacked-out thoroughly against the threat of air raids, and with the surrounding sky darkening, only the moonlight revealed its contours. In a tiny garden to the front and side the scent of flowers combined with the rays of the moon, bestowing an ethereal quality.

Jane wished the moon away for its reminder of the mission that Adrian must undertake, and the danger which might have been lessened, if only he would use her assistance.

'This night was made for romance,' he murmured, drawing her into his arms again, tracing the line of her cheek with kisses. 'We will talk no more of war, and not at all of separations. I forbid all seriousness – we should pretend we're younger than we are, *carefree.*'

If only we could, thought Jane, trying to will away dread, and to acquire once more a little of the love of fun which, ages ago, had enhanced what free time she'd found amid all those years of studying.

And suddenly Adrian's kisses seemed more tentative, exploratory, as they might had this really been the end to a meeting between strangers.

'I am pretending, you see, just for a while,' he whispered huskily, echoing her emotions. 'It's been our first date, you can't invite me in, your mother wouldn't approve, we must content ourselves with a kiss or three – or three hundred.'

Jane laughed softly, kissed him back, tested his teeth with her tongue. She was embraced more fervently, heard her own groan of suppressed passion, and now Adrian chuckled quietly, in triumph.

'You do need me as well! You're good at this, my Yorkshire. How ever shall I let you go when the time comes for parting?'

'If this were a date, and we *were* younger, free of this dreadful war, we'd be arranging where we'd meet again. Or would you make me wait, keep me guessing about a phone call that might never come?'

'I don't do that, I haven't ever.' His voice was hard, no pretence now that they might be other than the persons they were. Their brief suspension of reality had ended swiftly.

Jane felt too perturbed to say anything.

'I'm always straight with people I like, especially those for whom I feel more than liking. Count on that, Jane, count on that until – well, until whenever.'

'The certainty I need most right now is that you're not taking unnecessary risks. And you could be sure of one thing, if you chose – that's having any help I can provide on this trip of yours.'

'Don't suggest that again. Jane, you mustn't.'

'It makes sound sense.'

'To have you put your neck on the line . . . You don't know what you're saying. This is war, don't forget, against an enemy far better equipped than our forces.'

'Then you should ensure you're cleverer than their best, by amassing more information, if only to lessen his possible advantage.'

'Bless you, Yorkshire, but no. I cannot let you persuade me.'

A further hug, then a kiss, and he left. Jane listened while his running footsteps disappeared far into the night.

Mrs Carter, her landlady, was almost asleep in a chair in the tiny living room. They said goodnight as soon as Jane had been asked what time she wanted tomorrow's breakfast.

In her narrow bed she could not sleep, thinking of Adrian's

mission to France, convinced that she should not have him fly off so ill-prepared while she was being willed to use her knowledge of the Loire region. For Adrian.

Still finding sleep impossible, Jane prayed that he would be safe, and again – because the idea would not leave her – that some means might be found for her to accompany him.

It was a vain hope, she feared, but surely prayers existed for seemingly intractable situations.

Nine

E xhausted by lack of sleep and increasingly uneasy about Adrian's planned flight to France, Jane trudged along the road to the airbase. Following the brief inspection of her pass, she went through to join her colleagues. She was thankful to have a job which should occupy her fully.

Today the team was scheduled to begin to create mock-ups of vehicles for the perimeters surrounding the fake airstrip. Evidently, the motor company making inflatable dummy trucks was inundated with requests and hadn't yet supplied all their requirements.

Greeting the other members of her team as they scrambled on to the lorry transporting them to the site, Jane resolved to get to know the men better. The previous day had passed in such a blur of assimilating the things she had to learn she'd been unable to concentrate on personalities.

Jane was trying now to muster her ideas of how the new task might be accomplished. She had been shown the canvas and fibreboard on which they were relying. Constructing some kind of metal frame would be necessary, and so long as the covering materials were painted and the whole resembled the shape of a vehicle this could – from above – delude enemy aircraft.

'You're good at drawing, I believe,' Grant said from beside her as they clung to the frame of the lorry bouncing along on to the site. 'We need someone who can draft something more advanced. Got to have enough dummy aeroplanes around to make the place convincing. They'd have to be constructed in sections, you could draw the necessary parts from photos of aircraft.'

This sounded very different from creating the more rectangular shapes of trucks. Jane frowned, decided she ought to admit to her limitations.

'Well – oh, I'm not sure I could do that. I don't know enough about planes.'

He laughed, she suspected he enjoyed issuing her with a challenge. 'They need only be roughly to scale – just accurate enough to fool the Luftwaffe.'

'On a very dark night?' she suggested wryly.

'And when the moon's full,' David Grant responded swiftly. 'Pilots rely a lot on the moon.'

Jane could have done without that reminder. 'I'll have a go at it, of course.'

Hadn't she yearned to use her ability to draft plans, and visualize so clearly that the final construction was recognizable from her design?

'You'll find all you need in the workshop. And the lads will be ready and able as soon as you've got the plans drawn.'

The photographs of Spitfires and Hurricanes were enough to start her off, but they were depicted from the ground; she needed constantly to bear in mind that the most convincing aspect of the dummies had got to be the aerial view.

Jane examined the canvas and fibreboard to be utilized, and decided that only a few draft sketches would be necessary before she could risk drawing on the actual materials the outlines to be cut. Any other method would be a waste of time, and of paper. Since so much seemed to be based on estimates and sheer guesswork, anyway, calculated risks might be permissible.

'A *calculated* risk, eh?' someone said behind her into the telephone, and laughed, grimly. The instrument had been ringing, Jane would have been too absorbed in her work to notice its being answered if the person taking the message hadn't echoed the very words she was thinking.

She was astonished when David Grant announced the call was for her.

'Hello?' she said into the receiver, wondering if this might be some joke at her expense devised by her teammates.

The caller was Adrian and, from his tone, he was anything but joking. 'Jane – just listen, will you – and consider what I'm saying. About the job I mentioned last night. You don't have to agree, I surely won't think any less of you for declining. The thing is, they're threatening now to call the trip off, claiming it'd be foolhardy to go ahead without possessing more knowledge of the local terrain. However, you mustn't underestimate the extent to which this operation would be risky . . .'

'But it would be a calculated risk,' she put in quickly when Adrian paused, evidently unable to go on. And it's not into the occupied zone, thought Jane, but didn't mention that lest it revealed too much. Telephones could be intercepted.

'It ought to be tonight,' Adrian continued. 'But the next would serve, if you need time to think this through.'

'I said I was willing, I still am. The only problem's my work here – I've just started on something fresh, it seems important.'

'You'd be back in a couple of days, less maybe. That isn't a difficulty. I can square it for you there, but this is serious – are you really aware of what you're letting yourself in for?'

'Something more useful than whatever I've done in the past ten months. I want to have a go . . .'

Adrian asked to be put on to the man in charge, spoke to Grant for several moments, then was handed back to Jane.

'Be ready tonight, I'll pick you up from the airbase there. You'll have to travel light, I'm afraid, nothing with you that isn't essential. Wear the darkest clothing you have, I'll provide the flying suit to go over it. Only the guy in charge of your team is in the know, keep mum to everyone else. You might invent some crisis at home to explain your absence. To your landlady as well – don't want her reporting you missing.'

Adrian told her what time to be ready beside the runway. 'It'll be the Lysander again, yesterday was a trial run to get the feel of her. Keep your wits about you while you're waiting, there's likely to be other planes landing and taking off. If anyone questions what you're about, show them your pass, mention the camouflage lot, anything . . . Oh – and do you happen to carry your passport?'

'Oh, no! Does that mean I can't go . . .?'

Adrian's chuckle came down the line. 'I don't reckon we'll be required to show documents the way we're travelling!'

After checking with her one final time that she was aware of all the implications of the trip, Adrian asked to speak to David Grant again before ringing off.

Jane wandered in quite a daze back to her workbench, where she soon was waylaid by Grant. 'I guessed you were pretty extraordinary to be tackling a job like this – didn't realize it could be cover for being an agent.'

Shaken, Jane stared at him. 'Do I look like an agent?' she demanded, thinking how ludicrous the notion was.

'That's the whole point, isn't it? *Not* looking like one's essential.'

When they broke for a snack at lunchtime, she hurried as far as the village. She was thankful to find Mrs Carter at home.

'I shan't be in tonight, and maybe not until the day after tomorrow. A – a problem's come up, at home. Family stuff. I hope it's all right with you, that you'll keep my room for me?'

'Of course, dear. Sorry you've got a bit of trouble. Family, you say? Not anything to do with that nice young man who brought you back last night then?'

'No, nothing to do with him,' said Jane, and turned to go up to her room. There were things she needed for that night, but more urgently she had to recover her composure. Discovering that she and Adrian had been either observed or overheard was a shock.

The revelation of this made her forcefully aware of the need for discretion. The war here was so very substantial, totally different from the way that distance lent unreality to the hostilities while living in Yorkshire.

Thinking of her home was a bad idea. Jane remembered again about the bomb that had fallen out near Gorple. But that wasn't the only threat to her family – she was conscious of the inherent danger of her plans, of the impact if the worst were to happen. Her mother had been alarmed when Jane first had visited Montrichard. In peacetime. She could guess how horrified she'd be if she knew of this venture.

The time during the rest of that afternoon and evening behaved strangely. For a while after returning to her workbench Jane found the minutes dragging. The rest of them had been told she would be taking a day off to attend to a personal matter, they weren't surprised that she continued to work on after their stint finished.

She made certain of a solid meal, suspecting that refinements like eating might get overlooked after take-off. Adrian hadn't said how long the flight could be, another of the matters where absence of any substantial information provided Jane with plenty of conjecture.

No word had been said of where they might sleep, and nothing either of where precisely in the Loire region they were scheduled to land. She couldn't believe this operation was planned without an arrangement made for a rendezvous with some person over there.

The minutes began rushing by while Jane ate in the mess set aside for any civilians working at the base. She had intended devoting this time to running through in her mind the hasty instructions Adrian had given. She'd hoped also to try and recall from the previous night any facts about the trip.

As it turned out, however, she was joined at her table by a girl arrived only a half-hour earlier, destined to join the WAAF. Despite Jane's attempt to direct her first towards the office where she should report, then failing that to the correct mess, the girl remained anchored to the neighbouring chair.

The potential WAAF was very evidently nervous but, sympathetic though she was, Jane would have been happier alone. When the girl's curiosity about Jane's purpose at the site grew insatiable, the situation became quite worrying.

She's too naive to be investigating what I'm about tonight, Jane told herself silently, but she did begin to feel uneasy. Instead of ignoring the questions which had seemed merely an irritation, she decided one or two must receive selective answers.

'It's all quite hush-hush, to do with camouflage,' she admitted when asked point blank what she was doing at the airfield.

'Painting different colours on aeroplanes, you mean? But why come all this way to do that? And why are you working so late?'

Jane forced a laugh. 'We don't work factory hours, nor office ones, you know.'

'But you're not in the WAAF, you say? Is it the ATS then?'

'Neither.'

'You're learning to be a spy, aren't you? Training to be sent behind enemy lines. I've read about stuff like that.'

Jane swallowed, managed to smile. 'Sounds to me like you've been reading too many stories – fiction, I suspect.'

'It was in the newspapers, and on the wireless.' The girl paused, thought of something else. 'I know – you're here to learn how to fly, aren't you?'

Jane shook her head.

'I read about it,' the newcomer persisted. 'They're going to want women to deliver planes, on account of all the proper pilots will be flying already.'

'No doubt that's what *you*'ll be doing,' said Jane.

She had finished her meal. She stood up quickly and hurried towards the washroom. Jane had seen the girl emerge from its doorway earlier, prayed that she could count on being undisturbed there now.

A leisurely wash made her feel a little refreshed, but did nothing to ease her mounting tension. One part of it was excitement, but the greater proportion was rapidly becoming dread of the unknown. She had never flown before, could not imagine that this venture out above a Europe engaged in war would improve the experience for her. There would be shelling, she knew, from accounts that she had read. There was more than a chance that they would encounter enemy aircraft even before they reached the far side of the English Channel. Hadn't she heard about the Luftwaffe attacking British shipping in the Straits?

Above the conversations and clattering of cutlery and dishes from the mess, Jane noticed the distinctive noise of an aircraft approaching ready to land. Hastily checking that she had all her belongings, she dashed out into the cooling air.

Dust was blowing around, stirred by the plane as it touched down and taxied towards her. Staring through the increasing darkness, she tried to make out the features of the pilot. Complete with helmet and goggles, he was unrecognizable. While she waited for a clearer look at him Jane glanced at the shape of the aircraft itself. Sighing, she shook her head, certain from photographs she'd studied only that morning that this was a Spitfire.

It might be wiser to make herself less noticeable. She gazed about her and hurried across towards one of the Nissen huts. She was sitting on the grass with her back against the hut after half an hour when Adrian's Lysander finally touched down.

He was only ten minutes later than he'd said, and told her the reason when he came striding over to greet her.

'There was a strong headwind sprang up after take-off. We can only trust that it gets no worse or we'll arrive behind schedule. Are you ready?'

It was darker in the shadow of the Lysander after Jane hastened over at Adrian's side to reach what she discovered was a ladder attached to the rear cockpit.

'For passengers,' he explained, destroying any misapprehension she might have about being seated anywhere near him.

He nimbly sped up the ladder, then passed down a bundle of heavy clothing. 'Your flying kit, Jane. It'll seem huge, but that's so it'll go on over civvies. We all do this, ensures we're less noteworthy at the other end. When you've got yourself into that, I'll fix your parachute harness, explain how it works.'

Jane swallowed, managed to contain her appalled echo of 'parachute'. Adrian must know that she'd never learned how to use one, and she didn't mean to provide him with any cause now for deciding it might be safer to leave her here.

He did smile reassuringly while strapping her into the chute.

'Do be assured that I've no intention of these becoming necessary,' he exclaimed, before glancing at the few belongings she was holding. 'Glad to see you're not carrying much baggage. That should be stowed under the seat. Put your flying helmet on now.'

Feeling grossly overclothed, Jane struggled to raise her arms as far as her head.

Adrian laughed, she gave him a friendly thump, and he pointed to the ladder.

'First, though, I'll see to your helmet,' he said, relenting.

When Adrian had fastened her helmet to his satisfaction, he kissed her cheek, one of the few areas that didn't feel clamped rigidly by the items she was obliged to wear.

Determined she'd not seek assistance, Jane clambered up the ladder and hauled herself into the passenger cockpit. Adrian demonstrated plugging her helmet into the intercom and then how the microphone switched on and off.

'So, that's about it,' he announced. 'Oh – one thing more,' he added and showed how the parachute could be taken off. But warned her to leave it intact.

While Adrian left her and strode round to the pilot's cockpit, Jane glanced about her in the faint remaining daylight. She hadn't known what to expect despite seeing the exterior of several types of plane during the past day or so. This Lysander seemed all too insubstantial from where she was sitting.

Adrian spoke over the intercom, confirming that it was functioning, before explaining he would now proceed through the pre-take-off checks. The engine soon began to tick over, startling Jane. She heard his laugh and realized the intercom was still switched on, relaying her sudden gasp to him.

Keyed up as she was, the checking seemed to take an age, while Adrian was smiling and giving a thumbs up to the guy standing ready to remove the chocks.

I don't want to do this, thought Jane, wondered if she might become airsick and wished with all her heart that she'd found out more about this flight.

She heard the tone of the engine altering, increasing, and with it her pulse, to say nothing of adrenaline. Briefly, Jane closed her eyes, reflected that she was making a habit of praying, and asked that she wouldn't make an entire fool of herself.

Sensing motion as they began taxiing, she swallowed, willed herself to summon at least a tiny degree of calm from somewhere. 'People have been flying for years now,' she murmured reassuringly to herself.

'True, Jane,' Adrian responded with a laugh.

I'm going to turn off that wretched intercom, Jane resolved, but she dared not. The thing she most dreaded was panicking, and in a panic she might not remember how to contact Adrian again.

'Soon be airborne now,' he assured her. 'The take-off's the worst bit.'

That didn't convince Jane. What about landing? And in a *field*? This good solid RAF runway felt terrible beneath their wheels.

Her stomach lurched, she seemed to be thrust back into her seat. The darker silhouette of some airbase building appeared slanting to her left, and she accepted that there could be no turning back. They were flying.

'All right back there?' Adrian enquired gently once he was no longer concentrating too completely for conversation.

'Fine,' Jane replied, and was astonished that she still had a voice.

'We're in for a long trip,' he reminded her. 'But it provides plenty of time for you to grow accustomed to all this, before we start to use your knowledge about our destination. Just don't try to be too tough. You might find flying a bit strange, you don't have to keep the proverbial stiff upper lip.'

'Especially while I'm throwing up,' said Jane ruefully.

'There's a bag for that, should have shown you where.'

Jane found the bag, immediately felt better, and resolved not to need the thing. She hadn't grown up with two younger brothers without learning all about not losing face. Then there had been the other students, and various builders employed on sites up and down Yorkshire. Not letting them see her daunted had been useful already today. She'd got up that ladder into this thing, hadn't she?

'If you look down shortly you should see the coastline,' Adrian told her. 'Then we tackle the boring bit till we cross the French coast near Cabourg.'

Adrian was hoping it would be boring. The worst thing about having Jane along was his dread of encountering enemy aircraft. He would never forgive himself if he took her into danger.

'So when do you need me to talk you through what the Loire region looks like?' asked Jane, determined to be useful as soon as possible.

'You can begin when you're ready. The maps I have aren't nearly detailed enough, so you might give me the general picture, to act as confirmation. Then you can start on possible landmarks.'

'The various châteaux ought to show up with a moon like this, they're of very pale stone, you know.'

'And rivers will provide a good guide, water's usually visible in good conditions.'

'Yes, I can even make out the odd glimmer of white on the waves beneath us now.' Only I don't like to think about the depth of all that water down there, and how cold it would feel, even in summer! she reflected ruefully.

'Tell you what, Jane – give me a rundown on the basic layout of the area we're heading for, I'll try and fix it in my mind now.'

'Well, where precisely are we to land? You didn't say.'

'Sorry – too much to think of before we set out. It's just south of a little place called Chissay-en-Touraine.'

'On the Cher, isn't it?' Jane was glad he was aiming for somewhere which felt quite familiar to her.

'You do know it then?'

'Stayed very close to there for a night or so.'

'And what's the surrounding countryside like?'

'Undulating farmland mainly, although there are still several hunting forests.'

146

'Should be able to avoid those.' They might provide cover, thought Adrian, if they became desperate.

'There are one or two hills, I suppose, near the rivers.'

'As you'd expect. I believe the chappie we're to meet with has selected a flattish spot. Trouble is, if the surrounding area is too flat we'd be quite exposed.'

'I'm sure we'll find the rivers useful for identifying exactly where we are,' Jane told him. 'It's not all that far from there where the Loire itself and the Cher converge. There's also the Indre, and one other river . . .'

'The Vienne?' suggested Adrian, studying his map.

'That's it.'

'Only wish this thing was larger scale. None of the places I really want are even marked.' He paused, thinking while he flew on.

'So – Jane, have I got this right? The spot where we're due to land is east of the place where some of these rivers meet?'

'Correct. You'll have Tours shown on your map?'

'Sure.'

'Then Chissay is almost directly east of that.'

'Fine. Although we can't assume Tours will be showing any more light than our own towns and cities at night.'

Approaching the French coast they met occasional bursts of gunfire which Adrian evaded without diverting too radically from their course.

Jane grew silent, scared yet willing herself to give no sign of alarm. She didn't doubt that Adrian was a skilled pilot, and if there were several places where she would rather be she could blame no one but herself. He'd given her opportunities for backing out. No one had compelled her to board this fragile plane to ride the cold night sky while moon and stars appeared uncomfortably close, totally devoid of their magic, which had enhanced the night when Adrian had taken her to London.

'Ours is the first trip of this nature, you know,' Adrian told her. 'We're not normally so ill-served with information. What we need most of all are large-scale maps of France. Difficulty is, trying to obtain those on the ground – you're never a hundred per cent sure who you're dealing with.'

'I know just the man, he's French and a cartographer,' Jane announced.

'How well does he know the Loire region?' Adrian asked. He wasn't certain Jane fully understood how intensely detailed their requirements were.

'He's lived in the area for years.'

'We'll have to see if Jean-Pierre can arrange a meeting.'

'If he can't I'm pretty sure I could.' She carried Henri's telephone number with her always. And now Jane admitted, if only privately, precisely why she had been so keen to accompany Adrian to France. If she'd believed initially that she was motivated by ensuring Adrian reached his destination safely, she'd deluded herself. This surging elation at the prospect of seeing Henri again said it all. This was proof that she hadn't forgotten – and perhaps never would forget – how completely he thrilled her.

'You have an address for him?'

'More than one, it'll be a matter of telephoning to discover where he is at present.' Jane was longing already just to hear Henri's voice.

'Sounds an affluent bloke – didn't know you moved in such high circles.'

Jane laughed. 'He's renovating the family château, part of it's ruined. His other home's quite tiny, an apartment.'

'But neither place is in occupied territory, I trust? We could be in enough trouble landing over here, without seeking difficulties.'

'One's certainly south of the Loire.' Jane couldn't recall any finer detail of where exactly the boundary between the two sectors of France was drawn.

I hope to goodness the Bodin château *isn't* in the occupied zone, she thought. Whatever would happen to Henri, to old Bernadette, and to the boy?

'Where did you say this chap lives?' Adrian enquired, suspecting that Jane knew far more than she was telling. He was acutely aware of the need for utter secrecy on this mission, could not risk taking any chances. Even to acquire suitable maps, possible further information.

Adrian's evident cautiousness made Jane reflect on the danger to anyone on the European mainland who was unsure of a stranger's allegiance. She knew nothing that confirmed whether Henri supported the Free French or those who had done a deal with the Germans. All she did know was how fond of him she remained, she mustn't attempt anything that might compromise his safety.

'I suppose I could take you to his place after we've landed,' she said carefully.

'Why are you sounding as though you're unsure of me?' Adrian demanded. 'You know I serve with the RAF, isn't that enough – plus the fact that I'm undertaking this mission?'

'But I don't know what's really behind this flight, do I?'

His sigh over the intercom revealed rueful amusement. '*Touché*. Then I guess we each need to establish a bit of trust in the other . . .'

Jane had been interested to see the outline of the French coast beneath them, more than a little relieved. She couldn't really get used to feeling that the Lysander was too light to hold them up, had hated the thought of all that water far below.

Adrian had grown silent, and she used the absence of any distractions to try and recall as much as she could of the countryside surrounding the Loire. If she herself had possessed a map tonight, she might have felt better, she couldn't estimate how far they were from their destination.

'How many miles to go yet, Adrian?' She'd seen her watch had stopped and now felt to be travelling through a vacuum, losing touch with time as well as place.

'Not feeling too good, eh?'

'Nothing like that, I want to be prepared for approaching the region.' She was determined she wouldn't let him down, especially now he wasn't her only concern.

'Providing I remain on course, we've another hour's flying time. You might try looking for landmarks after about half of that. Depends how wide your knowledge of the area extends.'

Jane was feeling quite tired, remembered how exhausted

she'd been at the beginning of that day, but knew she could not even doze. The noise of the engine was shattering, too powerful to ignore, plus there was some degree of vibration. She'd also identified a further sound, one she assumed to be the wind through which they were pressing forward.

Disturbing her most of all was this possibility of seeing Henri again. It seemed such an age since she had stayed in his home, an age during which so much had happened. And even she couldn't pretend his letters had revealed his feelings.

Jane shivered, and knew the cold surrounding their plane wasn't solely responsible. Being elated at the prospect of their meeting was tempered now. Would she recognize any of the original affinity she and Henri had shared? Or would he seem unfamiliar? As unfamiliar as his château might from the air? Jane wondered, and began gazing towards the ground below them.

'I'm pretty certain that's Angers just to the north of the river there,' said Adrian at last. 'Do you know it?'

'Not really, too far north for me. But if you're correct, that river is the Loire. If we can follow its course we'll pass over the confluence with the Vienne. Chinon won't be far away then.'

Jane would recognize the castle at Chinon, she felt certain, its ruins would distinguish it from the many châteaux of the region.

Beneath them the terrain was tinged bluish by the light of the moon, its rivers revealed by the glinting of their surfaces, forests appeared darker than fields, and many larger houses were rendered visible by the pallor of their walls.

'There's Chinon,' Jane exclaimed, thrilled to have identified their first landmark. 'We ought to head north-east now, until we encounter the Loire again. If that's somewhere near Tours we'll find the Cher takes a line just to the south.'

'Parallel to the Loire, do you mean?'

'For a short distance, then the gap between them widens out. I'm hoping then we'll recognize Chenonceau that's the one constructed with an integral bridge that spans the river. It fascinates me, makes any architect wonder how they achieved a building like that all those years ago.'

'There's some châteaux in my sights now,' Adrian told her. 'Which one, do you reckon?'

The moonlight there was particularly bright. Jane could see alongside the huge stone buildings an array of formal gardens with even their pathways highlighted.

'If I'm not greatly mistaken, that has to be Villandry, we're almost at Tours now, so not far at all to Chissay. Can you follow the Cher, the narrower of the two rivers – the one further south?'

Jane had never felt more excited in her life. Like a map spread below them, the landscape was proving as recognizable as ever she could have hoped. In what seemed only a few more moments there was beautiful Chenonceau. It was no less splendid with only moonlight to reveal its walls of palest cream, and that magnificent bridge reflected back from the water.

'We're nearly there, Adrian!' she exclaimed, and then ahead was the little town of Montrichard, barely discernible due to being blacked-out. 'Sorry, that's Montrichard down there, we've somehow flown past Chissay, I didn't realize how quickly we were travelling.'

'So, it's what – about halfway between this town and Chenonceau?' Adrian checked with her.

'Might be a bit further than that now.'

'That's all right, got to circle in order to land into the wind anyway. This field we're looking for is to the south of the river. Same side as the château?'

'No, and Chissay is set among trees. Think that's why I didn't spot it.'

'We'll keep our eyes peeled,' said Adrian as they swung around in an arc.

'How will the field be lit?' asked Jane. 'With flares, or something?'

His snort was rueful. 'Don't I wish! Three torches, otherwise we risk giving the game away.'

Jane caught a glimpse of the château's walls, the roof of a turret. And then she saw them – tiny pinpricks of light barely discernible just beyond the river bank.

'Is that it?'

Adrian was descending already, the altered note of the engine witnessing to the manoeuvre.

'Sit tight, Jane. Afraid this will be bumpy.'

Bumpy was a gross understatement. As soon as the Lysander touched down it seemed to rock and bound along earth which felt to be rutted.

Adrian laughed. 'Well, we made it. Your navigating was first-rate. Don't move till I tell you now. Got to be sure about our reception first.'

Jane discovered she had been holding her breath during landing. Before she recovered completely she could see a darkly dressed man running towards them.

'Jean-Pierre,' Adrian called over to him.

The man ran even faster to reach the aircraft as Adrian opened the roof of his cockpit.

Easing stiffening limbs out of the cramped space, Adrian sprang down on to the ground. He told Jane to emerge, then turned away to shake the Frenchman's hand enthusiastically.

'Not bad for a trial run, eh? *Comment allez-vous?*'

Struggling to clamber out of her tiny cockpit and find the ladder with feet that were feeling quite dead, Jane ceased listening to the two men. She only hoped they would remember that she was unfamiliar with everything about this mission, and could hardly see a thing beyond the Lysander and the shadow it was casting.

Jean-Pierre was older than she'd expected, his shoulders rounded beneath the coat he wore, hair white under his dark beret. He was, however, gallant, kissing her hand when they were introduced, and enquiring in fractured English how she had found the journey.

Jane grinned. 'Quite an adventure, but interesting. I'm only glad to have been a bit of use.'

'And Jane promises more assistance tomorrow,' Adrian told

him. 'She knows someone who might provide all the maps we need.'

'Indeed? Some person who resides in our region, yes?'

'Yes. I'm going to contact him as soon as it's daylight.'

Adrian turned aside again to speak with Jean-Pierre about the Lysander. 'There is a barn, I understand, shouldn't we be making a move to stow her?'

'The men who work my farm are waiting to do that. You are to come with me immediately into the house. My wife made a pot of soup before going to her bed.'

Although pleased about the soup, Jane was troubled by something more urgent than hunger. As they were ushered into the farmhouse, she turned to Adrian.

'Do you think – would you mind asking him if I can go to the toilet first?'

Jean-Pierre was listening, and smiled. 'Mademoiselle wishes *pipi*, yes?'

He halted just inside the house, grasped Jane by the shoulder and led her back outdoors. A few paces away stood a wooden shed of sorts. Opening its door, he indicated that she should enter.

Unable to see a thing, Jane hesitated. Jean-Pierre handed her a torch, and left her to it.

The beam of light revealed an indentation in the ground, identifiable all too evidently by its odour. There was no refinement of any kind, certainly nothing resembling the expected chinaware, much less a seat. But Jane was desperate.

At least Henri will provide something a little more civilized, thought Jane, and her soaring heart told her that how much she would relish seeing him, quite regardless of any possible facilities. Her see-sawing emotions had overcome any misgivings. She was beginning to sense that her visit would delight Henri.

In the meantime, despite the basic simplicity of his home, their host couldn't do too much for them by way of a welcome. Following the soup and bread eaten at the huge kitchen table, she and Adrian were each conducted to a humble room over what appeared to be the stables.

Jane slept as though she had not slept properly for weeks, and awakened only when Adrian called her to breakfast next morning.

'Where did you say that cartographer works?' he asked. 'It is near here?'

'In Montrichard, if he's at the apartment. Just a few miles down the road. I'll ring through first to check that he is there.'

'Not possible, I'm afraid. The phones aren't working. It seems the system's overloaded since so many government people have evacuated to this region.'

'Oh, I see.'

'You mustn't worry, Jane, if we don't manage to contact him. I've been delighted to have you with me this flight, and you've helped so much.'

Adrian smiled into her eyes, and grasped her hand as it lay on the table.

Jane didn't say anything, but she had hoped all along that he wasn't reading too much into her eagerness to come to France with him.

'It's all organized,' Adrian went on. 'One of Jean-Pierre's workers will drive us over to Montrichard on the cart. No problem at all, you see.'

'I'm sure you're right, and Henri is a lovely person, he'll be only too pleased . . .'

Ten

'Good God – *Jane*! What on earth are you doing over here?'

'Hello, Henri. How are you?' Falling back on pleasantries was being evasive, she knew, but she really wasn't sure how to respond to his curt reaction.

The ride towards Montrichard on a farm cart had been horrible. Already aching from sitting in that tiny cockpit for hours the previous night, the rattling of the cart had located bruises that Jane hadn't known existed. And all the while Adrian seemed to be loving every second of the experience.

'We made it, Jane!' he'd declared repeatedly at intervals since she had joined him for their hasty breakfast following her no less hasty wash.

She had gathered earlier that their flight was to test out the viability of such a trip, and could understand that Adrian was elated by proving it could be done, but she suspected that his enjoyment was enhanced by every incident witnessing to her discomfort.

'This French chap's someone you met while you were training, is he?' he'd asked en route to Henri's apartment that morning.

Jane hadn't enlightened him. She was too preoccupied with trying to sort the words for explaining to Henri. Unable to make that preliminary phone call, she felt this was all so disorganized it was tarnishing the exhilaration of their reunion. And now they were standing at his door Henri was looking shaken, in no way delighted to have her there.

'This is Adrian Stewart, Henri – we flew out here last night. Adrian – this is Henri Bodin, the cartographer I mentioned.'

Two pairs of eyes narrowed as the men surveyed each other calculatingly. The men shook hands. Ominously, neither spoke.

'It's lovely to see you again, Henri,' said Jane, and realized that she was babbling for the sake of inserting something into this crisis of awkwardness.

'I think that you must come up to the apartment,' said Henri at last.

Jane felt Adrian's hand grasping her shoulder, possessively, as they followed their reluctant host. The staircase through the old building was narrow, was it only because of the gloom that it also seemed forbidding?

Henri marched into the room and to his desk where he immediately turned face down every map that lay on its surface.

'Adrian is a squadron leader with the Royal Air Force,' said Jane, sharply, sick with hurt at their being mistrusted. 'You can trust us.'

Henri shrugged. 'Placed as we are here, one cannot be too cautious. The fact that we are not, as yet, occupied does *not* mean there is a total absence of collaborators.'

'Jane told me what your work is,' said Adrian. 'That's the reason we're here.'

'Not the only reason. I wanted to see that you're all ri—' Jane began.

She was interrupted by Adrian who hardly seemed to notice she was speaking.

'The flight last night was – experimental. I can't elaborate, but once we're fully operational we'll be helping your people as much as anything. We can't operate successfully without more accurate information about the terrain.'

'Large scale maps, you mean?' Henri began to look interested.

'Largest scale you can provide. Of the unoccupied zone, initially. Could later require something similar relating to the rest.'

'Beyond the demarcation line?' Henri's dark eyebrows soared. 'I assume you do know what you're about?'

Adrian's blue eyes narrowed, he straightened his shoulders. 'I'm not a fool.'

'And nor am I. In supplying such maps, I could be jeopardizing my situation. I suggest that, for safety's sake, you take anything you require with you today. You must forgive my reluctance to invite continuing contact with any member of the British forces.'

'But Adrian's a friend of mine,' Jane put in. She was determined to break through this mistrust between the men.

Henri gave her a sharp glance, grey eyes glittering. '*C'est formidable!*'

By the time Jane translated that as "How nice for you!" it was too late to correct any of Henri's misapprehensions. Adrian was taking charge again.

'You're saying you have such maps in stock?'

'A few. Of every region of France, if that is what you need. I can supply one range sufficiently detailed that you may reproduce copies from them, enlargements too – assuming you have the necessary equipment.'

'I am very well equipped,' Adrian responded, with a secret smile.

'I am sure,' said Henri, his voice wry.

He avoided glancing towards Jane who was frowning at the descent into double entendres. Striding past her across the room to a tall cupboard, Henri took a key from his pocket. Behind the cupboard doors stood steel cabinets where each drawer also bore a lock.

While Henri worked swiftly, removing maps from suspension files, Jane noticed that Adrian was smiling to himself, well pleased. She'd have had to be especially dumb to fail to interpret Adrian's remark about equipment, and she disliked him for it. He couldn't know what kind of relationship had existed between herself and Henri, but he was fully aware that she had never consented to any intimacy with Adrian himself.

Henri was stacking the maps, sealing them into a capacious folder.

'How much do we owe you?' Adrian enquired.

Henri shook his head. 'We have too much in common for considering any charge.'

Jane felt his grey gaze resting on her, and was too embarrassed to meet his eyes. Could he really be believing that she and Adrian were lovers?

'You did not obtain them from me, please to remember that,' Henri added, sounding suddenly very foreign, coolly dignified.

Realizing her one opportunity to put right the misunderstandings with Henri was slipping away, Jane smiled towards him.

'It is lovely to see you again, you know. I have worried about you ever since the war started. And how are Bernadette and young Louis?'

'They are quite safe, *merci*,' said Henri stiffly.

'At the château?' Jane persisted, longing to be able to picture them there.

Henri sighed. 'I can see that you fail to understand how it is to live in my country today.'

Jane felt a strong masculine arm go about her shoulders, and wished with all her heart that she could summon the guts to tell Adrian simply to go.

He was smiling towards Henri. 'Thank you very much for what you have done to assist us.'

'Yes, thanks ever so much,' Jane added. She couldn't leave it at that, must dash across the few paces separating them to kiss Henri.

Adrian's fingers were digging into her shoulder holding her back.

Henri inclined his head slightly. 'I am pleased to have been of service.'

Adrian contrived to hustle Jane ahead of him, only releasing his grasp on her as they began descending the stairs.

'We'll see ourselves out, don't trouble,' he called back over his shoulder, preventing Jane from making a final effort to at least restore a pleasanter relationship with Henri before departing.

Her emotions were in such turmoil that she was surprised to see the farm cart awaiting them in the narrow lane. So much had been implied and inferred between the two men that she felt battered by the experience. How had she let Adrian's insinuations about their relationship stand? She wouldn't have believed that she could remain silent for so long, making little attempt to set the record straight.

I've been manipulated, she realized, and disliked Adrian for that. Toying with the idea of refusing to ride back to the farm with him, she remained motionless at the side of the road. Should she make one last effort to show Henri the truth? She only need turn back now.

Still indecisive, Jane felt Adrian's hand on her arm. She was about to brush it away when he picked her up bodily, set her down in the cart, then kissed her firmly on the cheek. As he clambered aboard he called to the farm worker to drive on.

Jane felt certain she could sense Henri watching them from the upstairs room.

'You didn't have to suggest that we're – well, *together*,' she snapped.

'Any more than you had to omit telling me from the start that there was another man in your life,' Adrian retorted, his voice cold, very angry. 'We could have had something good between us, Jane. *I* believed that we had that already. There are enough uncertainties in my life right now, I only needed to feel sure about one person. About *you.*'

'I never *hinted* to you that you were the only man in my life. And if you must know, I wasn't certain how Henri really felt about our relationship. Do you think I'd have been so friendly with you if I was engaged or something?'

'I really couldn't say – don't know, do I, how you behave?'

'Well, not like that! And not the way you did back there either – implying that you're my lover or some such.'

'Don't be such a child, Jane – it doesn't suit you. You're the woman who had the guts to fly over here with me, remember. Not some soft little twerp who's frightened of having two men interested in her. You were keen enough to come with me on this trip, after all. How do you expect me to interpret your eagerness?'

Abruptly, Adrian fell silent. No longer punctuated by his words the lurching and clattering of the old cart seemed to Jane to be drumming home the harsh truth that her relationship with Henri was ruined.

Adrian's sudden laugh jolted her into looking at him. He ran his hand over his golden hair, shook his head.

'I suppose I also must have been somewhat naïf, for not scrutinizing your motivation in coming with me. It was all manipulated in order to see him, wasn't it? Wasn't it, Jane?'

'Not initially, no. I did want to do something towards fighting this war, and I also wanted to help you make the trip succeed.'

'As it has.' He patted the package of maps. 'Far beyond expectations. So, why don't we call a truce? You're relying on me to get you back to base, aren't you? May as well put on an agreeable front about it. And as for Henri, if he'd been truly committed, he'd have made sure I was left in no doubt as to his intentions towards you.'

That particular line of thought had already occurred to Jane, along with the knowledge that, whatever Henri might once have felt for her, his cold grey eyes seemed to confirm that little that was good remained between them.

'There is another possibility worthy of consideration,' Adrian went on moments later. 'The frosty reception your friend gave you may be due to a far less *personal* commitment. The borderline siting of his apartment may be more than fortuitous. And his reluctance to welcome us proof that we're wrong to believe his allegiance lies with the Allied cause.'

'How dare you even suggest that! Have you forgotten that Henri gave you all those maps in order to help British forces?'

Adrian shrugged. 'I'm merely saying there is that possibility.'

Jane was still preoccupied with Adrian's insinuations about Henri when she was disturbed by hearing of plans for their swift return to England.

'We'll take off as soon as it's dusk. That means we'll be well on our way by the time the moon is up. I shall spend the rest of today studying Bodin's maps of this region, familiarizing

160

myself so that any landmarks will be fixed in mind for further visits. You'd do well to have a look too, that way you'll be more useful when we're airborne.'

Jane sighed. She was struggling to push from her memory all the elation with which she had anticipated landing near the Loire.

When Adrian spoke again his voice was warm. 'You did assist me very well on the outward flight, as I've said. You might allow that there are several things we can feel pleased about.'

Jane willed herself not to soften under a few kind words, nor the odd compliment. Adrian had contrived to finish whatever had existed between herself and Henri, and he had known what he was doing. She wouldn't readily forgive him, and nor could she resign herself to going along with this proposed amiability.

The meals at the farm were as plain as the previous night, and equally substantial. Jane was glad to wash, if in the cold water that appeared to be all that was available. And she steeled herself to use the grim toilet arrangements.

Adrian was in a teasing mode again, and ribbed her about her reluctance to avail herself of anywhere so primitive. 'You should have made use of your friend Henri's facilities. Pity we can't call in there en route to the plane.'

If we could, thought Jane, it would be for something far more imperative. If I could have another meeting with Henri, I would ensure that he didn't doubt the reality of my feelings for him. That he knew how very little Adrian matters to me.

Jane carried the package of maps as they walked out towards the aircraft while Adrian insisted on humping the rest of the gear. The evening was turning cool with a pleasant lightish breeze, and while the sky began to darken the moon hung there already amid a few early stars, promise of a good flight ahead of them.

'Come on, Yorkshire, time we were pals again,' said Adrian as they reached the Lysander, which had been moved out of its concealing barn by the farm labourers now departing after a cheery wave.

'Give me those while you clamber up the ladder.' Adrian took the maps, and grinned towards Jean-Pierre who'd remained to see them off. 'Time you got over your mood, Jane, settled for being agreeable. You'll not get better company than me this night, you may as well accept that.'

If he hadn't adopted a jocular approach, Jane might have gone along with him. But none of this amused her. She could still see Henri's hurt expression. She couldn't – *wouldn't* leave him like that.

'I'm not coming with you,' she announced firmly. 'I'm glad you've got the maps you need, and I hope you get back safely. But you can count me out.'

'Don't be a little fool. Think this through – I provide your only means of returning to England.'

'Not quite true – oh, about tonight, yes. But yours can't be the only flight that'll make it to France. And maybe I care less about getting home than about someone over here who's important to me.'

Adrian tossed the pack of maps into the open pilot's cockpit and faced her again. She felt his fingers grasp her chin as he jolted her face upwards. His blue eyes were unflinching, yet in their depths she read something close to pleading.

'Don't do this, Yorkshire my sweet.'

If he had thought his pet name for her would influence Jane, he was right about that, but the influence was against him. She wouldn't be coerced by anyone who believed that she would change her decision on the strength of that bit of affection.

'I have to,' she asserted.

As Adrian's hand slid from her chin, she swung away from him and began to run. Behind her Jean-Pierre called something to Adrian from the front of the plane where he'd waited to remove the chocks.

'No, let her go,' was Adrian's reply, and that was followed by the unmistakable sounds that he was stowing their baggage and climbing into the cockpit.

She *was* a fool, Jane realized: she had left behind her own personal belongings, which Adrian had been carrying. Something else I've bungled, she thought, completely overwrought. Nothing would induce her to turn back.

Jane had forgotten about the farm workers who had moved out the aircraft from its barn. Because she was running she caught them up before they had reached the outbuildings surrounding the house. One was the person who'd taken them by cart into Montrichard.

'*S'il vous plaît,*' she began. '*Je dois aller encore à* Montrichard.'

The man turned to his companion and shrugged, both laughed, then separated to indicate that Jane should hurry ahead of them.

Determined not to be deterred by the refusal to take her towards the town, she continued to run. Eventually, she slowed to a jog only when she was out of their sight around a bend in the lane.

Jane heard the aircraft engine starting up, smelt its fuel on the night air, and imagined that Adrian would stare down at her after take-off. The Lysander did indeed seem to pass right over her head as he circled before setting his course towards the coast. Towards England.

Her throat was aching with the effort of running, a pain which seemed to her exacerbated by the stench of aircraft fuel. Resolving to get herself right away – from the pollution and from reminders of what she had done – Jane quickened her step as much as she was able.

From what she recalled of that morning's ride and from the map, Montrichard couldn't be more than two or three miles away, four at most. She was fit, well able to travel that distance, and in little more than an hour.

Jane glanced at her watch, thankful that today it had kept going. It was a few minutes after nine o'clock, she ought to be with Henri long before he would be turning in for the night.

The moon that had aided their original flight to France assisted her now, illuminating the lane ahead of her even to the degree that the potholes – of which there were many – were visible. Jane stumbled, nevertheless, several times as she grew progressively weary. It seemed a very long time since she'd left England.

Once, a cyclist overtook her on wheels silent beyond her own laboured breathing. Startled, Jane leapt for the narrow verge, paused there to recover and curse her own neglect. Didn't she know France well enough yet to remember which side of the road was used by every mode of transport?

She had noticed the river Cher over to her left in gaps between the trees and hedgerows. Glinting in the moonlight, it seemed to reassure her with promise of her arrival in the outskirts of that little town on its northern bank.

Sure enough, Jane at last walked along the lane the cart had travelled earlier that day, and glanced across to the hotel where once she had stayed. The moon was reflecting back from the still water, along with the bridge and the strange building that looked like an inn. She had learned from Henri that it was a *maison du passeur*, constructed in the sixteenth century to control traffic across the river Cher. She wondered if, today, it might be utilized for checks on travellers.

A little way past the junction of her lane with the road that crossed the bridge Jane reached the old farm building where Henri had his apartment.

Arriving at his door she halted, inhaling deeply, as much to summon composure as to breathe easily enough to allow her to speak.

She rapped sharply on his door, prepared to wait . . .

The door was flung open at once. Henri stared incredulously at her.

'I was going out,' he announced baldly. 'What is wrong now? If he has sent you for further supplies, I cannot oblige.'

'This is nothing to do with Adrian. He's gone.'

'Gone? Then how do you plan on getting back to England?'

'I don't know, don't care. I'll tell you what's wrong, these misunderstandings between *us*. There was no need to jump to the conclusion that Adrian and I had some sort of a – a romance going. There was nothing like that, ever.'

'That was not the impression he conveyed. However, this is no time for standing arguing out here. I do have something important that I must do. I am afraid that you will have to return at some other time.'

'And where do I go meanwhile?'

'Jane, Jane – have you left your senses in England? This is no area now for a lone woman with no place to sleep, a *foreign* woman.' He shook his head, as though hoping to clear space for inspiration about his next possible action.

'You will have to come with me, I suppose. Please walk along the road, heading towards the river. Wait in the shadows this side of the *maison du passeur* – but for God's sake don't venture out on to the bridge. I will come in my car.'

Jane was obliged to stand around so long that she began to fear that she had identified the wrong spot for their meeting. When the familiar car finally halted beside her Henri opened the passenger door.

'*Vite* – please to get in swiftly.'

'Whatever's wrong?'

He replied only after negotiating the narrow roads past the town and heading out to the east. Jane could not avoid sensing that Henri had some reason for feeling nervous.

'This may be the unoccupied zone, but it is the border region. No one must be fooled into becoming reckless. I have friends, Jane, who inform me that the authorities to the north are interested in the business that I pursue.'

'You mean those who're collaborating with the Germans who've taken over?'

'The same. Hence the care I engage whenever I travel to a place that matters to me. The château, for example.'

'Is that where we're going now? I'll love seeing young Louis again, and Bernadette. How are they? You would not tell me anything this morning.'

'They are well. Sadly, you will not meet them tonight. They are no longer in my château. No one is sleeping there now.'

'But it's in unoccupied France, isn't it?'

'Adjacent to the demarcation line. On the wrong side of it.

That is why I have removed those two dear people to a country where they may be safe.'

'Are you saying they're over in England? Where, Henri? I must see them.'

He snorted ruefully. 'Do you really believe that anywhere in your country is safe? Where is your intelligence, has it really deserted you? I have taken Louis and Bernadette to one country that should remain free.'

'Spain?'

His reply was hesitant. 'It is – healthier that you do not know.'

'Do you genuinely not trust me? After all we had . . .'

'You misunderstand me. Yet again. I am afraid for your safety, Jane, would not compromise that by giving you information that could place you in danger.'

At last he had said something that reassured her. 'Thank you. I appreciate that. So – tell me, Henri, how have you been?'

'I have a great deal of work, more people like your friend today are needing as many maps as I can produce. That is why I go to the château now, to remove from there the very last of my supplies of paper, plus all remaining documents.'

'But does that mean the place will be empty?'

'Empty of furniture, furnishings, no. As I tell you, there certainly are no persons remaining there.'

'How can you bear to leave it like that?'

Henri did not answer.

He could not speak. And surely not to this woman who meant more than the world to him could he talk of the ultimate rationalizing of all priorities. She should not be expected to comprehend the dread which had driven him to abandon his only real home, *everything* except the few persons whom he loved.

Approaching along the moonlit drive, Jane thought that the château looked already to have taken on the aspect of a building deserted, left to rot even, *surrendered to the unknown*.

She could have wept, felt emotion stinging her throat, still sore from the effort of running towards Montrichard. Towards this man. She blew her nose, hard.

'Contain the tears, please,' said Henri. 'There is not time enough for me to permit any emotions. We cannot be certain that this place is not being watched.'

He told her to wait in the entrance hall, cold that night despite the July heat that had pervaded the day outdoors. Jane listened as Henri sped from room to room, while she yearned to run with him, to glimpse however briefly a little more of this home which was to her so dear.

'Do you mind if I use the bathroom?' Jane enquired as he ran back down the stairs to join her.

'Of course you must – but do not linger. We should be away from here with all haste.'

'How can you bear to leave this place?' Jane asked again as he hurried with her to throw the things he'd gathered together into the car.

They were seated before Henri responded as he switched on the ignition. 'Can you not comprehend how it is for me? I can remove from danger my people, the accoutrements of the work that I must do. As for the rest, I am obliged to resign myself to the possible sacrifice. It is a lesson, after all, that we should not attach this great importance to possessions.'

If she had not loved him before, Jane knew that she loved him for those feelings. But that could not resolve the differences creating such an abyss in their relationship.

'Tell me about the dashing squadron leader,' he demanded.

Jane was struggling to find some means of convincing Henri of how much she cared about *him*, needed to dismiss Adrian from her mind. 'There's not much to tell. We met through a job I did, helping plan a Fighter Command place. Then he got me interested in other work, with a team providing camouflage.'

'Do you make a habit of flying around with him?'

'This was the only trip. And largely because I hoped I would be able to arrange to meet you again.'

'Not a brilliant time for socializing.'

'I didn't suppose it was. It was much more than that urging

me to come – like the need to know how you were. That you're still alive.' Her voice faltered.

'Right.' Henri sounded weary, rather than delighted or even relieved. 'This is still a bad time, though, Jane. The unoccupied zone of France may appear relatively safe, but appearances deceive. You must understand that whatever I might wish about having you here, I can only insist that you leave immediately.'

'You won't let me stay in the apartment, even for a short while?'

'There is too much already to attract attention in my direction. I can only suggest that we return you to – to wherever you and the squadron leader slept last night. I assume he did have a contact over here?'

'A farmer, Jean-Pierre Something. Just south of the river from Chissay.'

'Ah – at Parçay?'

'I wouldn't know. We landed in a field, it didn't possess refinements like a plate giving the name.'

Momentarily, a smile widened the grim line of Henri's lips. Jane experienced a wild longing to impress with her fortitude.

'It wasn't comfortable, but it served. And the arrangements worked like a dream. Adrian seemed pleased with the knowledge I supplied.'

'He would be.' Henri's smile might never have existed.

'I did let him fly off home alone,' Jane observed softly.

He reached out a hand to cover hers while he drove on. 'I know, *ma chère*, I know.'

She heard the platoon's marching feet before she saw their uniforms. Recognizably German, no more than a field's length away to the north, on a road parallel to their own.

'You see,' said Henri dourly. 'We are not permitted to forget. Worse, though, are our own nationals who seek favours of the enemy, and believe information will buy them a kind of – privilege.'

'Are there really French folk who would do that?'

'Several whom I could name. Unfortunately, they are capable of naming me, as one allied to the cause of a France that might be free.'

More alarmed than she wished to admit by witnessing evidence of the German occupation, Jane grew silent. However would she bear to comply with Henri's decision to leave her at Jean-Pierre's farm?

She sensed without being told that Henri would insist that she should refrain from contacting him again, no matter how long might elapse before she returned to England. Sadly, the truth was that she would be far more concerned for his well-being than her own yearning. She'd never refuse to agree to such restrictions.

'Do any contingency plans exist for returning you home?' he asked.

Jane shook her head. Before she could say anything, Henri drew in a sharp breath.

'*Merde!*' he swore. 'We are being followed.'

'By some of those Germans?'

'More sinister than that. A car which I have observed previously. A man I know slightly who has – as you would say – "turned his coat".'

Accelerating, Henri watched in the rear-view mirror, cursed again. 'As I supposed, he too accelerates.' After a moment's thought he spoke once more, urgently. 'Slide low in your seat, Jane, and prepare yourself. I must try to shake him off.'

Jane felt her eyes opening wide in fright, steeled herself not to cry out, and sank down as low as she could.

'This time, I believe, he will do no more than attempt to learn where we are heading. Please be ready for a circuitous route. It may be quite some time before you renew acquaintance with your host from last evening.'

Startling her, Henri sped off up a narrow track into the nearby forest. 'This may have provided hunting all those years ago,' he said grimly. 'I do not enjoy that we are becoming the hunted.'

Eleven

J ane hadn't realized earlier how greatly the moon's light
contributed on the ground as much as in the air. They were
driving between massive trees that robbed them of all but the
merest glimmer. She soon noticed that the headlamps of a
French car seemed just as well shaded as any she'd used in
England.

Henri was sitting forward in his seat, struggling to peer
through the encompassing gloom and avoid hitting obstacles.
From the lurching and thumping along of their car, Jane judged
that small obstacles were many, she only hoped that anything
larger would become visible before a crucial impact.

'There are deer around,' Henri announced. 'I trust that their
eyes, at least, will show in what bit of light there is ahead of us.'

'It's not anything ahead that's bothering me,' said Jane. 'Can
you see in your mirror, is that chap still on our tail?'

'I think not. And I do not really suppose that he will be
sufficiently concerned now to risk his smart vehicle in our
pursuit.'

'That sounds as though you know who he is.'

'Unless an accomplice has use of his car. He is a former
classmate, in fact, from my school years. Even so long ago, he
could be relied upon to take tales to the headmaster. Rumours
abound today, as you will imagine, and those concerning him
imply that he would ingratiate himself with the occupying
forces.'

'So what will you do now? Turn around, or do you think he'll
be waiting?'

'I must not assume that he will fail to wait for us. But you should not worry, I already have a plan. Our people here are not slow to prepare for contingencies. Our partisans are ready with their routes out of difficult situations.'

Jane sensed Henri's concentration and was reluctant to interrupt with questions. In any case, she had little idea of where they were by now, any answers he gave could mean hardly anything to her.

In and out of forests, Henri drove on, for the most part in silence while his darting glance told Jane that he trusted no one who might appear through the night to any side of them.

'There is a bridge close by,' he told her as they emerged from yet another forest. 'One that I use quite often, normally it is not controlled.'

'Which river is this?' asked Jane, whose sense of direction had vanished somewhere back among those many thousands of trees.

'The Cher once more. We soon shall be in French territory.'

Henri had barely finished speaking when he swore then sighed exasperatedly.

'That car again. Over there, in the alley between two houses. I can only think he has seen me use this way some other night.'

'What'll we do now?'

Henri gave a tight smile. 'We try out a route designed for just such a circumstance. But first we lose *notre chasseur*.'

After turning the car to double back along the lane bringing them to the bridge, Henri put his foot down hard, intending to evade the other driver, who might have failed to notice them. They didn't quite succeed, had travelled less than a mile when they heard him approaching. The pair of headlights reappeared reflected in the rear-view mirror.

'Are you sure it's him?' Jane enquired. She was exhausted, and she was hungry, couldn't face even a half hour's further travelling.

'I must assume it is he. I dare not risk believing it could be someone else.'

'Where can we cross to safety then?'

'I shall show you. Be patient, *ma chère*. We enter one more forest, and then you will see.'

This time, the pursuing car continued after them, but he was still some distance to the rear. When Henri abruptly turned off the track, hurtling between trees which Jane felt sure they must hit, the other vehicle remained behind.

Henri stopped in a clearing, told her to get out of the car and gathered up the things he had recovered from his château.

'I shall not leave these now,' he asserted. 'Ready? Can you run?'

He locked the car hastily, pocketed the keys, stretched out his free hand to grasp her fingers.

A hundred yards further on they emerged from the trees. Jane gasped. Magnificent in the light of the moon, stood a huge château, its stone gleaming so pale that it appeared almost white.

'This way.' Tugging on her hand, Henri urged her forward. 'We can't know that he isn't following on foot.'

Fear accelerated her heartbeat while she willed her weary limbs to comply. She mustn't let Henri down. She was certain that, but for her, he would have been at home in his apartment hours before this.

Running too urgently to spare the building another glance, they were hurtling through gardens, chasing across lawns, dodging around flower beds, crashing through clustered shrubs.

Finding gravel beneath her feet, Jane was glad, but then the loose chippings seemed to shift under her speeding soles, presaging a fall.

'How – much – further?' she gasped.

Henri smiled down at her, tightened his grasp on her fingers. 'See that tiny door . . .?'

Barely discernible amid the dark shadows contrasting with the pallor of the stone, the door looked no more than four feet high.

As they came closer, Jane saw it was taller than that, but the best feature was to prove its being unlocked. That fact surprised her, but not her companion.

'Our friends have organized everything,' Henri commented, ushering her inside and closing the door behind them.

'Doesn't it lock?' Jane enquired, worried that their pursuer might be running after them. The hairs at her nape tingled with dread that he might yet catch them up.

Henri shook his head. 'We must not deny other partisans its use.'

Allowing no time for recovering breath, he was pressing forward, along dimly lit corridors until finally he opened a heavy door.

The light of the moon streamed in through large windows set in deep stone arches to either side of a very long gallery.

'Quickly!' said Henri, sounding elated. 'The France that's free is waiting . . .'

Her feet were like enormous weights on legs rendered limp from running. The far end of the gallery seemed over fifty yards distant, she would never make it. But behind them somewhere was the man who'd pursued them through the night.

Jane sped on, her arm aching from Henri's tight hold that compelled her to try and match his pace. Her head whirled from tiredness, making the black and white squares of the floor dance and tremble while she dizzily dreaded fainting. She almost did lose consciousness, but Henri had noticed. Releasing her hand, he swung a steadying arm about her shoulders, supporting her the rest of the way to the steps where the gallery ended.

'We're across the Cher,' he announced as the cool air met them, and then he hugged her. 'That was Chenonceau, perhaps you did not recognize it.'

They walked on, slowly, through a glade of trees, discovered a fallen trunk and paused there to rest.

Henri drew her close to his chest, kissed her fervently. 'Forgive me for placing you in danger.'

'You rescued me, though,' said Jane. 'But what about your car?'

He chuckled. 'I may have to stand by what I said regarding possessions. But I am far more hopeful than that. The people here are watchful, and they do know me. The plans being devised are likely to include covering all eventualities.'

'So, you'll get it back?'

'Let us say that when I enquire where it is, they could well have arranged its concealment.'

'That is marvellous!'

He smiled. 'During long months, mindful of the inevitable occupation of certain parts of France, our people here have been preparing.'

'Aided by you, and the work that has become your life?'

Henri would not say, but his silence revealed to Jane an involvement that was earning her respect.

'I cannot take you to my apartment,' he told her regretfully. 'That devil who gave chase tonight knows where I live. I am afraid also that you are much too tired to walk as far as the farm where you slept last night.'

'That's true. I could sleep where we are.'

'If not on this trunk of a tree! I must see what I may find . . .'

About a mile to the south of the Cher they located a barn, delapidated, open to the sky, it still provided some protection. Her head against Henri's chest, encircled by his arms, Jane slept.

Wood pigeons were making a terrible racket. Worse than that, someone's flamboyant peacocks began creating their peculiar cacophony.

'I can't waken up,' Jane moaned. And she didn't wish to leave that blissful sleep where the comfort of Henri's nearness seemed to cocoon her in love.

Henri kissed her. On the cheek at first, then deeply full on her mouth. 'We have to go,' he said huskily, grey eyes troubled. 'If I take you to the farm where you stayed with the squadron leader is there any chance that more aircraft will fly in there?'

'I don't know, Henri. Some day perhaps. He was just trying out something new. Nothing was said about any regular landings.'

'And it may be some while before they are organized. Here, we have only a core of patriots who are beginning to ready themselves for utilizing the little freedom they have retained.'

'I don't have to hurry back to England,' said Jane tentatively.

'But you must. You should remember your British passport may not always guarantee you the safety you expect.'

'What passport? I didn't have time to go and pick it up from Yorkshire. But, listen – I might be some use to you, in your work. So long as I could telephone home, just to let them know that . . .'

'*Non,*' Henri corrected firmly. 'That would be most unwise. You have taken enough risks already. Now hear me, please, and understand. There are friends I have, not far away to the south. They know all the routes. You may not be comfortable, but you should be safe. Yes, please God, safe.'

'But I . . .'

'I do not argue with you Jane. We do not enter a discussion. Today I take you to Suzanne Royer, she will give you a bed until she has arranged the second stage of your journey.'

Dismally, Jane accepted that she must agree to his suggestion. As they began walking towards the morning sun, she wondered dejectedly if Henri could actually be glad to be rid of her. She had disrupted his plans by returning to him the previous night, his firm attitude now prevented her from believing she had gained very much at all by refusing to fly home with Adrian.

Henri was so pensive that they were scarcely speaking by the time he led her away from the lane, between rows of meagre allotments towards a strange looking house. He gave a brisk triple knock on the peeling paint of the door. It was opened instantly by a woman of around Jane's age, strikingly beautiful with black wavy hair to her shoulders, violet eyes and near-perfect features.

'Henri!'

'Suzanne!'

The pair kissed, on both cheeks, taking quite some time, while Jane waited.

Henri introduced them, and the woman shook her hand, and all the while he and Suzanne were speaking rapidly. Jane's French was good, but nowhere near adequate for translating such volubility. So tired that she already felt quite lost, she ceased trying to comprehend even a few of the words they were saying.

Henri turned to Jane at last, bent to kiss her cheek. Merely the one cheek, she noted. About to proffer the other, she found him instead intent on speaking seriously.

'As I have told you, Suzanne will make all necessary arrangements for you to move on from here. There will be others too for whom your safety will be paramount. Please try to be understanding, your journey will undoubtedly take far longer than you would believe from the flight which brought you here.'

'Naturally,' said Jane before thanking him for taking care of her. Henri need not have reminded her about the distance involved. Hadn't she driven here herself only a couple of years ago? His attitude now suddenly seemed – well, *patronizing*.

Henri might have gone with her into the house. For whatever reason of his own, he did not do so. Too exhausted to question anything, Jane gave a mental shrug and followed Suzanne through the door set in an extremely thick wall.

Her shock was total when she looked around her, and beyond into what appeared to serve as a kitchen. This place was hewn out of solid rock, resembled a cave more than any home that Jane had ever visited.

Watching her expression, Suzanne laughed. 'You have no experience of a cave house,' she remarked, in English so good that it came as a relief. 'We are troglodytes – you know the word perhaps? I think is the same in your language.'

'I've heard it, of course, but without really understanding more than that it had something to do with caves.'

'I show you, yes? Is ver' cool in summer, and good for storing the wine. For food also, while we have food!'

'Do you have rationing here, like in England?' asked Jane, following through to a room which was even more obviously carved out of solid rock.

'I do not know how it is in your country. Here, we grow as much as we can, always. But especially since we know the

Germans come to overtake part of France. They seize the best of all *comestibles*, you know, meat and so on.'

Beside the kitchen roughly carved steps rose to the left, lit by a window cut unevenly through the solid stone. Suzanne tapped her own head and then Jane's before turning to lead the way.

'Do not hit your – your *tête*.'

The steps were irregular, but wide and not very steep. When she emerged in a large bedroom Jane smiled approvingly.

'This is wonderful. I'd never have thought . . .' She paused, realizing that failing to expect somewhere this attractive was hardly a compliment.

Her hostess was smiling back, anyway. 'I enjoy to surprise, especially when I introduce persons to my kind of house first time.'

'You've certainly done that. And I'm ever so grateful you've taken me in like this, and so on. I hope I'm not causing a lot of trouble.'

'It is to be my work now, that I help to move across our country all of those who wish again a free France. And Henri – he is my friend from a long time.'

Jane was given food in the comfortable kitchen, and offered the bed for a few hours when Suzanne saw how she began to doze after her meal.

She did not sleep at first, though the goose-down bed felt welcoming to bones that ached from weariness. Distantly she heard Suzanne speaking over what sounded like a crackling radio.

When Jane awakened refreshed, Suzanne showed her where she might wash, and insisted on loaning her clean clothing.

'You will stay here tonight, and through tomorrow. Then with the darkness you will leave here. I could arrange perhaps that Philippe shall take you onward some distance towards the Spanish border while he carries his fruit to market. First, though, we must provide you with necessary papers.'

'That sounds very good to me, thank you,' said Jane. And wished that the prospect of such a potentially long journey did not fill her with horror.

'From there you could be met, it can be organized. And all along the route, with friends who are proud to assist our allies.'

'But I've done nothing,' said Jane. 'Nothing to help your cause. I've only become a nuisance.'

'We make these trial runs, you know,' Suzanne confided cheerfully. 'And so when the Germans will overrun the rest of our country we are prepared.'

'But they won't, will they? This zone is free.'

'For how long? We must ask ourselves that. And then they shall not catch us unawares.'

Suzanne took good care of her throughout the rest of the day before insisting eventually that Jane should go up to bed.

'I could sleep in a chair or something,' Jane protested.

Her hostess merely smiled. 'The bed is big enough for two. You should not worry so.'

Once again Jane could hear from the upstairs room that Suzanne conversed with someone over what she felt certain was some kind of radio link. Still exhausted, Jane felt sleep overcoming her and was thankful. If she had such a long and difficult journey ahead of her, she would only survive if she felt fully rested.

Jane was jolted awake, alarmed because she was startled by someone shaking her by the shoulder. The lamplight revealed Suzanne's face close to her own.

'What's happened?'

'You must get up at once – I am sorry, but you will be pleased when you learn the reason.'

'Is Henri here, after all?'

'Henri? No. But I have receive a message. From Jean-Pierre, where you were the other time. He is to have a pilot arrive there before morning, he will take you to England.'

'Is it Adrian Stewart? Is he coming back for me?' Jane was incredulous.

'I do not know the pilot's name, simply that he will be there for a short time only. We have to go at once. Do you ride a bicycle, Jane?'

She hadn't ridden for years, but she had learned on one of her brother's bikes, and was glad of that, the cycles Suzanne possessed were men's machines.

As she and Suzanne set out together over the moonlit lanes, one thing in her favour was the relatively flat countryside, which made pedalling easier than Jane was accustomed to among her West Riding hills.

The journey to Jean-Pierre's farm seemed only five or six miles and was accomplished swiftly. Suzanne appeared to have received detailed instructions. After leaning their bicycles against a wall, she led the way straight out to the field that Jane recalled so clearly.

The bulky outline of an aircraft reassured her that it had touched down without a hitch, then set her wondering agitatedly if Adrian was the pilot. What on earth would he say to her? They had parted so disagreeably, and he could not be happy about feeling obliged to come back for her.

Suzanne was hustling her towards the plane when Jane saw Jean-Pierre and the flier to whom he was talking. The man had removed his helmet, and had a mass of dark wavy hair. He also was several years younger than Adrian.

Jean-Pierre and Suzanne kissed, and the pilot was introduced as Simon to both Jane and Suzanne.

'You go quickly now,' Jean-Pierre insisted, and Simon pulled flying kit out of the passenger cockpit to thrust into Jane's arms.

'I trust you can get into this lot pretty fast. We've got to be over our own coastline before dawn.'

'Thanks, I'll do my best.'

As she scrambled into the outfit Jane thanked Suzanne profusely for taking care of her. 'And for your part in arranging this flight.'

'That was not really me, I take no credit for it. Only our system of passing on information made this possible when Jean-Pierre, here, spoke with me.'

Jane thanked the Frenchman in turn, as she strapped on her parachute. She then started struggling to climb the ladder into the Lysander. Simon was already in his seat, the sound of the engine increased, threatening to deafen her.

'Hope you're strapped in,' Simon called back to her over the intercom. 'You did fasten yourself into the parachute too, didn't you?'

'Yes, thanks.' Jane was glad to have had that previous experience which helped her to speed up tonight's departure.

Busy with indicating that the chocks should be removed, and afterwards with the actual take-off, Simon did not say anything more for several minutes.

Taking to the air was uncomfortable, to say the least. From what Jane recalled, landing on that improvised airfield had been bumpy, tonight's lurching along felt alarming before they finally soared above the hedgerows.

Simon appeared to have several tasks to complete once they were airborne, Jane waited with no degree of patience until she judged that speaking to him might not be too serious a distraction.

Eventually, she blurted out the question that had been whirling around in her brain since the moment that Suzanne had awakened her.

'Was it through Jean-Pierre that you were asked to come here to pick me up?'

'Nay, don't you know better than to ask a question like that? I thought you were friendly with a squadron leader! You should have learned by now that you ought never to enquire into details of RAF missions!'

'Sorry, sorry – I only thought – well, that it might have been something Adrian had arranged.'

Simon laughed. 'I've been told this is all part of my training, you'll have to be satisfied with that, same as me. Any road – what part of Yorkshire do you come from, Jane?'

'Hebden Bridge, but how did you . . . ?'

Another laugh interrupted her. 'Do you mean to say you hadn't noticed the way I talk, as well? I'll go to heck! I'll have to tell that to the lads on the base – forever ribbing me, they are, on account of my accent.'

'So, where are you from then, Simon?'

'Keighley, nobbut just over the moors from you. You'll know it, I reckon?'

'Naturally. Many's the time I've walked over the tops there, especially to Haworth.'

'Oh – I see. Bookish, are you? Love the Brontes, and so on . . .'

'Well, *Jane Eyre*'s my favourite. Then *Wuthering Heights*.'

'Happen it's Branwell I have more in common with,' Simon admitted. 'Especially since I joined up. A few beers is the best way of getting on with your mates. Have to watch it, of course, when we're likely to be sent aloft at a moment's notice. Take tonight, for instance. I was due to go with the girlfriend to the pictures. She's mad to see *Pygmalion*.'

'I hope she'll forgive you when you arrange another date. I'm certainly grateful you made it to rescue me. If you hadn't come they were getting me some false papers so I could be taken through to Spain.'

'You shouldn't be telling me that. The Free French have enough to contend with, they don't need one of us talking carelessly.'

'Sorry. I wasn't thinking. But then I trust you, don't I?'

'All the same – keeping stuff like that to yourself is a habit you must acquire. There really is no knowing who might be listening in. We're not the only side as have agents – be aware of that, won't you, from now on.'

'Of course, of course. I wouldn't want to endanger anybody.' She'd never forget how helpful both Suzanne and Jean-Pierre had been.

'So, how come you were over there in France. Are you an agent, Jane?'

'Anything but.'

'Joining the WAAF, are you? Afraid you girls won't get to earn your wings.'

'Some might, who's to say they couldn't?' Jane felt compelled to speak up for her sex.

Simon's easy laugh reached her again. 'All right, all right, don't get on your dignity. Doesn't matter either way to me. There'll be plenty to do afore long, no matter how many pilots complete their training.'

They flew on in silence for several minutes before he spoke again. 'So, what do you do in peacetime, Jane? Are you something in the textile trade?'

'Nothing like that. I'm an architect.'

'Whatever made you choose that kind of a job? Long training, isn't it?'

'It is that. But my family are builders, so it sort of just followed on from there.'

'And there aren't many female builders, eh?'

'Even fewer than architects!'

They laughed together and Jane realized that she was beginning to like Simon. She wanted to learn more about him, wondered what rank he was, but thought better of asking. She did enquire how long he'd been in the RAF, though.

'Since war was declared. I'd always fancied flying, but instruction wasn't something I could ever afford. I was a motor mechanic, though, that helped me pick up the technical side. I was the first in my batch to get my wings.'

Before they could discuss anything further, Simon's ability was tested. They had reached the enemy-occupied coastal strip, and encountered a succession of streaks that were flashes from German anti-aircraft guns.

When the plane darted about to avoid flak Jane was terrified, discovered she was holding her breath, and forced herself to inhale deeply to contain her fright.

At last Simon's sharp laugh came over the intercom, confirming that they had evaded the gunfire.

'Not scared, I hope, back there?'

He had only just spoken when Jane heard him swear. She saw the Messerschmitt then above and to their left, silhouetted against the moon, heading straight for them.

'Hang on to your seat,' Simon yelled, commencing further evasion tactics.

When the Lysander gave a sudden lurch as he changed course

Jane felt her stomach lurch with it. Praying there was a sick bag, she searched the darkened cockpit.

There was no bag and she tried to concentrate on her breathing in the hope that it would quell the urge to vomit. She was not going to disgrace herself.

Jane was still concentrating on refusing to be ill when Simon gave a shout of triumph. 'Lost him – maybe he's low on fuel and has got to head for base.'

The direction from which the 109 had appeared suggested it was participating in operations over the English Channel.

Still feeling queasy when they finally touched down on the RAF airstrip, Jane all but fell down the ladder after landing, and walked unsteadily round to thank Simon.

He grinned down at her. 'Even if the trip turned you green!' he exclaimed. 'Too much excitement, eh?'

'Could be. Certainly enough to last me for a while.'

Jane was obliged to find something to lean against while she took off the flying suit to return it to him.

'Do you have a bed here?' Simon enquired. 'Looks like you need one.'

Glancing about her in the thin light of dawn, Jane realized that they had touched down at the base where she had been working. Despite feeling ill, she smiled.

'I'm lodging just down the road.'

First though she must find out if the camouflage team were on site, and have a word with David Grant. She was hoping he would understand her need for a few hours' recovery before working.

Simon was preparing for take-off again, and gave her a final cheery wave as he taxied around.

Despite her sickness, Jane was glad to be back, already looking forward to getting on with her job, perhaps later that day.

She met David Grant in the entrance to one of the hangars. For a minute or so she thought his frown was on account of her pallor and general unsteadiness.

'Sorry about yesterday,' she began. 'And for not being up to par now. We had an encounter with a 109, Simon's diversion played havoc with my innards. I shan't take long to recover, though. Will it be all right if I start back with the team this afternoon?'

'Afraid not,' came the sharp retort, and Jane started to understand that more than her state of health was concerning Grant. 'Matter of fact, we shan't be needing you any further.'

'You mean the team's moving on? That's all right. I can travel anywhere . . .'

'No. Any stuff you had on site is in the locker there.' He gave her a key. 'Collect it now, then I want you out of here. Pronto.'

'But why, what have I done wrong?'

'Don't ask me. I only know we're not to employ you here. Squadron Leader Stewart's orders. He insists you're unreliable. Not something he'd say without good cause.'

Twelve

J ane was devastated. If anyone had suggested she couldn't be trusted to work on an airfield she would have been dismayed. Learning that Adrian was responsible for the decision tore at her guts.

The nausea already tormenting her increased until acid rose to scour her throat. Tears stung her eyes. She brushed them away angrily. Much as she felt like weeping, she would *not* give way on site. Venting her fury, she clattered around, cleared every last item of her belongings from the locker, slammed it shut, turned the key in its lock.

Grant was watching, she knew, but Jane could not compel herself to meet his eyes when she thrust the locker key into his hand. Willing still-fragile legs to keep moving, she summoned the effort to stride away towards the airfield perimeter.

Only when she'd hastened past the guard at its entrance did Jane slacken her pace. And then the tears came. She no longer cared to conceal them. Adrian was so unfair. He might have been disappointed to discover how attached she was to Henri Bodin, he needn't have retaliated for her refusal to fly back with him. And not so brutally by destroying her chance to do this work.

Hadn't she confided to him all her yearning to put everything she'd got into helping to win this war? To no one else had she ever said as much about her need to make a difference. Solely to Adrian had she admitted the difficulties she'd experienced before finding this work here that seemed to utilize her skills.

Having the sympathy of Mrs Carter her landlady from the

second that she opened the door undid the remainder of Jane's fragile composure.

'Oh dear – you've had bad news, I can see,' Mrs Carter began after one glance at Jane's miserable face. 'Family troubles, didn't you say?'

When Jane simply stared uncomprehendingly, the woman tried again. 'Some trouble at home, that was the reason you had to go off so sudden like, wasn't it?'

Dimly, Jane recollected her hastily cobbled-together excuse for departing. 'I'm afraid things aren't too good at all, I shan't be stopping here any longer. Sorry not to give you more notice about the room.'

'That doesn't matter, dear. These things happen. Specially in wartime. You will be staying tonight though?'

'Not really, no.' All Jane wanted was to get right away from here, somehow. To leave behind that wretched airfield and with it all the trauma of losing her job. To get as far away as humanly possible from the man who had caused her this massive upset.

'But you're done in, as pale as death. No matter who's taken badly, you're not going to be much use at home, are you, not in that state?'

'I've got to get away.'

Mrs Carter was scrutinizing Jane's expression. 'It's more than family stuff, if you ask me. Is it that young man who's upset you?'

'No man will ever turn me into a wreck like this.'

'I see, so he has done. Well, you'd best get a good meal inside you before you start steeling yourself to overcome – *whatever it is*.'

'You're very kind, and I'm terribly grateful, but I couldn't eat a thing.'

'No, well – that greenish tinge to your cheeks will soon pass off with a nice drop of brandy.'

'Or I'll pass out,' said Jane ruefully, a sliver of grim humour returning.

'That way, you would get a bit of sleep, at least. I'll still be around to cook you something when you come to, you know.'

The brandy did help, Jane began to feel capable of making the effort to climb the stairs to bed.

She awoke at seven that evening, no longer feeling sick and sufficiently recovered to decide she'd never give Adrian Stewart another thought as long as she lived.

After a meal of sausages and mash, together with substantial quantities of tea Jane insisted that she must pack her belongings.

'I'm going to be on my way now,' she explained. 'I need to get home, and there's no knowing how the trains will be running. I wonder – is there any chance you could arrange a taxi to take me to the station?'

'There's only the chap down the road does anything of the sort – and that isn't what you'd call a proper taxi. Some old motor, he has, it was ancient before the war.'

'Sounds fine to me, I'd be really grateful if you could contact him for me. Whatever the car's like, it'll be far superior to some vehicles I've ridden in these past two days.'

'Really? Do your people live way out in the countryside then?'

Jane stared at her, until remembering the reason she had given for her absence.

Her lift to the station was arranged, and arrived while she was settling with Mrs Carter for her stay at the house.

'If you come working down here again, you must stop with me, don't forget,' the woman insisted.

'I will, I will,' Jane responded, while praying that she would never have cause to be even reminded of any place in the area. She couldn't visualize a time when such associations would cease to tear into her whole being.

The journey as far as the station in a ramshackle car was only the beginning of a night of such discomfort that her only consolation was the thought that she was distancing herself from Squadron Leader Adrian Stewart.

At each stage of her journey trains were delayed, only to endure further hold-ups between stations along the line. Carriages were packed to capacity and most of the corridors so full that being wedged into a small space could be said to have just the one advantage of holding her more or less upright.

The case Jane had packed before leaving Yorkshire wasn't strong enough to bear her weight and provide a seat, it became a further encumbrance rendering her unpopular with other travellers. In the main, these were military personnel, some of them bearing scars or bandages witnessing to active service, while snatches of conversation conveyed that several had been among the troops evacuated from Dunkirk.

So much had happened in Jane's life during the past few days that she was surprised that men who had survived to be evacuated from the beaches were apparently still being moved around the country.

Towards morning she dozed, and awakened as dawn was breaking over industrial Yorkshire. Feeling that she had never before truly appreciated her home county, Jane sighed midway between relief and ecstasy. She would soon be home with Mum and Dad, best of all – would be able to put the past behind her.

'Eh, Jane love, it is good to see you.' Sheila was flinging the door open to welcome her. 'You should have let us know, I'd have got something special in for your dinner. We've had a bit of excitement, an' all – just this morning. Your Adrian telephoned. Wanted to know if you'd been in touch with us. You'll have to tell me what it's about. He said he'd arranged for some chap he knows to fly to some place I didn't quite catch. *To pick you up*, Adrian said.'

'Oh, no!'

'Whatever's up, love? That's nothing to get upset about, is it?'

'Just don't ask, Mum. The whole thing's altogether too complicated.' The last thing she wanted was to learn that she was indebted to Adrian for having someone fly out to France to rescue her. Hadn't she only just simplified her life by dismissing him from her mind for losing her that job?

Jane was relieved when Sheila's further questions were delayed. Hearing her arrival, her father was wheeling himself through from the workroom.

'I thought I heard your voice, this is a treat having you home again. How long have you got here this time?'

'I – don't really know. That job I was doing didn't – didn't quite work out the way I hoped. I've got to decide what I'll tackle next.'

Alfred was looking curiously at his daughter. 'Is it the WAAFs you're in, Jane? Your mother and me haven't quite understood.'

'No, it's not. I'm not in any of the services. And if I never see another airman until this war's over that'll be too soon! I just want to forget all about flying.'

Jane's need to put from her mind all connections with the RAF quickly became impossible. The Luftwaffe attacks on shipping in the English Channel were continuing, and alongside those their attempts to destroy British airfields had started. Day after day, she either read or heard on the wireless accounts of the destruction that threatened to put the RAF out of action. On occasions she learned of some airfield which narrowly had escaped bombardment, and sensed that the place might have escaped due to good camouflage or perhaps the existence of a local decoy base.

When civilian targets also began to suffer intensive bombing she agreed with her parents that they must be thankful that, so far, their own small area within Yorkshire remained relatively undamaged. Even there, though, they weren't immune to attack; incendiary bombs and flares fell on Southowram, Shelf and Norwood Green during August. In the following month Bell House Moor above Mytholmroyd was hit.

Henri had written to her, saying how greatly he hoped that she'd encountered no further problems during her journey home. He said how busy he was, trusted that she would understand this caused the brevity of his note. But he signed off with love. That was enough for Jane.

Since arriving back in Hebden Bridge she had thought about

Henri constantly, and every night had felt afraid she would not sleep unless she could feel his arms around her. But sleep she always did, quite frequently to dream of that one night which they had spent together.

Jane was still having difficulty adjusting to her life in Yorkshire when Hitler's bombing of civilian targets increased. Although the worst hit areas were London and the South-East, several of the large northern cities also were damaged.

Jane's big surprise came on the day that her old boss Hugh Dunstan rang to enquire where she was working. Learning that she was simply assisting in the family firm, a smile warmed his voice.

'Then I can use you. I'm struggling alone since that son of mine went into the forces. There's work in our own line now, reconstruction aplenty. Suddenly, architects have a use again, if only to assess where it's feasible to rebuild and what must be demolished.'

Jane wasn't certain that such a job was what she must do. 'What I wanted was to become more directly involved in struggling to win this war. I was thinking along the lines of joining the ATS, or going into a munitions factory.'

Hugh Dunstan groaned. 'Are you certain about that, Jane? They'll introduce direction of labour for women before too long, you could be sent anywhere then. This sort of work could stop them forcing you to do anything like that. Think about it – isn't it a sin to fail to utilize all that training?'

She would give it a try. If, as seemed possible, they might be working as near home as Sheffield, she could be to hand fairly often, able to keep an eye on her parents.

So little news was filtering through about men in the forces that Sheila continually worried about first one of their sons and then the other. Alfred naturally was anxious too, he also was feeling the lack of any incentive to continue with the beautiful carving that he loved. With no new buildings going up, and stipulations for any renovations based on pure serviceability, he couldn't justify using his diminishing stock of *tuffeau* stone.

Alfred appeared quite relieved on the day that Jane told him Hugh Dunstan wanted her to do some work connected with architecture.

'I might not be so far away, Dad, if you do need a bit of help with the books or something,' she added.

He smiled. 'Nay, Jane love, I'll manage. Happen I'll be glad to have more to do in that way. I'll be happy, an' all, to know you're using all the stuff you learned.'

Now that his son was serving overseas, Hugh Dunstan seemed a different boss: content to have Jane working with him again, and pleased to let her show what she could tackle.

Jane discovered that she loved some of the jobs. They were the ones where expert inspection of a building confirmed how it might be saved by reconstruction. Others where the damage rendered them structurally unsafe, fit only to be condemned, depressed her. She hoped that, in time, she might become involved in planning any rebuilding, but too much was happening to look very far ahead.

Hull and Liverpool were among the first places where she worked, and having had Sheffield badly hit by bombing made Jane alarmed that the Luftwaffe were bringing this war close to her own home. She was anxious about her parents, how ever would Sheila cope during an air raid, with the practicalities of getting a man so badly disabled to the safety of a shelter?

The test of Sheila's capability came on the occasion in November 1940 when their area suffered. Following one bomb in nearby Halifax eleven people died, ten were treated in hospital and over 500 houses were damaged. Telephoning to check after that night, Jane was relieved to learn that her parents, with help from neighbours, had both managed to reach their air raid shelter.

Now that she often was working where the situation was far more serious, and seeing so many ordinary people rendered homeless or, worse, bereaved, Jane grew increasingly conscious of the very real dangers. The only good thing about any of it was feeling that she was participating fully in the wartime situation.

This sentiment that she was doing her share was one thing which would endure throughout the rest of the war, and somehow helped to sustain her whenever any particular job felt wearisome and unspectacular.

Jane followed the international news avidly, hoping especially for additional details regarding the situation across the Channel in France. Since the day that Marshall Pétain had set up his own form of government in Vichy France, Jane had realized that this 'free' zone was by no means so ideal a contrast to the region occupied by Germany as people might suppose.

After she'd replied to Henri's letter assuring him of her safe return to England, she had to wait several anxious months before hearing from him again. Once more he wrote briefly, little more than a note. Unsurprisingly, Henri gave no clue to what he was doing, but he did mention that he had heard that young Louis and Bernadette were well. He also passed on to Jane good wishes from Suzanne.

Initially pleased that the French woman remembered her after so short an acquaintance, Jane soon became perturbed. The reminder of the hazards daily to be faced in the Loire valley did nothing for her peace of mind. A more personal disturbance was wanting to know just how well Henri really knew Suzanne.

When she heard in the July of 1941 that all holders of British passports had been ordered to leave France, Jane understood how grave things had become over there. She felt she ought to write only occasionally to Henri, wasn't there a possibility that any envelope bearing an English stamp could draw attention to the recipient?

She had seen for herself the existence of so-called friends who were ready to betray their compatriots, she could only trust Henri's safety to his understanding of what he was about, and hope he consistently remained aware of potential hazards.

The decision not to write to him wasn't an easy one to fulfil. Busy though her own life continued to be, Jane found the scarcity of direct news from Henri difficult to bear. By the summer of 1942 the situation over there had deteriorated. Word came through of German forces allowed to enter Vichy France and hunt out radio transmitters used by Resistance workers. Jane had trouble quelling her panic.

Worse followed a few months later when Germans and Italians began to occupy the Vichy zone. Jane felt terrible. She had been relieved and surprised to hear from Henri only two weeks previously, but realized now that she should not expect further letters from him until this seemingly endless war was over.

Jane's only consolation came in hearing that the BBC was broadcasting morse-code bulletins daily to the French Resistance fighters.

That last brief letter from Henri soon became something to treasure, and rereading its last two paragraphs was all she had to see her through the anxieties of the war years:

> I think of you often, Jane, and pray that you are safe. Whenever I hear news of events in England I take comfort in learning that your home region is some few miles from cities such as York which was bombed so heavily.
>
> It is difficult to look ahead too far while these present days are so demanding, but I do hope sincerely that the peace for which we strive may somehow grant me the opportunity I need. We have left so much unsaid between us, I yearn for that chance for us to have some time to devote to each other.

Jane, along with many local folk, had been shaken when York was attacked and felt heartened that Henri was following news about England. Strangely, her next substantial first-hand news of the situation across the Channel came when she finally agreed to meet Adrian. He had written to her several times, the first almost as soon as her mother had told her about his telephone call. She had destroyed every one of his letters, but the first had somehow stayed in her mind.

Beginning with profuse apologies for losing her the job with the camouflage team, Adrian had tried to explain how angry and upset he was when she'd refused to fly back to England with him.

He confessed to being jealous already after witnessing how keen she was to see 'that Frenchman'. Evidently, her refusal to board his plane was a tremendous shock as well as a disappointment.

Adrian admitted that he was wrong to react in such a vindictive way, but tried to justify that by adding that he had for just a short while thought that she might not be entirely dependable.

Jane was surprised that he'd tried to put things right by having another word with David Grant, who had endorsed his suggestion that she ought to be reinstated as a member of the camouflage unit. Adrian concluded by saying that he hoped she would wish to remain his friend.

Jane was only sorry that she couldn't bring herself to go back to that airfield. She let months pass before she began to even contemplate seeing Adrian again.

Although initially she persisted in refusing to see him, trying to ignore his letter wasn't wholly successful. She couldn't help being impressed by his frank apology. More importantly, she hadn't forgotten that Adrian had sent that young pilot to the Loire to bring her back to England.

During those months while Adrian's letters continued to arrive, if only at irregular intervals, he also telephoned her home number. On the first three or four occasions Jane wasn't there, and she was relieved to merely receive a message through one or other of her parents. Messages that she could dismiss.

Inevitably, one weekend in 1942, she was at home when Adrian again rang through. Hearing his voice made her spirits surge with excitement. When he chuckled, 'Caught you, at last, Yorkshire!' Jane felt her resolve weakening.

Without further preamble, he told her that he was about to set off south after leave in Scotland. He wanted to stop off en route, in order to see her.

'I'll take you for a meal, or we could have a day out some-where, walking.'

It was a sharply cold day in December. Jane had no intention of spending hours trudging the moors with Adrian while he plied her with reasons why she ought to forgive him. The meal out might have been the more comfortable arrangement, but her own reaction to the surprise of hearing his voice alarmed her. Surely, all her reservations about seeing him again still existed? Facing Adrian across a table somewhere could tax her see-sawing emotions. No matter how much she had wanted his friendship, she'd developed a feeling – however superstitious – that seeing him might diminish her chances of being reunited with Henri.

Remembering that she and Hugh Dunstan were scheduled to set out on a job very early on the following day provided an excuse. When Adrian sounded deflated Jane reflected that if he ceased contacting her that might be for the best.

Perversely, all too quickly, Jane began to wish that she had agreed to see Adrian, if only the once. She badly needed someone to talk to. Life at Hebden Bridge felt very stressful. Her brother Jack's unit evidently had been posted to join the fighting in North Africa. Phil, meanwhile, was somewhere at sea, so rarely in touch that the three of them at home seemed perpetually anxious, a state which appeared to be eroding the spirit of Jane herself as well as her parents.

Jane hadn't known Adrian intimately, but she did know him sufficiently to believe his positive attitude could have been a tonic. It felt such an age since she'd been able to talk through family anxieties with anyone. But she didn't only want to make use of him. Her private feeling that such a hasty refusal to meet had done him less than justice was gnawing into her, urging that she put things right.

She was continuing to feel quite guilty about Adrian on the day that Hugh Dunstan received bad news. Jane was at the Dunstan home waiting to set out with Hugh when the telegram came.

Hugh's son had died as he crash-landed his Spitfire after an encounter with a Heinkel somewhere over the English Channel. Utterly distraught, Hugh refused Jane's offers of help and sent her off instead to the job they were scheduled to tackle, while he braced himself to break the news to his wife.

Jane's journey to the site near Liverpool was miserable, once there she was hardly able to give her attention to the work awaiting her. A massive factory had been hit by incendiary bombs, creating a fire which had destroyed the roof of one large section, together with some timbers of the part adjacent to it. Her task was to assess the state of the area that was less severely damaged, and advise on the safety aspects of any potential reconstruction.

The fact that the factory produced aircraft parts didn't help her to try and forget the loss of Hugh's RAF son. And nor did it allow her to dismiss suddenly increased fears on Adrian's behalf. She had learned enough to be aware that his task was likely to involve more than missions to bomb enemy territory or to ward off attack while piloting some RAF fighter. Hazardous though such operations were – Jane had sampled one of his flights – no one would convince her that he wasn't engaged in missions to Europe that frequently involved the gravest risks.

Hugh Dunstan returned to work far sooner than Jane had expected, earning her respect for his composure while making her suspect that he was glad to have something to occupy him. He talked quite a bit about his son, and although Jane had never especially liked the young man during their years of sharing an architects' office, she began to appreciate the spirit with which he'd taken to air-force life.

'His mother never wanted him to fly,' Hugh confided. 'I was the one who encouraged him into it. Can't say much at home now, or I get my head in my hands. Trouble is, I'm afraid I'd still do the same if we had that time over again. I knew my son, he'd not be satisfied if he wasn't doing his bit.'

'There are lots of folk like that,' said Jane. 'We can only try to let go, allow them the freedom to do their best.'

Just don't let it be Adrian who gets killed, though, she thought. I do care, even if I'll never be madly in love with him.

It seemed more than coincidence that he wrote to her that week and, without saying anything very special, conveyed his need for their friendship to continue. He had stayed at the pub run by Eileen and Tom. *I miss you, Jane.*

This time, she hadn't the heart to refuse to write to him. Ever careful, though, she reminded herself that this war wasn't going to go to *her* head. So many people of her age, and younger, were rushing into relationships, marrying *friends* hastily, under the threat that someone dear might be snatched from them. Those left behind in Britain were fed too little information about the war for gleaning comfort, and at the same time too many stories which made picturing the dangers all too easy.

When eventually she and Adrian met it was after a more or less regular correspondence in which he pleased Jane by asserting that her letters brightened many a day when news of colleagues could only be described as utterly depressing.

Adrian drove to Hebden Bridge from some aircraft factory not far from the Lancashire coast where he had discussed special requirements in a certain type of aeroplane.

Delighted that he evidently was respected for his expertise, Adrian was in good spirits when he arrived. He was welcomed as enthusiastically by her parents as by Jane herself, and soon needed to apply considerable tact to extract himself from Sheila's eager hospitality.

'I can't share you with anyone else,' he confessed as Jane got into the familiar car while he held the door for her. 'We have so much to catch up on, Yorkshire. And I've only got today before I start the long drive south again.'

'Let's hope we don't get any air raids to spoil things then,' said Jane. And then she wondered what to say next. Had all ease between them disappeared?

Adrian's not wishing to share her company was slightly alarming, but she'd been determined she wouldn't hammer home the fact that there were limits to her feelings for him.

She couldn't send him off afterwards to the war accompanied by such stark reminders of the situation.

'I've seen Henri Bodin, and he is well,' Adrian said, and astonished her while he calmly started up the car. 'As you will guess, he's supplying maps that our people require. Can't say more than that, except that there is considerable traffic now between his region and Britain. So you see, Yorkshire – our little expedition established a precedent. Plus several other routes. All top secret, of course.'

'Are you sure you should be telling *me* this?' asked Jane. And wished instantly that she hadn't. His earlier misgivings had been explained, she had forgiven them.

'Touché! However, I do want to assure you that Henri and his compatriots are receiving whatever assistance we are able to deliver. And that does please me – despite the factor of your evident affection for him, and my understanding that nothing but this abominable war would keep him away from you.'

'I don't know quite what to say,' Jane began.

'That I'm a good bloke who deserves your friendship?'

'Well, of course.'

Glancing sideways, she saw his private smile that confirmed he wasn't oblivious to the fact that she hadn't until recently relented towards him. But Adrian did not mean there to be any resentment between them. He began talking easily about their surroundings, the hills which they both loved, the walking they might do when there was more than one day in which to enjoy each other's company.

It was September now and Italy had capitulated. There were signs that these wretched hostilities might not last for ever. But countless difficulties still lay ahead, both Adrian and Jane were conscious that endurance was going to be expected of them. Not to mention courage.

'There's a pub I know where we'll have lunch,' Adrian announced. 'If the day stays as bright as it's begun, we can sit out in their garden.'

He needed to talk. The little Jane knew of that first mission to France would supply background enough to enable him to speak of his fears, the exhaustion encountered, without any risk of telling too much.

'Confidentiality is a burden heavier than ever I understood,' Adrian began when they had ordered from the limited fare available and were seated outdoors.

'Only with a handful of fellow pilots at the base can I ever discuss the job. Rank doesn't help, senior officers aren't permitted to show any degree of alarm in front of the rest. Being set that little apart doesn't agree with me.'

'Do you have no friends outside the RAF?'

'Aquaintances, rather than friends. A girl, from time to time, rarely the same one more than thrice.'

'And you can't talk to family?'

Adrian sipped his beer, shrugged. 'I'm too fond of my parents, wouldn't mar my rare leaves home with anxiety about my work. They have unease enough without my prompting.'

'What's your home really like? Tell me more about it.'

'Quite a lot like yours, actually. Scottish through and through, of course – but with parents who care perhaps rather too much. Another burden, good thing the shoulders are broad. Can't let them suspect that the depth of their concern for me creates additional problems.'

'Are you their only son?' Jane didn't recall if he'd ever told her.

'Only child, worse still. Come the end of this war, that will scarcely matter. Or wouldn't if I hadn't set my heart on flying civilian aircraft. I guess I'll have to emphasize to them the relative lack of hazards.'

Jane smiled across the table. He *was* the good bloke which he evidently hoped she considered him. *If* there had never been anyone else . . .

She shook her head at her own meandering thoughts. Surely it was no compliment to any man to suppose that he came second in her affections. Jane applied herself to tackling the food placed before them. Perhaps Adrian would be encouraged to confide further now that she was with him.

'I believe an airline pilot's life will suit me well. Satisfying my yearning to travel and, being single, I can indulge any whim that accommodates my schedules.'

He was emphasizing that he'd no intention of settling to married life. Jane didn't wish to learn his reasons, yet was relieved to be freed of the dread that he could visualize commitment to her. She just wished he didn't make her suspect that, were circumstances different, he wouldn't be remaining single.

It was the only difficult moment, the rest of the day felt like a holiday, time taken off from the troubles of war, a release from emotional turmoil.

'Now I've behaved so well,' he said in the car, 'I expect you to reciprocate by agreeing to let me take you out again.'

He was driving back to her home. As he drew up there, he turned down her suggestion that he spend a few minutes with her parents.

'Sorry, Yorkshire old love – only because *you*'d regret it. I've seen that look in your mother's matchmaking eye, I'll not expose you to the opinions she's likely to inflict upon you!'

Jane laughed. 'If I didn't know you better, I'd call your self-assessment as husband material arrogant!'

'And if I didn't know you so well, I wouldn't be insisting that by keeping in touch with me you'd receive any reports I could relay from France to you.'

'I won't ask you to give him my love.'

'Better not, Yorkshire! There are limits.' He kissed her, firmly, affectionately, on the cheek.

Jane liked Adrian more than ever before for his honesty that day, for his remarkable understanding.

After they had said goodbye she realized that Adrian had, indeed, lightened the strain of the war for her. She could look forward to seeing him again, and relax, knowing that he wouldn't expect more than the friendship that seemed so good for them both.

Whenever her own work or the international situation depressed her, she thought about their next meeting. The phone calls he made, irregular though they were, usually made her smile and somehow renewed her with their promise of seeing each other *one day.*

Jane later became thankful that she couldn't have known that she and Adrian would not meet again throughout the remainder of the war. Perhaps because they were the only link between them, each telephone conversation they shared became important to her.

Only to Adrian did she ever confide her real concerns about the dangers her brothers faced, especially around D-Day when what little they were permitted to say conveyed sufficient to convince that they both were involved in the invasion.

Alongside her perpetual concern for Henri, the effect that the absence of Jack and Phil was having upon her parents was worrying Jane more than ever. Sheila had aged twenty years since 1939, and Alfred seemed increasingly to dwell within his own world where the dread visible in his eyes must be contained. Being confined to the house, he'd little to take his mind off fears regarding his sons. Whenever Jane had the time to help him update the family business Alfred appeared to become more animated. But she had her own work, often elsewhere about the country where sites that had been bombed were being salvaged.

Again, Adrian was her safety valve, listening while Jane explained how inadequate she felt while trying to care for her parents had to take second place. If it had not been for him she would have felt very alone. The jobs she undertook, usually among people far worse off than herself, didn't lead to making friends who could be burdened with her difficulties.

Whatever happened, Jane decided, when this war finally ended she would make certain that Adrian Stewart fully understood how much he'd done for her morale.

Thirteen

The telephone did not ring. Jane sat there far into the night, refusing to believe that Adrian had let her down. Eventually a little after three in the morning she trudged slowly up to bed.

The initial elation of knowing she would see him again, and so unexpectedly, had been surprisingly tiring but not so greatly as these subsequent hours of wondering what had gone wrong. She was too exhausted to lie awake, yet too disturbed to sleep. Even reminding herself that they were now enjoying the first year of peace was failing to have its usual effect of calming her unease. Her mind would not rest, insisted on playing back and replaying all the circumstances of their arrangement.

Adrian's call had been only the second since the war had ended. Months previously Jane had concluded that he'd either finally decided that friendship wasn't enough between them, or had met some other woman who resented the understanding which he and Jane shared.

Hearing him on the line speaking excitedly of walking the Pennine Way with her had delighted Jane. He had sounded exactly like the old Adrian. She still couldn't believe that he hadn't even rung through now to explain his failure to arrive.

The urgent knocking at the front door made her sit upright in bed while she was submerged in drowsiness. It was six in the morning. This could be Adrian – extremely late, but just as keen to see her. Wishing to prevent her parents being disturbed, Jane thrust on her dressing-gown and rushed down the stairs.

Smiling, prepared to welcome him with an enthusiastic hug, she opened the door.

The two uniformed policemen looked too old to appear so afraid of her reaction.

'Miss Townsend?' the taller officer enquired, then swallowed hard.

'Yes? What's wrong? Has something happened to my brother Jack?'

They both shook their heads.

'May we come in?'

Before they had followed her through the hall, they asked Jane to sit.

'There's been an accident, I'm sorry to say, miss,' the smaller of the two began.

He was turning his helmet round and around in front of him. Jane steeled herself not to tell him to stop fidgeting.

'Who is it then, Jack's wife – Cynthia? My other brother, Phil?' But Phil was here at home, surely? Distress was rendering her irrational.

The policeman who had first spoken continued, slowly, 'I believe you knew Squadron Leader Stewart – Adrian Stewart . . .'

'Yes,' said Jane, but only a croak emerged. 'Yes.'

'I'm afraid his plane came down, only a few miles from here, as it happens.'

'God! Is he badly hurt?' Adrian was so energetic, would hate it if he were disabled. She couldn't bear to think he might be crippled like her father.

'It's bad, Miss Townsend. I'm sorry. As bad as it gets. The wreckage caught fire, you see. Didn't have a chance.'

'Was he – was he flying alone?'

'The other chap baled out. Can't be sure, but it looks like your man was sticking with it. Might have been intent on avoiding towns. A lot round here, aren't there?'

'Where – where did you say he is?'

'Not so far from Top Withens.'

'You wouldn't be thinking of going out yonder, Miss Townsend?' his colleague said quickly. 'Should leave it for a while, eh? The Air Ministry or some such will be taking everything in hand. Don't think they'll let anyone near the – the, er . . .'

'The wreckage?' Jane suggested, determined that already she would face the truth.

'The site,' the officer finished.

'How – how did you know to contact me?' Jane enquired. Among all this confusion of impressions – *horrible* impressions – she needed to fix a few of the facts. She couldn't comprehend any of this.

One of the officers cleared his throat. 'There was a letter of yours, I believe, that survived.'

'Together with his ID disc,' the other added.

Jane saw that he flushed, wondered if very little of Adrian's belongings had withstood that ghastly fire . . . If very little of Adrian had . . . ?

'Do you know how to contact his family?' she asked, over-whelmed with sadness for their loss. They, like her, would have been feeling so thankful that he'd survived the war.

'The RAF folk will attend to all that.'

'I need to see his parents,' Jane asserted.

'Someone will be able to let you have their address.'

'I have it already.'

'Is there anything we can do to help, Miss Townsend? Want somebody with you, or owt?'

'Thank you, no. Mother and Dad will be up and about before long.' And she needed desperately some time alone before being obliged to convey the dreadful news to anyone.

Her father came through as she was seeing off the police-men from the door. By the appearance of his disordered clothes, Alfred had pulled them on hurriedly after hearing voices.

'What's up, Jane? Was that the police I caught sight of?'

'Aye, Dad. I'm afraid so. It's not family, but it is bad . . .'

'You'd better tell me then. Sit down, why don't you, love.'

Jane remained standing. If she gave in to sinking on to that chair again, she might never get up. Her legs were feeling so peculiar.

'Adrian's crashed. Near here, over the moors. The plane caught fire.'

'You mean – he's not . . .?'

'Not made it. I wouldn't be half as upset but for the bloody irony. After all the risks he had to take throughout the war!'

Tears sprang to Alfred's blue eyes. 'Eh, dear. I am sorry. He was such a grand lad. I took to him, you know, right from the first.'

'I know, Dad, I know.' Both of her parents had loved Adrian. More freely, she had thought, than she'd loved him herself. Today, she was unsure, knew only that among the myriad of feelings Adrian aroused there had been a kind of love. It seemed now that somewhere deep within her – beneath this numbness that shock created – would always lie a massive sense of loss.

'I'd better go and have a wash,' said Jane, wanting no company, even that of her father.

'Wouldn't you rather have a cup of tea first?' he suggested gently.

'It'll take more than tea to do me any good. But I'll be all right, I shall, Dad, really.'

She thanked him for coming to discover what was wrong, bent to kiss him, and escaped up the stairs.

Her mother was at the door of her room. 'What's going on, Jane? Summat's up, isn't it?'

'It's Adrian, there's no easy way of telling you – he's been killed. A plane crash. Do you mind if I don't talk about it just yet?'

'Adrian? That lovely man? Oh, no! He was always so nice, so appreciative. A proper gentleman. His poor mother . . .'

When Adrian's father telephoned her on the following day, Jane didn't quite catch his opening words. In her confused state, she believed she was speaking to someone connected with the air force until Mr Stewart said how they couldn't have wished to have a better son.

'He was very fond of you both, deeply attached to his home,' Jane reminded him.

'Aye, well . . .' the all-too-reminiscent Scottish voice continued. 'We've never had an excess of material things, you ken, but we like to think we compensated wi' the upbringing we gave our lad.'

'We've just been saying – my parents and I – how Adrian was a fine man.'

'And we're intent on providing a fitting tribute. It'll no' be a big funeral, there's no' so many of us here. But I hope we may expect to see you join us, Jane.'

'Thank you, I want to have a part in that.'

Travelling to Scotland, Jane was thankful to have her emotions controlled. Over the intervening days, she had alternated between outbursts of weeping and a feeling of weary unreality that hung like a heavy fog about her.

That unreality, now sufficiently familiar, felt to be an acceptable accompaniment to this journey. One feeling which, she trusted, would remain throughout that day and the next. She was invited for the night, Ted and Margaret Stewart insisted that she would stay with them, to be ready for the morning's interment.

'We always thought, as a family, we'd go for cremation,' his father had told Jane. 'Somehow, we couldn't bear the thought of that, not when he'd known flames already. There's still space for one in my father's grave, the lad shouldna' be lonesome.'

But I shall be, thought Jane while the train carried her north. Even more lonely than I'd expected in a world bereft of Adrian Stewart. They had not met often, and had never been lovers, yet there always had been some kind of affinity. She would rely on that today, as she prepared to try and be *something* to the squadron leader's family.

Their home rather resembled her own, comfortable without attempting too much style, welcoming in its equating well used with well loved. The room she was given might have been *his*, though she suspected that would have possessed more artefacts of his interests, and would be sacrosanct.

Through the enduring fog of unreality, Jane observed less

than would have been her custom – and felt that was right. She had no wish to take away with her more memories to increase the ache that would be inevitable.

'I'm not very good company,' she admitted during dinner that first night, and found Mrs Stewart smiling back at her.

'And do you suppose we shall be? Nay, Jane, we needed only that someone who mattered to our Adrian should be with us. You'll do fine, the way you are.'

The blue of air-force uniforms distressed her as much as anything in the tiny kirk. She had been told the RAF would be represented, but the hurt that would cause proved unexpected.

His parents were wonderful throughout the simple service and the actual interment, taut-faced, staunch in their determination not to be overcome with tears. Jane saw in them echoes of Adrian's self-possession, admired the dignity supporting their composure. Afterwards in their home, they took good care of her, ensuring she was introduced to the air-force officials, that she met the few members of their family.

Although relieved when the time came to leave, Jane thanked them warmly for asking her to be with them. She was thanked in turn. It was then that Margaret Stewart revealed what they had been thinking.

'We are wondering if you might help us, Jane. We want to mark in some way the spot where it – *happened*. In Scotland, we would erect a cairn. Dad and I thought maybe a small monument of stone, quite simple, carved with his name.'

'That's a lovely idea. Would you like to come down to Yorkshire, we could visit the – the site together, discuss your thoughts.'

Sheila and Alfred would not hear of Adrian's parents staying anywhere except with them. Although pleased to be offering the couple a warm welcome, Jane was slightly uneasy. She was well aware that her mother especially had been very fond of Adrian, and hoped she wouldn't create the impression that Jane and he had planned any future commitment.

Jane herself had been particularly careful to ensure that her visit to Scotland had not left his parents under any misapprehension about her relationship with Adrian.

Ted and Margaret Stewart arrived one Saturday morning, and Jane was relieved to notice that her mother's welcome, although warm, was not followed by any expression of whatever hopes she might have entertained about Adrian as a potential son-in-law.

Initially, Alfred Townsend was quiet, as he so often seemed with strangers since his accident. Following a late lunch, however, he asked Ted if he would be interested to see his workroom.

When the two men emerged, still talking, Jane felt any relief begin to wane.

'Your Adrian was such a good chap, and he was good for our Jane, you know. She seemed to relax – able to just be herself whenever he was here.'

Ted Stewart was smiling. 'He certainly spoke well of your daughter, had plans to bring her home to meet us, you know. Throughout the war, he mentioned Jane quite regularly. First time he's done that with any lass he's met.'

'That's one reason we wish to have this simple memorial of him so close to your part of Yorkshire,' his wife added from the door of the kitchen where she'd been chatting with Sheila.

'I've got a suggestion to make about that,' said Alfred. 'As you see, I still do what stone-carving I can. If you'd allow me to, I'd love to tackle the wording you want on that stone.'

They were both delighted, and Ted insisted that his wife be shown some of the carving which Alfred had in his workroom.

'What kind of stone did you have in mind?' Jane heard her father asking as Adrian's parents both followed his chair into the workroom.

'If they choose granite Dad will never manage to work that!' Jane exclaimed to her mother, 'I hope they don't have too many fixed ideas.'

Before deciding on the actual materials, Ted and Margaret needed the landowner's permission to erect the stone where Adrian's plane had come down.

The officials in charge of investigating the crash were sympathetic to the idea of a memorial stone, put forward the suggestion on their behalf, and soon confirmed that such permission was granted willingly.

It was windy over the tops when Jane drove Adrian's parents to the site. The breeze began tossing their hair as soon as they left the car. The air-force people had marked the scene, unwittingly, as they had tramped about in the course of their investigation. Jane wasn't sorry about that, with heather and turf flattened in that way the central area, which at her first visit had looked severely scorched, was becoming fractionally less obtrusively evident, if no less poignant.

She noticed how his parents stood a little apart from each other while they gazed, sensed they were dreading contact which might accelerate emotions. Gently, she approached the pair, slid a hand into arms that seemed held woodenly to their sides.

Together, they moved forward, pressing Jane's hands against their bodies, as though to include her in what they were feeling.

His father spoke. 'Aye, this is something we must do. For the part of him remaining in this place. Yorkshire.'

Jane sobbed. That one word, *his* private name for her, reaching her ears on a voice that surely *was Adrian's*.

'Sorry, sorry,' she moaned, regretting her loss of control. She had been determined to remain composed, for them.

They turned simultaneously to her, perturbed by her grief.

'You couldn't know, he often called me that,' Jane confided. 'At first, it made me mad, but it didn't stay that way.' Just as so much she liked about Adrian Stewart had grown out of the fun he found in challenging her.

'You should have called him Scotty,' Ted told her.

'I did actually.'

It was Jane who found the tiny scrap of metal, perhaps part of the fuselage.

'Do you think the accident investigators will want this?' she asked Ted when he looked at what she was holding.

'Nay, I shouldna' think it'll be any use to them. They'll have all they require. You keep it, Jane.'

She shook her head. 'No, no. I was wondering if you'd maybe . . .'

Ted took the metal fragment, thrust it into a pocket. Jane was thankful. She had wished immediately that she hadn't picked it up. There would be memories of Adrian, of course, but this place would be her only shrine to him.

Before the Stewarts left for Scotland they discussed with Alfred further details of the memorial stone they visualized. They would send him a sketch, together with their chosen wording.

On the day that the sketch arrived Alfred became concerned. When Jane came in from the architects' office that evening he immediately confided the problem.

'It's rather bigger than I expected, love. That's put me in a bit of a quandary. Trouble is, I haven't got a piece of *tuffeau* stone left that's large enough. I don't know how I'll break the news to them, or ask if they might modify their ideas.'

'We can't do that, Dad.' She wouldn't have that for Ted and Margaret's sake. And nor would she for Adrian's. 'I'll take a day or two off, tack that on to a weekend so it's worthwhile. It shouldn't be all that difficult now to travel through France. I'm going to obtain the finest piece of stone that the Laigret brothers can offer.'

These days, she felt freer to go off like that, Phil had surprised them by being glad to leave the navy when the war ended. The West Riding and a secure job in the family firm seemed more attractive to him since meeting a Yorkshire girl who'd served in the WRENs. Renewing acquaintance with his greatly matured son was putting fresh life into Alfred Townsend, a new incentive to restore the success of the business. And for Sheila the wedding the couple planned was providing rare excitement.

Townsend's seemed now to be on its way to becoming a major building firm, with ever widening contacts. Jack's decision to set up home in the south of England was providing several advantages. Evidently remorseful about his father's initial distress, Jack was happy to emphasize his new branch's link with the original business, and he'd agreed a percentage of his profits would come to the parent firm.

Alfred and, to a greater degree, Sheila were even more delighted that Cynthia had produced their first grandson. They were already counting the days to a visit from Jack and his family.

Jane set out determined that she could not go to France without seeing Henri – so long as she succeeded in finding him! She had heard from him only the once since his telephone call assuring her he was still alive when the war in Europe ended. The letter he'd written eventually had told of his intention of travelling to Spain to bring home the old housekeeper and Louis.

I've got to see them all, thought Jane yet again, and admitted to herself that Henri was the one who mattered most to her. The most of anyone in the world.

She didn't make comparisons between Henri and Adrian, she never had, their places in her life had been very different. But Adrian's death had compelled Jane to examine her own feelings. She might have known this already, but she now was certain how deeply distressed she would be if Henri were ever to die.

Even seeing him as rarely as she had, his entire being dominated her thoughts. So many situations throughout that wretched war had brought him repeatedly to mind, but she had never needed such reminders. Henri Bodin was a part of her life, no matter what separated them. Jane only wished she knew how she might ensure there would be no further separations. But she didn't even know that Henri wanted anything of the kind . . .

He never made anything any easier. His long silences, many of them stretching across months, always made Jane feel that he was too busy with other things to be really concerned about her. The ending of the war had done no more than remove one cause of her deep anxiety about his well-being. So often now these long periods without news of him set her wondering if he could be ill. And if when she'd eventually heard from him again relief surged through her, that was dulled by sensing that he should not have left her so long without any word. Had all those early sensations that he really cared about her been no more than her own delusions?

Monsieur Laigret came rushing from his office to greet her effusively, kissing her on both cheeks before exclaiming how delighted he was to have her call upon him.

'I hope you still have good supplies of your lovely stone,' said Jane as she recovered from the surprise of his eager welcome. 'I need the best piece you've got, just let me find my note of the dimensions.'

A suitably large chunk of *tuffeau* was found, and he took details of the additional supplies requested by her father. And then the elderly man invited her to sit beside his desk while she drank a glass of the wine produced locally.

'You will be visiting your friend Henri Bodin, while you are in the region, *oui*?'

'I hope to, yes. Only he's not expecting me, and I'm not sure whether he's at the château, or still in that apartment near the Cher here.'

'He is returned to the château, living alone there, I believe. It was badly damaged during the fighting, barely habitable so that Bernadette Genevoix and the boy are lodging with neighbours.'

Poor Henri, thought Jane, he will be dreadfully upset about his home suffering further damage. She wondered why he had not written of that to her, surely anyone felt better for sharing distress with a friend . . . ?

Unless, she thought suddenly, dismally – unless he already has the only friend he really needs. During all these years she had never quite blanked out her unease about the possible truth of his relationship with Suzanne Royer.

All the way to the château Jane was too concerned about the coming encounter with Henri to take in very much detail about her surroundings. The many fields to either side of her meandering road did look different, however, with some evidence of bomb craters, and great swathes of ground spoiled by the tracks of tanks and gun transporters. Some farms were damaged, making her wonder how gravely the many historic châteaux had suffered.

Henri's home looked quite intact from the road. Jane halted the car, and gazed towards the building, praying that she would find the right things to say. So many times with Henri she'd seemed inarticulate. Too frequently uncertainty about his true feelings rendered her incapable of beginning to express the depth of the affection that kept her love for him alive.

Still no more sure than ever of where she might begin, Jane drove slowly towards the château and parked beside the front entrance. As soon as she switched off the engine she heard the noise of someone chiselling stone.

Following the sound, Jane walked around one side of the building which she now saw had been hit by either bombs or shelling. And then she had reached the rear. She stood for a minute or more, watching.

Henri was stripped to the waist above a pair of ragged shorts, his skin was bronzed by days of exposure to the sun, glossy with perspiration. He was wielding the chisel aggressively, shaping a hunk of stone to match what appeared to be a succession of similar stones. Preparing to form the arch over what had been one of the dining room windows.

'Can you use an architect perhaps?'

Her question startled him totally, absorbed as he was and with ears ringing to the noise from the tools he was using.

'Jane! By all that is marvellous!'

Henri dropped the chisel as he swung round to face her, sprang to his feet from the ground where he'd been kneeling, and ran to hug her.

Jane noticed as he ran the limp in his left leg, but then she was in his arms, lips rough with dust from the stone were kissing her repeatedly.

'You should have said you were coming to France, I'd have been clean at least!' said Henri ruefully, steadying her against him.

'It was all done in a bit of a rush. Dad wanted more *tuffeau*, for – for a memorial stone.'

'So, this wasn't only to see me.' He sounded deflated suddenly, as uncertain about her feelings as she'd so repeatedly felt about his.

'But I am here. Because I knew I'd got to see you.'

Henri held her closer still. She felt the perspiration on his skin moisten the thin cotton of her dress while his heart hammered against her chest. Jane kissed him, deeply, lingeringly.

'Jane *ma chère*, come into the house.'

'What happened with the leg?' She had seen when he moved that a mass of flesh was gouged from the shin where scar tissue witnessed to one or more operations.

'The bullet that met its target. Could have been worse.'

'When was that?'

'Last year. When the Germans knew that their time was up, they took revenge as they retreated. The Resistance were at their busiest then, mining bridges, sabotaging railways, that kind of thing. Naturally, some of us didn't quite escape damage ourselves.'

One day he would tell her about coming upon the final minutes of that battle of the bridge at Montrichard. Jane would understand his distress over arriving too late to aid the one local youth who sacrificed all that he had. She would appreciate that his own wound, a retribution by the retreating Germans, seemed a small price. His lasting witness to that gallant resistance against enemy attempts to mine the river crossing.

'But you survived. Thank God.'

'Had to. There was this chance that you might come back.'

'I'd have been here sooner. You only had to say . . .' There was to be no pretence, and that meant she wouldn't conceal the hurt that hearing so rarely from him had caused her.

Henri gave an elaborate shrug. 'Things needed attention. Repairs take time.' He tapped the injured leg, grinned. 'And to my home as well.'

Jane nodded, looked about her. They'd entered by a side door, she could see through into the dining room where the furniture, some heavily damaged, was stacked against an inner wall.

'Looks as though someone undid all your restoration work.'

'Plus more besides. Means it's unfit as a home. How could I offer you a place here, Jane?'

'You would have done so then, if – if things had been better?'

Henri drew her to him again. 'Marrying you has been one prospect that has kept me alive. But I could not even ask you, until there was something worth sharing.'

'Like your life here? Don't you know that'd be enough?'

Henri laughed aloud in sheer delight, startling her. 'Then marry me now, don't leave me again.'

'I'd marry you today, but weddings have to be organized. And this is a very hasty trip, Dad's waiting for that supply of stone.'

'For a memorial, you said? For someone in your family?'

'Not family, a friend.' Jane would not mention Adrian's death, would provide no reason ever for Henri to even suspect that he himself might not have been the only man she really wanted. Once was enough to see him hurt by believing she could love some other person.

'You will stay at least one night with me? Give me a moment to wash, and we must talk.'

Talking took second place as soon as he emerged from the bathroom. Their speaking of marriage was enough, no reason on their earth now would prohibit the love enduring through seven years of separation.

It seemed fitting to Jane that her longest wait of all – to be loved by Henri should end in a bliss no less complete despite the war-damaged room of his home, even despite the pain from his leg which he almost managed to ignore. She had known perfection could not exist, couldn't be happier to accept this close approximation.

Tomorrow they might laugh over the occasion's romantic shortcomings, but they would have tomorrow – this future, a future of laughing together. But first must come the renewal of her acquaintance with old Bernadette, and time to absorb the changes in Henri's adopted son Louis.

Her hand in his, Henri walked with Jane to his neighbour's house, where they both were rewarded with Bernadette's affectionate greeting. Louis, whose child's memory failed to conjure forth her name, was more reserved – but only until Henri provided reminders of her earlier visits.

'You are to stay with us now, yes?' the boy suggested. 'To make a family?'

Jane smiled, bent to hug the boy. 'A real family, yes.'

'Papa is mending the house for us. Soon it will be better.'

Henri's thin lips curved into a smile. Bernadette laughed, as though she had not laughed in years, tears coursed down her lined cheeks.

Jane went to put an arm around her shoulders. 'It will come right, Bernadette – I mean to see that it does.'

Louis tugged at Jane's skirt until she turned to him again.

'Papa will not be *sérieux* any longer. We might have fun if we all live here together now.'

Henri sighed. 'Louis, *non!* You must not expect too much of Jane.'

Jane shook her head at him. 'The boy is right. Your trouble is never expecting enough.'

'But you have seen – the house is a wreck . . .'

'But you are not – none of you dear people are anything but whole – entirely what I need.'

Gradually, Henri's grey eyes brightened. His smile seemed to light every feature of his weary face.

Climbing slowly, pensively and alone, Jane left the road behind and tramped on across tussocks of open moorland. The day had started bright enough with September sunlight warming the walls of the house, now though, clouds had filled the sky, rain was slanting down on to darkened surrounding hills.

A breeze had sprung up and was tugging at her hair, flattening her skirt against legs which despite this exertion were chilling, until she felt hampered. Or was reluctance diminishing her steps, impeding her progress far more than the local elements?

She hated goodbyes, especially those which she knew would be eternal. If Jane had told anyone of her intention, their thinking her mad would have been justified.

It was something she had to do. The earlier farewell accompanied by his parents had been devoted to them, her only concern for *their* well-being. The tranquillity she sought could not be found in company.

The stone looked large, crowning a hillock, virtually at the summit of the moor. Hewn quite roughly, as the Stewarts had wished, and soaring to a point. Pointing to the skies where he had found his purpose, fulfilled his ambition.

Against the blackening clouds the stone appeared white already, as it would in reality with a few seasons' weathering. Fine and strong, staunch as he had been.

Jane wept over the fate that had deemed him mortal.

Rain splashed down, wetting the back of her neck as she bent to read her father's carving. A name, a couple of dates relating birth, death, but nothing of the true nature of this man whose life was surrendered here.

'I loved you, Scotty,' she said out loud. 'Even if never enough.'

She hoped he was at peace, believed her own peace rested on his having understood that he would have mattered more, *if* perhaps they hadn't met too late.

Jane sighed, touched the stone affectionately. She must not linger. Henri was on his way from London, heading north with Louis and old Bernadette: heading towards tomorrow, and their wedding.

Her fingertips traced the rain-washed letters set in the stone's surface, she sensed that they would last through many a Yorkshire year. Even though she herself would need nothing to remind her of him. From her new home, in the valley of the Loire, she would picture this place, as much a part of her past as her family home here.

She would feel happier about Adrian Stewart after this day. With time she might come to understand completely that this spot among her native hills was where he'd found eternal freedom. She could let him go, believe that his spirit would soar to *his* skies. Or, if memory remained with him into that further life, he might walk again over her beloved hills towards limitless horizons.

Jane knew that life was strewn with regrets, but Adrian's death reinforced how fortunate she was. She had survived, and so had the love that had proved as enduring as if it were carved into stone like this – the stone which had first taken her to Henri Bodin.